THE
Confidence
GAMES

THE Confidence GAMES

Tess Amy

BERKLEY

New York

BERKLEY
An imprint of Penguin Random House LLC
penguinrandomhouse.com

Copyright © 2024 by T.A. Willberg OÜ Ltd.

Library of Congress Cataloging-in-Publication Data

Names: Amy, Tess, author.
Title: The confidence games / Tess Amy.
Description: First edition. | New York: Berkley, 2024.
Identifiers: LCCN 2023048267 (print) | LCCN 2023048268 (ebook) |
ISBN 9780593642504 (trade paperback) | ISBN 9780593642511 (ebook)
Subjects: LCGFT: Thrillers (Fiction) | Novels.
Classification: LCC PR9369.4.W54 C66 2024 (print) | LCC PR9369.4.W54
(ebook) | DDC 823/.92—dc23/eng/20231013
LC record available at https://lccn.loc.gov/2023048267
LC ebook record available at https://lccn.loc.gov/2023048268

First Edition: July 2024

Printed in the United States of America
1st Printing

Book design by Ashley Tucker

For Tarryn

Before

AT THE TIME IT FELT INEVITABLE THAT I'D WIND UP HERE: SIT-ting on the front steps of our Chelsea apartment, everything I owned stashed in one suitcase and two cardboard boxes, a court summons crumpled in my hand. Without realizing it, I'd reached the age of reusable shopping bags and cellulite, of home loans and bad debt and long-buried insecurities. The age when things start hurting, especially hearts, when all the stupid choices you made in your twenties finally catch up with you. Like getting engaged to your boss, like thinking you could trust him, like key-ing his car and egging his office when you find out you can't.

The front door of our apartment slammed and I twitched as Joel shoved past me on the stairs, our house keys jangling in his hand. Six years together and he couldn't even bother to say good-bye.

On that balmy August morning in London, I should've been on my way to work at Green Fields Insurance Firm, preparing to analyze the likelihood of my latest client getting taken out by a madman on an e-scooter or some hitherto unknown dreaded disease. But, of course, my actuarial position at Green Fields had vanished along with my fiancé, home, dignity, and all my future plans the moment I walked in on Joel straddling his PA like something out of a B-grade Western. And now he was suing me for everything I had left. Partly because I'd ruined the paint-work on his twenty-thousand-pound Tesla. Mostly because he wanted to remind me that men who cheat can be forgiven but women who go nuts must be ruined.

I wiped the tears from my cheeks and looked down at my ridiculous outfit—puppy-dog-print pajamas and pink fluffy slip-pers, the ensemble I was wearing when the police popped by to hand me the court summons. No point getting dressed after that, I figured.

A middle-aged woman with a pug under her arm flashed me the side-eye as she hurried past, like I was a gory car crash: hard to look at but impossible to ignore. I didn't blink, didn't look away, just stared right ahead, at her, at nothing, blank-faced and feeling numb. At some point I'd have to get up and move, be-cause if Joel found me sitting here when he returned from work, he'd no doubt call the police and have me arrested. But where was I supposed to go? I still had enough money in my savings account to survive without a job for several months, but if Joel won the court case (I'd have bet my life he would), I'd need it all to pay him damages (Tesla paintwork redone, office de-egged, ego reinflated . . . you get the picture).

I was desperate. For help. For love. For a place to stay and a shoulder to cry on. For a friend, most of all. And sure, judging by my social media you'd think I had those in droves: work col-leagues, university buddies, schoolmates I hadn't spoken to in decades. But now that everyone had heard about my egging/ keying incident, I doubted very much whether any of them would even pick up the phone. As it stood, my options were:

move back in with my parents (that's assuming they remembered they had a daughter), find a rat-infested flat share somewhere in the cheaper part of London and hope I didn't end up getting stabbed or robbed, or, I don't know . . . join a cult?

I looked left, toward the bus stop. Joel was still there, his back to me. My toes curled in my slippers as I considered—albeit briefly—tackling him to the ground, snatching back the house keys, and forcing *him* to move out instead. But since the apartment was technically his, and I was a blubbering wreck, I knew my chances of making that work were one in ninety thousand, at best, about as likely as being hit by a meteor, or ever being happy again.

So I got up and started walking, leaving behind my suitcase and cardboard boxes. Down the stairs, onto the street. I stopped as I reached the middle, closed my eyes. A car hooted. I didn't move. The sun beat hot against my forehead. Exhaust fumes. The trickle of sweat on my arms. A driver cursed at me; someone else screamed. I heard the roar of a truck's engine, brakes screeching, so close I could smell the burning rubber.

I counted to ten, hoping that was long enough for something to happen. And it was.

In a blaze of moving light, I saw the rest of my life unfold as if I'd already lived it. I saw dazzling sunsets in foreign skies, bright nights in strange cities. I saw myself in a thousand different places, none of which I'd been in before: old forests and ancient cobblestone streets, town squares and rolling hills. Morning rain, the sun in my eyes. Stars, a trillion miles away. I saw skyscrapers and church spires, the Eiffel Tower, the Colosseum, the Blue Mosque—all the wonders I'd never got around to seeing in my short, chaotic, empty life. I can't say it was a premonition. Maybe it was a waking dream. But if I had nothing left to live for because I had nothing left to lose, then why did I feel so afraid to lose this?

I opened my eyes, took a step back. The truck swerved just in time. I stumbled onto the pavement, picked up my suitcase and boxes. I took a breath.

Start again.

MINUTES LATER, POSSIBLY hours, a black cab pulled up directly beside me, hazards on. I waved it off without thinking, but when the back door opened and a waft of cool air hit me in the face I said, "Fuck it," and climbed inside.

"Destination, ma'am?" the driver asked.

"Anywhere," I said.

"The Savoy, please," said a woman in the front passenger's seat, whom I'd only just noticed. Her voice was strange, almost put on, yet somehow familiar. "That all right with you?" she asked.

I didn't answer.

"I like your pajamas, by the way," she went on. "Where'd you get them?"

"Umm, I . . . I can't remember." I knocked my head back against the seat. The cab hadn't started moving yet, but I was still too numb to ask why.

"What's in those boxes?" the woman in the passenger's seat asked next. "Are you moving or something?"

"Sorry?"

"I know this amazing moving company called Cherry Logistics, in case you're interested? They nail the whole thing, seriously."

I was about to tell her to shut the hell up when something

sparked in my head, a memory. I straightened in my seat. This was a trick, wasn't it? One I recognized too. The rapid-fire list of random questions, designed to make me think of only two things.

My heart beat faster.

"OK," she said, now in a voice I recognized completely, "think of a color and a tool and I'll read your mind."

I gasped, childhood memories flooding my head: mind games we used to play to read each other's thoughts, warm summer nights and breezy autumn afternoons, secrets and promises, always just the two of us. I leaned forward, and together we said, in unison, "A red hammer." It'd been two years since we'd seen each other—the longest we'd ever been apart—and yet she'd just read my mind as well as ever.

Nellie Yarrow smiled as she turned to face me, her dark-blue eyes and champagne-blond hair like something out of a Maybelline ad. But to me she was the girl I'd met at school all those years ago, the girl who'd nicked money from our teacher's pocket to buy me lunch when my parents forgot to give me any, the woman who knew me better than anyone else, the first friend I ever made, the only friend I had left.

"Hello, Em," she said, reaching for my hand, fingers looped with silver and diamonds, perfectly manicured nails. "Sorry I'm late."

"When did you . . . I thought you were . . . You didn't tell me you were back in London!"

"I wanted to surprise you."

"But I thought you were staying in Cambodia for another three years."

She squeezed my hand a bit tighter. "Yeah, well, I changed my mind when I got your email about Joel. A code red, if ever I heard one," she added, referring to the phrase we used whenever either one of us had been upended by a member of the opposite sex. "I've missed you, Emma Oxley. So much. The last few years have been fun, but it feels weird doing life without you. It's not the same playing mind games with anyone else."

I laughed and wiped my eyes as she opened her purse and pulled out what looked like a very expensive men's watch. I knew right away she'd stolen it, probably in the same way she'd nicked that lunch money from Mrs. Morrison's back pocket.

She dangled the watch in front of my face, close enough for me to see that it was a Rolex. And one I recognized.

"Oh my God, is that . . . ?"

"Yep," she said. "I bumped into him at the bus stop just now."

I looked up, scanned the bus stop. But Joel was gone. I turned back to Nellie, my eyes wide with horror.

She laughed, ran a finger along the watch's gold strap. "I reckon we could get about ten thousand for it, minimum. Just short of what he's suing you for."

And I guess that's how the whole thing started.

PART I

Five Years Later
LONDON

IN A CRAMPED ROOM ON THE THIRD FLOOR OF A NON-descript building opposite the Ritz hotel, a man turned on his laptop. He logged into his profile, username ENT00X, on the dark web listing platform he and thousands of others across Europe used to buy and sell stolen merchandise, and stared a moment at the item he'd pinned to his home page under the FOR SALE tab. Four thousand preliminary bids had already been made, one for nearly sixteen million pounds by someone who called themselves Mr. L. But in order to pocket that sixteen million, ENT00X first had to actually take possession of the item. And that's where *they* came in.

He clicked on the joint profile of Annie Leeds and Janet Robinson, the platform's most followed members and—undoubtably—Europe's most infamous luxury jewelry purveyors. He scanned their recent listings: Rolex watches, Versace cuff links, David Yurman rings, all one-offs, custom designs, every item with a price at least six times its original value. He worked his jaw, seething. No one else on Goods Exchange International was able to sell these items at these prices, but there was something intangible Annie Leeds and Janet Robinson possessed that buyers lusted after. After many weeks of tracking the duo's every move, studying their profiles, obsessing over their techniques and tactics, he'd finally come to the conclusion that if he couldn't beat them, he might as well join them.

Although his master plan would be set in motion tonight, in reality it had kicked off weeks ago. And now Europe's most brilliant con artists were about to get duped by their own tricks. Proof, he supposed, that no one was immune to mind games.

He checked the time—nine p.m.—and walked over to the window, where he waited. Thanks to his extensive intel, he knew the duo were booked into a room at the Ritz for several nights. He even knew which room. And sure enough, right on cue, a cherry-red MG convertible pulled up outside the hotel. Two women got out, handed their keys to the valet, and disappeared into the lobby.

ENT00X picked up his bag, threw in a roll of duct tape and several cable ties, and headed for the door.

1

NELLIE AND I PULLED UP OUTSIDE THE RITZ IN PICCADILLY, handed the MG keys over to the valet and our luggage (and ancient tabby cat, Sir Sebastian) to the concierge, and stepped inside the hotel's glitzy lobby. It was March, the busiest and most important month in London's black-market jewelry trade: four flashy weekends of prestigious exhibitions at galleries all across the country, the most renowned of which—Tiffany & Co.'s *Serenity and Splendor*—would take place next Saturday.

Everyone who was anyone would be visiting London this month—celebrities, royalty, journalists, politicians, influencers. And one thing every good con artist knows is that where there's money and flashing lights, there's opportunity.

Tonight I wore my favorite ensemble, just subdued enough to make sure no one took any notice of me: a charcoal knit dress, black leggings, black blazer, and clunky ankle boots. The only touch of glamour I allowed myself was some sparkly copper eyeshadow to complement my pale green eyes, a teardrop necklace, and one opal-encrusted hairpin that held back my sleek auburn mane.

One of the many ways Nellie and I differed was that, for her, being seen was nonnegotiable. Dressed in a stylish yellow satin trouser suit and silver block heels, she was tall, blond, and tanned—all lean muscle and hourglass curves. Posture dead straight and unyielding, she strutted, never walked, moving with the air of someone who knew her place in the world. But if you looked closely, if you knew her like I did, you'd see the scar above her left eyebrow, the divot in her chin, the misshapen knuckles on her right hand, and you'd know how hard she'd struggled to get there.

We walked hip to hip through the hotel's revolving doors, Nellie's trouser suit rustling at her ankles, the diamond choker she wore as a knuckle-duster twinkling under the milky light of the crystal chandeliers. Heads swiveled as we moved, eyes passing over me, settling on her.

I preferred it that way. Gone was the Emma Oxley who cried in public and moped around in puppy-dog pajamas and pink fluffy slippers. In the last five years I'd learned to cry in private and hide my weaknesses, to blend with the shadows as Nellie and I swept through Europe like wisps of glittery smoke—Paris, Rome, Prague, Barcelona, and back again—chasing opportunity and swerving around infamy. Together we were an indestructible force, the perfect double act, the dream team. Bonnie and Clyde without the guns and murder. They called us swindlers, fraudsters, tricksters, cheats. But make no mistake: we never crossed anyone who didn't deserve it.

Nellie had come to believe in things like karma, cosmic justice, and the unbending laws of the universe, and was therefore very particular about the targets we duped. They had to tick all the boxes, so to speak (think dating checklist, only better).

1) They had to live in the city we were passing through (ten-mile radius, max).

2) They had to be rich (I'm not talking Elon Musk rich, just goes-on-a-three-month-summer-holiday-every-year rich).

3) (and this was a deal-breaker) They had to be the sort of person who deserved their place in the Games: that sleazy estate lawyer, that shady investment banker, that corrupt politician. But while Nellie was out to exact revenge on every lowlife she ran into, I was in it for the anonymity, the disguise of a hundred different names: the masks I hid behind.

"MS. ROBINSON, MS. Leeds?" the head butler said as we approached the reception desk and his colleague hauled our collection of Bottega suitcases and hissing cat up the grand carpeted staircase that led off from the lobby.

"Hi, yes," I said, "that's us."

If Nellie was the star player in our Games, I was coach and referee, the master puppeteer who pulled the strings. I knew every detail of every Game we had scheduled: the names and backgrounds of our marks, the items we planned to steal, and their black-market values. There was nothing—or almost nothing—I left up to chance.

"Welcome," the butler said cheerfully, though his eyes fixed on Nellie alone, as if I weren't even there. "And you've booked our Green Park signature suite, correct?"

"Yep," Nellie said.

"Wonderful. Then you're in 101, first floor." He handed Nellie a black-and-gold key card. A beat later, he remembered there were two of us and handed me one as well. "Follow me, please," he said, extending a hand in the direction of the staircase.

Nellie slipped her key card into the secret pocket of her trouser suit—one of many she'd had sewn in, especially for Exhibition Month. "Actually, we'd like to grab a drink before settling in. Which way's the bar?"

The butler gestured to the colossal French doors on our left, the entrance to the famous Long Gallery. "Just through there. The Rivoli."

"They're open still?" Nellie asked.

"Until ten thirty. But of course there's a minibar in your suite, fully stocked. I can arrange anything extra as well. Wine, whisky, whatever you request."

"Perfect, thank you," she said, then leaned in and whispered to me, "but a nightcap in our suite's not going to cut it, is it? It's Exhibition Month and we're staying at the Ritz. We *have* to celebrate!" Before I could protest, she seized me by the shoulders and flashed her megawatt smile, the same one she'd used to convince me a life of crime was my destiny.

ARRIVING AT THE Rivoli, we settled in a pair of snazzy low-back chairs and ordered two double vodka sodas and a plate of overpriced snacks: deviled eggs, fig and olive tapenade crostini, caviar on toast, filo pastry tarts filled with Brie. The bar was crowded at first, but by our third round of drinks, the late-night guests began to filter out, one by one, until it was just me, Nellie, and the barman.

I leaned back in my seat, my vodka soda resting on my thigh, and as I realized it was nearing ten, my thoughts drifted to tomorrow and what we had planned for the evening—our first take of Exhibition Month. Like all our Games, it would be an old-fashioned street con, repurposed and polished to a high shine. Sure, we could've made a lot more money dabbling in the vast ocean of online scams and high-tech trickery that were currently all the rage. But that was risky. Too risky, by my calculations. Besides, it gave us an unequaled sense of satisfaction to know that amid the constant advancement and ultrasophistication of the modern world, simple mind games worked just as well now as they had a hundred years ago.

Play would kick off at a pricey cocktail lounge nestled inside the Biltmore hotel in Mayfair, which we happened to know was hosting a number of Exhibition Month's most esteemed attendees. Including our first mark, thirty-eight-year-old investment banker Arlo Taylor. Taylor had money, obviously, and he liked to spend it on expensive cars and watches. More importantly, though, he had a string of very well hidden sexual misconduct allegations to his name. Safe to say, he ticked all our boxes.

"Cheers to us," Nellie said in a bright voice, raising her glass. "Together, always."

"Always," I repeated. "Nell, can you believe it's been almost five years since we started?"

"Hardly. And what better way to celebrate—"

"—than by screwing over a few entitled dickheads? Speaking of which . . . we should go over the plan." Nellie grumbled at that, but I insisted. It was all very well being able to finish each other's sentences, but preparation was the key to our impeccable record, rehearsing every move, every step, until we could do it all without thinking.

I pulled out my miniature marble chess set and arranged the board—white for me, black for Nellie—placing each piece with surgical precision in the middle of its appropriate square. It might've looked like it, but we weren't about to play any normal game of chess. This was a game of focus, thieving, and deceit, and the winner would not be determined by which king fell first, but rather by who snagged the highest number of possessions from the other without them noticing. I was pretty good at chess—the regular kind—but Nellie had been playing dipper's chess with her late great-aunt, a legendary pickpocket herself, since she was eight. That made her basically unbeatable.

"All right," Nellie began, her sharp blue eyes moving across the board. "It's tomorrow night, seven p.m. We're at the Biltmore. Arlo has just arrived. He's waiting in the cocktail lounge for his Tinder date, the one and only Ms. Janet Robinson."

I gave her a theatrical bow.

Days earlier, Dax Frederick—our tech sidekick (in training) and all-round assistant—had set up a Tinder profile on my behalf, using the photographs of a woman he'd found online who—at a stretch, a *major* stretch—looked vaguely like an airbrushed, two-stone-slimmer version of me. I mean, Janet. Arlo would no doubt think he'd been catfished when he met me, but hey, happens to the best of us.

"Has Dax confirmed the profile looks legit?" Nellie asked.

"He has."

A subtle frown creased her forehead. "You sure? We should probably double-check that. This is Dax we're talking about . . ."

WE MET DAX on a chilly autumn day in Bucharest, four years ago. Nellie and I had spent two long hours at a sketchy internet café trying to persuade a pockmarked teenager to recover files from our laptop, which had been, for the second time that month, blocked by ransomware. Though this was an apparently to-be-expected side effect of dark web trading, it wasn't something we'd been prepared for or knew how to deal with. In any case, the teenager was no help whatsoever.

"Impossible," he announced after a brief inspection of our laptop. "Either you pay the hackers the ten thousand or your files are toast."

"Or we pay you half that and you fix it for us?" Nellie suggested hopefully.

The teenager's cheeks flushed red with excitement. But after some thought he shrugged and said, "I wish. But this is top-level stuff. You'll need to hire an ethical hacker."

"A what?" I said.

"You know, one of those dudes who—"

Before he could finish the sentence, as if summoned by prayer, an ethical hacker popped out from the café loo, and less than thirty minutes later, Dax had recovered our files and restored our software, free of charge. He vanished before we could offer to pay him for his services (or ask for his number—did I mention he was gorgeous?). But late the next evening, as Nellie and I were strolling through Izvor Park, a bit drunk from a night at the ballet—*Swan Lake* and too much Țuică—we happened upon Dax sleeping on a bench. He said he was there by choice, spinning us some long-winded story about how he worked part-time for the internet café and part-time for some tech company based in the Bahamas. We believed him right up until we noticed the scuff marks on his shoes and the holes in his sweater. As it turned out, he was unemployed, homeless, and dead broke. This might've been the point when most people turned away, but there was nothing Nellie and I respected more than a good-hearted person who knew how to lie. So, naturally, we offered him a position, and it was only several months later that we realized his computer skills were limited to very specific ransomware recoveries and not much else. But he could learn on the job. And besides, we were far too fond of him by then to let him go. Translation: I had a crush.

"ALREADY DONE," I said now, confirming I'd double-checked Dax's work. His skill set was steadily expanding, but it never hurt to take extra precautions.

Nellie raised an eyebrow. "Meaning you've actually spoken to him? I thought . . . after the *Incident*—"

"Like I said, I've double-checked." No need to mention it was a great relief that said double-checking did not require any face-to-face interaction between the two of us, because, as Nellie was pointing out, the last time we'd seen each other had been one of the most mortifying nights of my life and I'd been avoiding him like the plague ever since. I accepted the fact that, since we were colleagues, we were going to have to talk about the *Incident* at some stage. I just hoped it wouldn't be for another hundred years.

"Anyway, Janet is thirty-one years old," I said forcefully, shaking off the memory, "and works for the Levi's UK social media team." I wriggled my shoulders and flashed a grin. Being Janet Robinson never failed to give me an instant surge of confidence. Funny that I knew exactly who I was when I wasn't being me.

"Cool. So, Janet walks up to Arlo," Nellie said, "introduces herself, lets him order her a drink, then another and another."

"But she's not really drinking them," I added, "so Arlo's the only one getting tipsy." I moved a white pawn two spaces forward.

Nellie followed with a French Defense, handing me control of the center of the board while she built up a wall of protection with her pawns. Control for me, protection for her. Whether or not we did this intentionally, it was a perfect metaphor for our lives.

She flashed me a conspiratorial smile. "Three drinks in, Annie Leeds shows up."

I leaned back in my seat, arms folded tightly over my handbag, my mind skirting from the chessboard to Arlo to what Nellie was about to nick from me. They say women are good at multitasking because we're born to be mothers. I say: con artists. "Annie approaches Arlo and says, 'Oh, hey, Arlo! You're Elaine Taylor's son, aren't you?'"

Nellie moved another pawn forward. "Arlo nods, a bit confused, and Annie holds out her hand to introduce herself and explain, 'Our mothers know each other from book club.'"

"Arlo doesn't contest it," I supplied, moving my bishop forward, "even though he's never heard of Annie Leeds or this alleged book club."

Nellie smirked. "After all, Annie knows his name, and his mother's name—"

"—which subconsciously makes him inclined to trust her," I added. "I mean, why would she lie, anyway?"

Nellie took a long and languid sip of her drink, a glint in her eye. She shifted her pawn one space up to attack my bishop, which I moved quickly out of the firing line. "Annie walks off. But as soon as she's out of earshot—"

"—Janet will lean over and whisper in Arlo's ear, 'Shit, *shit*, I think that's her!'"

Nellie frowned, feigning confusion. "*Her?*"

"'HER!' she'll repeat frantically, 'That con woman from the

news!' Janet will look down at Arlo's wrist, touch his swanky new Patek Philippe, and say, 'Oh. My. God! I knew it. She's taken it. She's stolen your watch! This is exactly how she operates!'"

We were taking a teeny-tiny gamble here, assuming Arlo would actually be wearing his custom-made Patek Philippe on date night, but since he'd been posting about it all week on Instagram with the hashtag "ImThatGuyNow," it was a gamble we were comfortable with. By the way, the posts were geotagged, too, which was how we knew he was staying at the Biltmore. Tut-tut. Rookie error, Arlo.

Nellie spoke in a mocking baritone while moving her queen three blocks forward. "'What are you talking about, woman? My watch is right here on my wrist!'"

I laughed. "'No, no,' Janet will say. 'That's a fake. A perfect replica. She swapped them! Look. *Look!*'"

"At which point, Arlo glances over and spots the Patek Philippe in Annie's clutches," Nellie added. "He'll doubt himself for a moment. But then he'll notice the clasp on his watch has been loosened. Weird. How did that happen?" She fluttered her fingers at me.

"And because he's acting on emotion, not logic, he'll march over to Annie, fuming," I concluded.

"And demand a swap," Nellie added. "None the wiser. Easy."

"Easy," I echoed. In fact, the only thing easier would be nicking the watch without all the foreplay—Nellie could do that with her eyes closed—but whenever possible we liked our marks to willingly hand over their possessions and assume *they'd* won the Game, not us. That way, we reduced the chances of them coming after us. Or worse, going to the police. Call it good sportsmanship.

"HE'S CUTE, RIGHT?" Nellie said sometime later, while shifting one of her bishops five spaces diagonally. The bar was quiet, the lights dim, and the alcohol swirling through my veins was making me drowsy. She tilted her head subtly to the right. A man in a deep-navy suit had just entered, briefcase at his hip, phone in hand.

The old me would've swooned at the mere sight of him, but now I barely looked over, blinking dully, just to make it perfectly clear to Nellie and the man in question I wasn't the least bit interested. "Maybe."

"And no ring," she observed.

Or he's just taken it off for the night. "Right," I said, keeping my voice flat.

"Also, that suit's Valentino."

"OK."

Nellie rolled her eyes. "*OK?* That's it? That's all I get?"

"Gah! *OK*, I agree. He's rich and cute."

Rich, cute, and perfect, actually—tall, surly, dark-haired. My type. Everyone's type. But so what? I had zero percent chance of catching his eye while Nellie was around, especially if he was the kind of man who liked to wear tailored Valentino suits. And even if I did catch his eye, and we got chatting, and he asked for my number, and a date, and a coffee back at his place . . . then what? Would I tell him I was a professional criminal who made a living swindling dirty men? Or worse, end up falling in love with him, trusting him, letting him pierce through my tough exterior and inspect the weaknesses beneath? No, thanks. I'd made that mistake before. I knew how it ended.

"One day," Nellie said, placing her glass on the table like a judge with a gavel, "you're going to meet the man who sees through all this. Like I do."

I snorted dismissively, hoping she was wrong. After all, the idea of being seen was just as terrifying as the reality of being ignored. "We should get the bill," I said suddenly.

She nodded, but of course we weren't quite done yet.

I popped an olive into my mouth and sucked off the bitter flesh as I surveyed the area for something of Nellie's I could get my hands on. I stretched out my legs beneath the table, only then realizing she'd kicked off her silver block heels. Not perfect, but it would do. Using my left hand, I moved my knight over her pawn while I used my right hand to pass her a plate of deviled eggs, all the while using my feet to slide one of her heels toward me under the table.

Meanwhile, the bill arrived in a neat leather folder. Nellie came to sit beside me.

I tensed.

She reached for the bill with her right hand while her left moved subtly backward.

Something silvery flashed in my periphery. I felt a strange warmth whip past my cheek but was too distracted by Nellie's next chess move to pay attention to what it was. Her black queen materialized diagonally in front of my king; her rook stood to his left.

It was over.

"Checkmate, babe," she chirped, showing me the necklace glittering in her palm. *My* necklace.

Quickly, I looked down at my feet, expecting to see at least one of her heels clamped between my boots. That would've made it even.

She shrieked with giddy laughter as she bent over to tighten her ankle straps.

I toppled my king in graceful defeat and raised my glass while we laughed together at how masterfully she'd bested me. "I *will* beat you one day. That's a promise."

She got to her feet, threw 150 pounds in cash on the table, then handed me back my necklace. "Nightcap at the suite?"

"I'll meet you there," I said, starting for the loo.

I'd just reached the bathroom when I heard the familiar ring of our burner phone. I spun round, spotting Nellie just as she pressed the phone to her ear. I shook my head in admiration and laughed. When and how she'd plucked *that* from my bag, I had no clue.

2

IT COULDN'T HAVE TAKEN ME MORE THAN TEN MINUTES TO finish up in the loo and reach our suite on the first floor—a six-hundred-square-foot, two-bed apartment with a tented silk ceiling, gold-leaf fittings, and a sprawling view of Green Park and Piccadilly. Our suitcases were waiting for us in the entranceway, along with Sir Sebastian, who was curled up on a custom-designed gold-thread pet bed that Nellie had ordered in Paris last month.

Closing the suite door behind me, I gave Sir Sebastian a scratch between the ears (which earned me a hiss) and strolled past the shower—which was on full blast—and into the dining lounge. A silver tray with two empty glasses awaited me, alongside an unopened bottle of champagne. Nellie's half-unpacked suitcase was lying open on the settee—designer heels and dresses spilling out onto the floor, mixed up with boxes of incense and the small collection of miniature stone Buddhas she carried with her everywhere. A memory caught me off guard, of the years we'd lived together in our twenties while I attended university and Nellie worked as a sales assistant at Selfridges.

The memory was pleasant enough, but it made me flinch. I couldn't think about those years in isolation, forgetting Joel and the pain that had come after. And now, amid the mess, I noticed an old dress of mine, one Nellie had helped me pick out for my university graduation party. Flamingo pink, figure hugging, low-cut V-neckline. I was so sure I'd binned it, though, along with everything else from my past life. And since it was a few sizes too big for Nellie, I couldn't understand why she'd salvaged it. It might've been my favorite dress back then, but I wouldn't have been seen dead in something so glaring now.

I drew back the silk curtains and peeked outside. The street-lights twinkled, and in their glow I could just make out a large grayish shadow that was the boundary of Green Park. This time tomorrow, Nellie and I would be returning here from our Game with Arlo at the Biltmore, a brand new Patek Philippe in our collection. Maybe we'd sneak into the park for a late-night cele-bratory drink?

"Coffee or tea?" I called out. The excitement of tomorrow's Game would make it hard to fall asleep now, so I planned to stay up a few more hours, running over our plans—just one last time. "Or fizz? I could do with a glass, to be honest."

No answer.

I put the kettle on, turned on the TV, and flicked through to the evening news. Something about an ongoing investigation into a hit-and-run near Paddington station from a few days ago, an MP squabble in Parliament last night, a cold snap expected for the week ahead. I hardly paid attention to any of it. Listening to the news made me uneasy, always vaguely concerned Nellie and I would one day see our faces glaring back at us.

I flicked over to *E! News* and only had to watch for five min-utes before a piece came on about the world-renowned *Serenity and Splendor* exhibition happening on Saturday, hosted by Tiffany & Co.

"London's answer to the Met Gala, am I right?" one of the hosts declared.

I turned down the volume—just as the hosts began running through the purported guest list and "who" they might be wearing—opened my laptop, and logged into our profile on the dark web trading forum Goods Exchange International. Seventy new profiles had followed us overnight, bringing our total count to ninety-eight thousand.

A quick scroll through the platform's buy-and-sell catalog showed me the most popular items at the top of the page. Someone had just listed an apparently "brand-new" Yacht-Master Rolex for five thousand quid, similar to one Nellie and I had sold a few weeks ago (after nicking it off a seedy MP at a fundraising event in Edinburgh). But in less than two seconds and without even zooming in, I could tell it was a cheap knockoff. The lens wasn't magnified, there was no engraving on the winder, the crown was bare. And most importantly, no criminal worth their salt would sell a genuine rose-gold Yacht-Master Rolex for less than one-third of its retail price. I smiled at the post, though, because it was amateurs like these who made professionals like me and Nellie the hottest ticket in con town. After thousands of happy customers, nearly ten million quid in sales, and an unblemished reputation for offering high-lux goods at unreasonable prices, we were without question the most trustworthy swindlers Goods Exchange International had ever seen. In fact, in all our years of trading, we'd only ever had one blip—a sale of cuff links that fell through at the last minute. Not bad for five years on the job.

And the best part? Despite all the prestige we'd garnered, we still managed to keep our true identities completely concealed. Thanks to Dax's hard work (albeit with a few speed bumps here and there), Nellie and I now had a digital footprint as clean as the driven snow: no bank accounts, no smartphones, no photos anywhere on social media. We sold our stock in cash or crypto; we used encrypted email addresses and VPNs and real-time operating systems. To anyone outside the dark web, we didn't exist at all.

But how did we nick the items we sold in the first place?

Well, it starts with understanding that we're all the same—susceptible to a touch of coercion and a smattering of manipulation, so long as it comes from someone we trust (though trust me, no one can be trusted). And while everyone would like to believe they can tell the difference between the truth and a lie, here's a little something I've learned over the years: it's the storyteller who counts, not the story. It doesn't matter what you tell someone, it doesn't matter how outrageous it is, how obscure or far-fetched, as long as you tell it well. And rest assured, Nellie and I could spin that yarn better than Rumpelstiltskin himself. We'd tell you exactly what you wanted to hear, soothe your fears, confirm your biases, and give you something to believe in. We'd smile and nod in all the right places, and by the time you realized what we were really up to, we'd be fifty miles away, painting our nails and sipping Dom Pérignon in our MG.

I minimized my current tab, opened a new one for Facebook, and logged in to the fake account I'd set up under Janet Robinson's name, which I used to track and suss out our marks. As usual, a bombardment of posts flittered across the screen: engagement rings, fetal ultrasound scans, family portraits, all from Janet's one hundred and ten "friends." An unwelcome lump rose in my throat, a longing I didn't wish to explore. After the Joel ordeal, I'd made it my mission to rebuild my life exactly the way I'd always wanted it—unsuitable for marriage, babies, family, love. It was a life of power, free of the fear of losing all the things I had once craved.

I was about to do some last-minute research on tomorrow's mark when something on my home page caught my eye. A post by Joel Beck, whom I'd friended (as Janet) a few months earlier in a moment of weakness and too much tequila. It was a picture of a golden-skinned, bright-eyed couple at the Cliffhouse in Uluwatu, Bali. I knew the place because I'd been there six years ago scouting it out as a potential wedding venue. But now Joel had taken someone else, his new fiancée, my replacement, a twenty-five-year-old Instagram influencer with platinum-blond hair and perfect eyebrows. I stared at the picture for a minute straight without blinking. Something was happening inside my chest, but I wasn't sure what it was. Not pain or jealousy—I'd long since buried all that. Frustration, probably.

I slammed the laptop shut and marched over to the steaming kettle. But I wasn't in the mood for tea. I popped the cork on the bottle of champagne, tipped some into a glass for Nellie and a bone china saucer for Sir Sebastian, and knocked back a mouthful myself. The cat dipped his trim pink nose into the bowl, took one lick, stretched his legs out in front of him, and wandered off to Nellie's side of the suite without so much as a thank-you.

Outside, the night sky had darkened further and a swift wind now tapped against the windows like a metronome. Time passed in slow ticks. My eyes drifted to the shower door, then to the time on the carriage clock in front of me: 11:05, more than thirty minutes since Nellie and I had parted ways at the hotel bar.

My heart rattled; 11:06.

Sir Sebastian was staring at me intently, and the image of Joel and his fiancée in Bali was swirling around my brain at a dizzying speed, distracting me from the plans I was supposed to be fine-tuning for tomorrow. But these weren't the reasons I now felt so on edge.

I walked over to the shower, skin tingling. The water was still going full blast. But you know how when someone is washing themselves, you can actually hear it? There isn't just the sound of an incessant stream of falling water; there are other sounds mixed in too. Like feet shuffling against wet tiles, the swish of limbs and the general clink and clang of things moving about. But I heard none of that now. Just the water gushing and my heart thumping.

I yanked open the door, blinked into the steamy abyss. The shower was on full blast. But Nellie wasn't there.

3

NELLIE ISN'T HERE. SHE LEFT, WALKED OUT ON ME.

Those were my first thoughts. Knee-jerk, irrational, bleeding out from old scars I'd so hoped had healed.

But no. She hadn't left me. Impossible. There had to be another explanation. She'd probably just left the suite to stretch her legs or to fetch something from reception. Or maybe she went down for another drink at the bar. *Alone? But wasn't it closed already?* Or maybe, like she'd done the last time we were in London, she'd gone to Mayfair to test-drive the latest Aston Martin. *At eleven p.m.?* And maybe she just left the shower running by mistake.

I recited all these options to myself as I left the suite, marched down the hotel corridor, to the bar, the restaurant, the Palm Court, the lobby, and even halfway down Piccadilly Street in a howling gale.

But Nellie was nowhere to be seen.

Sucking in increasingly ragged breaths, nerves jangling, instincts screaming that something was off, I made my way back up to the suite, closed the door behind me, and crossed into the lounge.

OK. If I really thought about it, it wasn't out of character for Nellie to run off somewhere in the middle of the night. Often, when we were staying in a foreign city, she'd leave me lounging in our hotel room with the latest *Hello!* magazine and a bottle of wine while she went off to dance the night away with a bunch of strangers at some swanky cocktail lounge. She also used to do it when we were kids, lots, like all those times she'd slept over when my parents went on holiday without me. Pillow forts, tea parties, *Harry Potter* by torchlight, and when we ran out of things to eat, she would skip off to buy us sweets and crisps with the money she'd nicked from Dad's back pocket. But still, not once in all our years together had she ever gone anywhere without telling me.

"Something's definitely not right," I muttered nervously to myself, surveying the room.

The TV was still on *E! News*, which was now running a report on Leonardo DiCaprio's new supermodel fling. I glanced again at Nellie's half-unpacked suitcase, then checked the time—11:36. What was I missing? Maybe she *had* told me where she was going before she left the hotel bar; maybe I just hadn't been listening. And what about that phone call she'd received just as she'd left? Was it a call from her brother, Jack? Or her parents? Unlike my family, the Yarrows *did* actually keep in contact. But no, it couldn't have been. Nellie never gave out our number to anyone. Neither did I.

Theory squashed, I turned again to examine Nellie's belongings, hoping to find some sign of where she'd gone.

And then I heard it: footsteps—a soft, quick *pat-pat*—coming from the corridor. Closer. Closer.

I tensed. Not Nellie's footsteps, not the certain, steady pace I knew so well.

Click.

The suite door swung open. I gasped, took a step backward.

A young girl, around nine or ten, dressed in faded pajamas patterned with sleeping dinosaurs and sporting a mousy brown pixie cut, skidded to a halt in the foyer, a worn blue backpack slung over her shoulder and a mix of surprise and relief on her face.

"Hello," she panted, her pale skin glistening with sweat, a slight tremble in her bottom lip and puffy red rings encircling her eyes, like she'd been crying. She shuffled forward, then back again, as unsure of me as I was of her. "I'm . . . I'm Sophia."

I stared at her, my mouth hanging open.

"Sophia Keeling," she added breathlessly when I didn't react.

"Oh. Hello. And what—" I looked past her, at the door, which I was very certain I'd locked. Yes. Definitely. I'd locked it. So how did she get in? I put a hand to my neck, the throb of my pulse rapid under my fingertips.

"I have a message for you," she explained, lowering her voice and edging closer. "It's urgent."

"Sorry?"

Sophia glanced furtively over her shoulder and repeated, "A message. From the bad man."

"Bad man?" I echoed, marching past her toward the door, still completely baffled by whatever was going on. Nellie, who'd grown up around a gazillion cousins and knew how to deal with kids and the strange things they say, would've almost certainly known what this scruffy child was getting at. I, however, hadn't the foggiest. "What bad man?"

Sophia huffed, like I'd just asked a really dumb question that she didn't have time to answer. "The one who took your friend!"

I was frozen for a moment, unable to speak or move.

The one who took your friend.

Surely I'd heard wrong. I watched the girl through narrowed eyes, trying to decide what to make of her. My parents had always scolded me for being too trusting of strangers, which was a fair criticism back then since I'd once let a kind-looking gentleman (who turned out to be an ex-con in need of a TV and some irreplaceable jewelry) into our house on one of the many occasions I'd been left home alone. That side of me, though, was dead and gone.

I slammed the suite door shut and locked it—irrefutably—then drew the heavy silk curtains over every window, dimmed the lighting, and turned off the shower. I peered through the peephole at the carpeted corridor outside. All clear. No bad man about. I marched over to the street-facing window, parted the curtain just an inch, stuck my face through, and surveyed the pavement below. Nothing suspicious there either, unless you counted the haggard lady in the purple jumpsuit who was lingering outside the hotel and appeared to be talking to herself. Next, I reached inside my handbag and scratched around for my phone. But of course, I remembered then, Nellie had nicked it off me at the bar during our game of dipper's chess. Instead, I picked up the suite's landline and dialed the cell's number, which I knew by heart. But it was all just ring, ring, ring, voicemail, nothing. What on earth was going on? Leaving the shower on, not answering her phone. It was almost as though she didn't want me to find her.

Out of options and more confused than ever, I turned back to the girl with the cropped hair and tattered pajamas. I raised a dubious eyebrow and, at a loss, asked, "OK . . . so what's this message you have for me, then?"

She took a long, frustrated breath, as if she'd been wondering when I'd come to my senses. She handed me a crumpled note from her pocket.

I received it hesitantly, smoothed it out with trembling fingers. The note was handwritten, though definitely not in Nellie's elegant script.

The one side was inscribed with my alias, Janet Robinson, and the other with a simple instruction: *Meet me at Denmark Hill Station at 1 a.m. Lock the girl in the bathroom. Any tricks and your friend's dead.*

I swayed a little, stammered, "B-but . . . what . . ." I dug my fingernails into my temples. *Focus! This is a joke, right? It has to be a joke!*

Sensing I needed some further explanation—ASAP—Sophia said, "I was with the bad man when he phoned your friend and told her to meet him outside." She narrowed her eyes and added, "It was a trap, I think."

"He *phoned* her?" I shrieked, stupefied. "Meaning . . . he has our number? How?" I thought of the phone call Nellie had received just as she'd left the bar. But if that call had been from this alleged bad man, then . . .

He had to know who we were, where we were staying, *and* how to contact us. Yet that was impossible. Nellie and I were always so careful to cover our tracks, to use burner phones with alternating SIM cards, fake online profiles, encrypted email addresses, and secure browsers. It was inconceivable to me that someone had dug through it all to find us. Then again, I thought with a spasm of worry, Dax was the one responsible for cleaning our digital footprints, and let's be honest, he wasn't exactly the best in the business.

I blinked dumbly at Sophia as she pulled a black-and-gold

Ritz key card from under her sleeve. "This was in your friend's pocket," she said. "The bad man gave it to me, saying I had to use it to fetch you."

I reached out and grabbed the edge of the settee, sitting down before my legs gave way.

"You look scared," Sophia pointed out matter-of-factly as I looked up at her, my eyes wide, trying to process what this meant and whether I was going to survive it.

"I know how it feels," she went on despite my silence. "I'm scared too."

I got up, started walking, itching to move. Sophia trailed me back into the lounge, her short legs moving fast to keep up with my frantic pace. It was only when I paused and turned around that I noticed she'd extracted something from her backpack. A tattered hardcover book of some variety.

She pored through the book, a finger trailing across the pages until she found what she was looking for. "Here," she said, reading a passage out loud with a strong, assertive voice, as if trying to steel herself as much as me. "'If scared, take a few deep breaths, close your eyes, and remember: sometimes it takes the scary things to show us how brave we are.'"

I stared at her, then the book, not breathing very deeply at all, thoughts swirling, anxiety rising. *Where did I leave my Xanax?*

"This is the only copy in the whole wide world," Sophia added, tapping the book's spine proudly. I noticed a handwritten title on the cover: *The Book of Good Advice*. "Daddy said I should always carry it with me, especially when I'm alone." She paused thoughtfully. "Which is often now."

Sir Sebastian, who only then seemed to notice our visitor,

leaped off Nellie's bed and slinked over to Sophia with his chin held high. He curled his body around her legs and started purring.

"Hello, kitty," Sophia cooed, momentarily distracted as she ruffled what was left of the fur behind the ancient cat's ears. "You're so pretty." She examined the name tag dangling from his jewel-studded collar. "*Sir Sebastian*, it's a pleasure to meet you. My name's—"

Her introduction was cut short by the shrill ring of the hotel landline, which made all three of us—me, Sophia, and Sir Sebastian—leap a foot in the air.

"Hello?" I said urgently into the receiver.

"Mate, where've you been? I've been calling your cell for ages but no one's answering."

"Oh, Dax, hi," I said awkwardly. "Sorry . . . Nellie has it. And she's, well, she's not here at the moment."

"OK . . ." He paused. "Well, you need to get over here fast. To the office. Something bad's happened."

Same here, I thought. I hesitated a moment, wondering if I should say it out loud, because didn't saying something out loud make it real? "Nellie's been . . . she's been k-kidnapped."

"*What?*"

"We arrived at the Ritz this evening and we . . . I . . . we were having drinks at the bar and we split up for a second and now she's gone."

There was another long pause, so long that I thought we'd been cut off.

"Dax? Are you there?"

"Kidnapped? *Shit*, man. You serious? When?"

"About an hour ago. And yes, of course I'm bloody serious! I wouldn't joke about this!"

"It must be connected, then," he said.

"Connected?"

"Someone tried to break in here," Dax explained. "That's why I called. It happened just a few minutes ago."

"What? Break in where?"

"At *the office*," he whispered, as if afraid someone was listening in. "You've got to come over and check it out. It's really . . . weird."

"No. Wait. Dax. The kidnapper asked me to meet him at Denmark Hill and he seems to know everything and—"

But the line clicked, dead.

I replaced the receiver, looked at my handbag on the dresser, then at the note Sophia had given me: *Meet me at Denmark Hill Station at 1 a.m.* It was already 11:55.

I was beginning to feel sick, the kind of sick you get when you realize you're about to make a life-or-death decision for someone you've only just met.

"Please don't leave me here," Sophia said in an urgent whisper, Sir Sebastian now cradled tightly in her arms, his eyes bulging slightly from the firmness of her grip. "I know that's what the note says, but . . . I'm really scared."

I pressed the heel of my hand to my forehead and closed my eyes to think.

Lock the girl in the bathroom. Any tricks and your friend's dead.

Did *not* locking Sophia in the bathroom count as a trick? I had a feeling it did. But if I left her here alone, what sort of fate was I subjecting her to? Would she be here when I got back, or would the bad man send someone to fetch her while I was out?

I stared at the girl for several seconds, trying to think of an alternative solution, one with a lower risk profile. I really didn't want to put Nellie's life in jeopardy for some random ten-year-old girl. At the same time, leaving the kid here alone and afraid made me feel a bit too much like my own neglectful family.

Hesitating a moment, I crouched, took the girl's hand in mine. The skin on her palms was cold and calloused and she smelled like she hadn't had a shower in some time. She pulled back stiffly, so I let go.

"Where do you live?" I asked, thinking out loud.

"Nowhere."

"But you have a house, don't you? Where is it?"

"No, I don't have a house. Daddy and I were living in a shelter. We're poor, and . . ." Her words fizzled out on a sigh.

I opened my mouth, closed it again. There was obviously a story there, but I didn't have time to hear it right then. "A shelter. Right. Where?"

"Don't know."

"What was it called?"

She looked at me but said nothing.

"Right, never mind. Then we'll just . . . let's call your dad. How's that?"

She shook her head sadly. "I don't know Daddy's number."

I took a deep breath. "OK. And what about the other people in your family? Grandparents? Aunts? Uncles?"

"Daddy doesn't have any brothers or sisters or parents," she answered glumly. "And Mummy has left for someplace that has a beach." She contemplated me for a second, a small furrow forming on her forehead. "Where are your mummy and daddy? Maybe they'll know what to do? Do you want to call them?"

Caught off guard by the question, I stammered. "Well . . . no, I don't think they would. And anyway, they're not . . . They're somewhere . . . over that way." I pointed in the general direction of southwest London, though to be honest, I had no idea where Harold and Jude Oxley lived these days. Probably on a barge sipping margaritas, like they always said they would've done if I hadn't come along.

Sophia nodded slowly, as if she understood this in full. "I see, yes . . ."

I swallowed, checked the time. It was exactly midnight now and Dax's "office" was in Camberwell, which was basically on the way to Denmark Hill station. I took it as a sign. "All right," I said, making up my mind. "Come on. I have a plan."

"Where are we going?" Sophia asked, knees shaking slightly.

"To my friend's place."

"Friend?" She wiped her eyes with the cuff of her sleeve. "Is she nice?"

"*He.* And actually, he's not really a friend. We work together. But yes, he's very nice."

She stared down at her book thoughtfully. "Daddy says friends are important. But . . . he doesn't seem to have any."

"Well, that's because it's hard to make friends," I said automatically, then realized it wasn't exactly true. Emma Oxley hadn't struggled to make friends, not at school, not at university or even the insurance firm. In fact, one could argue that she used to make friends too easily, trusting even those who'd proved themselves fickle. But, of course, Janet Robinson knew better. I stole a glance at myself in the mirror. My pale, unsmiling face looked back at me, a face that seemed to scream, *Stay away*, shoulders hunched, neck muscles flexed, ready for battle. I forced my shoulders down and turned back to Sophia, who—along with Sir Sebastian—had been watching me watch myself. They looked uneasy and I could hardly blame them. I wasn't exactly a picture of confidence, and confidence—I suspected—was exactly what they needed now. Lucky for every-one, I'd always been good at pretending.

"Righto. All good, kids," I said, pulling myself together with a clap of my hands. I shoved my laptop and the MG keys into my handbag and led the way to the door. "Nothing to be afraid of. Let's go."

4

TAKING SOPHIA WITH ME TO DAX'S OFFICE INSTEAD OF LOCK-
ing her in the bathroom was probably very stupid, but I calmed
myself with the notion that—if asked—I could just say I'd taken
my eyes off her for one second and she'd run away. Not my fault.
In statistics we call this a null hypothesis, in other words, true
until proven false through experimentation. And so (after a
painfully long argument about why we had to leave Sir Sebastian behind and that he'd probably be happier without us
around), I wrapped Sophia in one of my enormous raincoats
and Nellie's Burberry scarf, and off we went.

Maybe thirty minutes later, I parked the MG outside a drab
block of studio flats in Camberwell, extricated Sophia from under
the dashboard, and got out.

I smoothed my dress against my thighs, scraped back my
frizzy hair. I looked up at the seventh window on the second
floor, remembering what had happened the last time I was
here—*that kiss*—and cringed inwardly. Except it wasn't just
shame I felt now, but a horrible sense of unraveling. Everything
that had happened tonight was making me feel more exposed

and self-conscious than I had in years, as if a crack had formed in my armor, small still, but widening fast. But then I remembered: Janet Robinson was confident and in control and she knew exactly how to get Nellie back. There was nothing to worry about.

"Are you *sure* there's nothing to be worried about?" Sophia asked, eyeing me uncertainly and apparently reading my thoughts. "Because you look quite worried to me."

I smiled tightly. "I'm sure. One hundred percent. Everything's under control."

"Is this your friend's place?" she asked next, her gaze flitting from me to the flat and back again.

"I told you, he's not a friend. More like a colleague."

"What's a colleague?"

I steeled myself, locked the car, and got walking. "A person you work with."

She trotted after me as I made my way to the block's entrance. "What do you do for work?"

"I'm a . . ..a . . ." *I shouldn't say criminal, should I?* "I sell watches and jewelry. Very expensive ones."

"To who?"

Scumbags, general riffraff. "People who like expensive watches and jewelry. On the internet."

She considered my answer with a frown. Why did I get the feeling she didn't believe anything I said?

"Daddy says the internet's where people go to feel better about themselves but come away feeling worse."

"He's talking about social media," I said, my mind suddenly drifting back to that post I'd seen from Joel and his new fiancée. *Goddammit, get a grip on yourself!*

"What's social media?"

I ignored her and rang the bell for flat 21, tilting my head a few degrees to the left to examine my reflection in the door's central glass pane.

"Are you worried about how you look?" Sophia asked.

"What? No."

"Well, I think you look nice, anyway."

"Oh . . ."

"You're very pretty."

It'd been a long time since anyone (besides Nellie) had called me pretty and, as it was a compliment of the severest kind, I wasn't sure how to take it. I settled on, "Umm, thanks."

She studied me intently for an excruciatingly long minute while we waited for Dax to buzz us into the building. When at last he did, I marched swiftly up the sticky linoleum stairs to the second floor, Sophia trailing several feet behind. As I reached the landing, I paused.

"Something's wrong again," Sophia stated, tugging at my hand. "Isn't it?"

I stared at the ugly, dark corridor ahead, my skin hot and itchy despite the chilly weather.

"I thought you said he was nice," Sophia piped up again.

"What?"

"Your colleague-friend person. You said he was nice."

"He is."

"So why are you so scared of seeing him?"

I took off my coat because I was hot, then put it back on because I didn't want Dax to think I was hot on a freezing-cold day. Dead giveaway. "I'm not scared, just—"

I was cut short when a tall, straight-up Herculean man with wiry black hair popped out from the second door on the left. Dax Frederick. Caribbean-born, London bred. Up until the night of the *Incident*, our interactions had been amicable and easygoing—a rare source of comfort and familiarity in my tightly controlled life. But then, in a flash of weakness I will forever regret, I'd dropped my guard and let him in and now we could hardly bear to look each other in the eye. How predictable.

Two weeks ago, he and I were sitting alone on the couch, here in his "office." There was a bottle of wine on the floor between us, Ed Sheeran's "Perfect" streaming out from the computer speakers. And because Nellie and I had just wrapped up a brilliant con at the Savoy, I was—for once—dressed to the nines in a cute little black Prada number with a pinched-in waist and six-inch Balenciaga heels.

Dax started off by telling me about the dead-in-the-water IT repairs business he'd tried to start up a few years before we met him, and what this failure had done to his already shaky self-esteem. I reciprocated by telling him about Joel, whom Dax pronounced—there and then—to hate more than anyone he'd ever known (*jealousy*, I thought, *good sign!*). And by two a.m., Dax and I had moved on to a lengthy philosophical debate on what exactly heartbreak feels like. "A thousand knives to the chest," Dax suggested simplistically. "No," I said, recalling in perfect clarity how I'd felt the day I sat on the steps of my Chelsea apartment, and all the days my parents had pretended I didn't exist. If anyone knew heartbreak in all its manifestations, it was surely me. "Like dying, like drowning in freezing water, can't breathe, numb, can't feel anything but the thing that's killing you, can't scream, or if you can, no one can hear you, and then, right before the end, when everything hurts so bad you actually *want* to die, somehow, you take a breath and start again."

Dax took my hand, saying nothing but communicating so much. I knew I wasn't in love with him, not in the way I had been in love with Joel. And yet I found him attractive and easy to talk to. Moreover, he made me feel *seen*, like I mattered, like if I disappeared he might actually notice. Which is probably why I decided, on a whim, to permit him a glimpse of the person behind the mask, the person I'd locked away for so long, who loved love and craved affection, who wanted to be seen and heard and needed—the antithesis of the person he knew me to be. And so, I—without any encouragement from Dax whatsoever—leaned over and pressed my lips against his. I mean, he actually let me kiss him *twice* (out of pity, I am sure) before he gently peeled himself away and mumbled something about not wanting to mix work and pleasure. If it'd happened to Nellie (not that it would've because nobody rejected Nellie), she would've laughed it off and never spoken of it again. I, however, burst into hitching sobs while I wiped the lipstick from Dax's chin. It wasn't like I was learning this lesson for the first time or anything, but just as a reminder: no one wanted Emma Oxley. Best to keep her hidden. After all, everything I had gained in life had come from leaving her behind.

"WHO'S THIS?" DAX asked now, eyes widening as he stared at Sophia in her oversized ensemble. Though I only realized it then, Sophia was just the distraction I needed to get through the encounter without him bringing *it* up. The good Lord really does work in mysterious ways.

"Sophia Keeling," came a tentative voice from somewhere deep within the layers of my raincoat. "Pleasure to meet you."

"Oh. OK," Dax said, then turned to me with a questioning gaze, surely looking for a more thorough explanation.

Just to keep my eyes from his, I checked the time: 12:40.

"Dax, listen," I said stiffly, "I've got to be at Denmark Hill station in twenty minutes. I just came to drop off—"

But before I could finish the sentence, Dax had turned on his heel and was leading the way down the darkened corridor and up to flat 21. "Come. You've got to see this," he said over his shoulder, trusting we'd follow.

Sophia trotted after him and, begrudgingly, I tagged along.

WE ARRIVED AT the flat to find the front door hanging precariously from its hinges, the lock broken. The carpet was ripped up at the threshold and the old wooden floorboards cracked in several places, like someone had tried to bash their way under the door as well as through.

"I thought you said *attempted* break-in!" I shrieked.

"Yeah, mate, I was softening the blow."

I stepped inside the office, aka the "Laundromat"—the storage facility for our stolen watches and luxury-brand jewelry. But now the Laundromat looked less like the back room of a shifty pawnshop and more like a bomb site. Cardboard boxes, paper, and packaging were strewn across every inch of the floor. Tiny pieces of glass and metal were scattered like ash on the couch, on the kitchen counter, even in the bath and on the toilet seat.

I gasped. "Dax!"

"I know, I know. It's all gone. And what isn't gone is destroyed."

I picked up one of the cardboard boxes that had been tipped over, scratched around inside. But there was nothing. I picked up another and another. Every single one was empty. I did a quick run-through in my head. Dax usually stored at least six weeks' worth of stock at a time, which meant we'd lost eighty thousand quid, minimum. Eighty thousand. Six weeks of hard work. I tried not to think about it.

"I was out with mates when I got the alert from my security system," Dax explained as I continued to stare at the mess. "We were at Opium," he added unnecessarily. "In Leicester Square. You been?"

"Umm, no."

"It's pretty wicked. They do this cool thing where they plan out the menu based on the signs of the zodiac." His shoulders twitched oddly, and I got the feeling he was speaking just to prevent any awkward silences during which we'd both be forced to contemplate our last uncomfortable interaction. "Theo introduced me to the place, actually. A while back."

I blinked. "Who?"

"Theo Fletcher. The graphic designer I told you about?"

I nodded, a vague memory of this conversation springing to mind. But since it'd taken place around the time of our embarrassing encounter, I'd shoveled it into a dark room in the back of my brain, locked the door, and tossed the key.

". . . really good at what he does. And he's cool. You'd like him, I think."

A bit confused, I said, "OK."

"Anyway, Opium's a nice place to take a date. You know, in case you ever—"

"I have to go now," I blurted out in an odd yelp, like I was in pain. Wherever Dax was going with that sentence, for the love of God, I could not bear to hear it. I already had more than enough to deal with tonight.

Dax faltered at my outburst. Sophia looked up at me with a frown.

"I just . . . It's almost one and I'm supposed to—" I mumbled, then handed over the note Sophia had given me. "It'll take me at least ten minutes to get there from here, I think."

Dax read the note in silence, then looked up, his pupils—which were already twice their regular size—doubled again.

"It's from the bad man," Sophia explained. "The one who kidnapped your friend." Dax's face paled. "And in case you were wondering, I don't know his name or anything. Daddy works for him and we've been to his house a few times but that's all. Daddy doesn't like the work, I think, which is why he's been trying to leave, but . . . but . . ." Her expression tightened with fear. "I haven't seen Daddy for a while now."

Dax looked at me, horrified, as he attempted to piece together this peculiar story. "I don't get it. Your name's on this note." He cleared his throat weirdly. "Janet Robinson, I mean. How does he know that name? And where you were staying?"

The skin at the back of my neck prickled. "Exactly what I was wondering." I thought for a moment, the prickling spreading down my arms to my fingertips. "Could it have been a data leak? Our laptop, maybe? What if it was hacked somehow? That's possible, right?"

"Well . . . yeah, sure, in theory. Have you clicked on any suspicious links recently? Opened random emails? PDFs?"

"No, of course not. I'm very careful about that stuff."

"Then I don't think a hack is likely. I've set up your laptop with all the best firewalls, secure browsers, anti-tracking apps."

I decided not to remind him that just a few weeks ago (back when we were talking and he'd had a bit too much vodka) he'd admitted how advanced the world of cybersecurity was becoming and how difficult it was to keep up-to-date with it all. His exact words were, "I worry I'm the worst hacker you'll ever meet. Maybe you should hire someone else."

"But I'll just run through some checks to be sure?" he asked now with a hint of uncertainty. "Do you have your laptop here?" I nodded, retrieved my laptop from my bag, and handed it over. He dashed off to his desk, sat down, and tapped something out on the keyboard at lightning speed.

I craned my neck to see over his shoulder. "Well?"

"Nah. Everything seems good," he said. "Doesn't look like there's a virus here, or any kind of tracking apps installed." He chewed his lip thoughtfully. "Unless . . . I dunno, it's something I'm missing, something super advanced. I should probably check again."

Aware of the time, twelve forty-five, I snatched back the laptop, hitched my bag over my shoulder, and made for the door. "No time now," I said. "But thanks for your help, anyway. I'll call you if—*when*—I find Nellie."

Dax leaped up frantically. "No, wait! Where're you going?"

I nodded irritably at the note I'd passed him. "Denmark Hill! I have to show up there in less than ten minutes."

"Yeah, but . . . you're not just going to waltz on up to him, are you? What if he's dangerous? I mean, he almost definitely is."

I was briefly tempted to ask him to come along with me. But that would sound needy and scared, and Janet Robinson was neither of those things. "I'll be fine."

He sighed, then nodded subtly at Sophia. "OK. But what about . . . ? Don't you think this bad man will come looking for her?"

"Yes. That's why I brought her here, Dax."

"But . . . what am I supposed to . . . I mean, who is she even?"

I watched the girl stare off into the distance, twisting the hem of her grubby dinosaur pajamas between her fingers, shuffling her feet. I almost reached out and took her hand, comforted her, but something stopped me. *Strangers*, I reminded myself, *should not be trusted.*

"Don't know," I said. "But she's related to this whole thing somehow, so we'd better keep a close eye on her."

5

I ARRIVED AT DENMARK HILL STATION WITH JUST ONE MINUTE
to spare. A million questions surged through my head as I parked
the car alongside the pavement. Did the kidnapper know what I
looked like, along with everything else he seemed to know about
me? Who was he? Would he come alone? Would Nellie be with
him? What did he want from me? But as I reached the station
entrance, these questions were wiped clean from my mind.

Despite the hour, the place was swarming. Though not with
civilians, I quickly realized. Five uniformed officers—transport
police—were gathered by the entrance, and three marked cars
were parked on the pavement. I ground to a halt and held my
breath, eyes scanning the throng for any sign of Nellie. Had the
person who sent the note done something to draw in the police?

Or . . .

I tried to recall the news story I'd heard back at the hotel—
about some unnamed pedestrian who'd been killed in a hit-and-
run. Was that why the police were here? But why now, if the
incident had happened several days ago? And had it happened at
Denmark Hill station, or somewhere else? I couldn't remember.

Five minutes passed, ten, twenty. I paced back and forth along the pavement, my gaze fixed on the station entrance. But nothing happened. The police remained in situ and the station barricaded off.

No sign of anyone who looked like he was there for a meet-up. No sign of Nellie. Eventually, after nearly an hour and a half of waiting, I gave up. The police's presence must have thwarted the bad man's plans, and the next best course of action seemed to be to drive back to the Ritz and await further instructions.

BACK AT THE hotel, I parked the MG around the corner and rushed up to my room, swallowed a Xanax, and locked the door. For a while I just sat there on the settee, staring blankly ahead, my fingers gripping the edge of my seat. But the longer Nellie and I were separated, the harder it was to pretend I knew what I should do next. Because without Nellie, everything unraveled. Without Nellie's support, I was back on those steps outside my Chelsea apartment, alone, lost, unsure of everything. Without Nellie's friendship, I had no idea who I was.

I swallowed a second Xanax, washed it down with a glass of champagne, but it seemed to make no difference at all. By four a.m., I decided I couldn't sit around and wait another second. I had to do something to get her back or I was toast. We both were.

I picked up the landline and dialed Dax's cell.

"Hey, you all right?" he asked anxiously, answering on the first ring. "Have you talked to the kidnapper yet?"

"No. I went to the station but he wasn't there." I paused, a dreaded thought crossing my mind. What if he'd called off the meeting because I hadn't left Sophia in the hotel bathroom like he'd asked? What if Nellie was . . .

"Crap," Dax said. "Now what?"

"I don't know. I thought maybe he would've left me another note at the hotel. But there's nothing."

"You could wait a bit longer?"

"No," I said sharply. "It's been three hours since we were supposed to meet. Something must've happened. I'll have to go out there and track him down."

"That doesn't seem like a good—"

"Please ask Sophia if she knows where the bad man's house is," I cut in, "the place she said she and her dad visited a few times."

"Mate, it's four in the morning. She's asleep."

"Well, wake her up! This can't wait."

"All right, hold on," he grunted. I heard feet shuffling, muffled voices, a short conversation, lots of sighing and yawning. "She says it was 'a big house somewhere,'" he said when he eventually returned to the phone.

"That's it?"

"Yeah, I mean . . . she's only ten. And half asleep. She doesn't seem to know the street name or area. She says it wasn't far from the Ritz, though. Maybe fifteen minutes by car."

Fifteen minutes from the Ritz in any direction. *Wonderful.* "Right, well, that's not much use."

"She can't give me any names either," Dax added. "I asked again and she just says there was more than one of them. Kidnappers, I mean. Two, apparently, plus her dad, Chris Keeling." He paused as if thinking. "Hey, do you want me to see what I can dig up on him, Chris? I'm not promising I'll find anything, but if I do, it might lead us to the kidnappers and what sort of operation they're running."

"OK," I said, my voice hopeless.

"Cool. I'll get back to you if I find anything."

I sighed and hung up, dropped my head into my hands. "Dead end," I announced to Sir Sebastian glumly. "Now what?"

He looked to the right and whacked his tail against the settee irritably.

I turned my eyes to Nellie's suitcase, still lying where she'd left it, about one cat's tail away from where Sir Sebastian was sitting. I wandered over, sifted through the mess. All her purses, shoes, and dresses were still there, including her favorite ankle-length Armani number that she'd once joked she'd like to be buried in (*no, no, don't think about that*). She'd also left behind her passport, driver's license, spare cash, phone charger, three packs of Marlboro Lights, a half-empty vial of J'Adore perfume, and her eighty-five-quid gold-plated Tom Ford lipstick in blood-drip red. In fact, the only thing missing was her diamond choker / knuckle-duster.

Did I feel any better knowing she had it with her? Maybe. But also . . . no. Despite the tough outer shell she showed the world, Nellie had fears and anxieties, just like I did. It would be easy to assume she strutted around with that choker in her hand to frighten people. That's what she would've wanted you to think, anyway.

NELLIE WAS EIGHTEEN when she met Kade Manson. Right from the start I knew he was trouble. That fickle smile, those roaming hands, the way he looked at me whenever Nellie wasn't around. He was older than her by seven years, had a job in banking, a motorbike, and the kind of swagger you only see in the movies. Broad shoulders, tousled black hair, sharp green eyes, daredevil— he was everything Nellie's indomitable spirit craved.

After less than three weeks of going out, she told me she was in love, and the next thing I knew, she'd moved out of her family home and into Kade's swanky new Canary Wharf town house. We tried to talk her out of it, obviously—me, her parents, Jack. But even the person whose opinion she valued above everyone else's—her beloved great-aunt, the famous pickpocket who'd taught her everything she knew about life—couldn't persuade her otherwise.

So I let her be. We all did. What choice did we have? It wasn't that I'd changed my mind about Kade. But having just started my first year at the University of London, and overwhelmed with the excitement of it all, I'm ashamed to admit I was too busy to spend my time worrying about my best friend's relationships. Besides, Nellie had always been so strong-willed, so absolutely confident in everything she did. I didn't think there was a person on earth who could frighten or manipulate her. Back then, I didn't know it was often the toughest people who were the most afraid.

It started with a cut above her left eyebrow—shallow, split skin, barely visible. I can't remember the excuse she made up— walking into a mirror, tripping on the stairs. But I knew, obviously. Women always know. Next it was a lump at the back of her head, a bruised eye, a broken finger. She started acting oddly, ignoring my calls, making up excuses not to see me, traveling farther and farther down a path I couldn't follow.

Then, one night, three years in, she crawled through my dorm window covered from head to toe in bruises and blood, clutching the diamond choker Kade had tried to strangle her with. Her nose was broken, her jaw dislocated, her left eye swollen beyond recognition. Seeing her like that was one of the worst moments of my life, and as I watched her slump to the floor, withered and broken, a bolt of pain surged through my chest. Like always, what happened to one of us happened to both.

"Code red," she muttered weakly, trembling as I wiped the blood from her lips. But when I picked up the phone to call the police, she stopped me. "Don't," she begged. "Please, Em. If we call the police, he'll know. He'll kill me."

"He'll kill you anyway," I said, terrified because I knew it was true.

She wrapped the choker around her knuckles—the first time I'd seen her do it. "I'm so scared," she admitted. "But I don't want to be."

I thought of telling her then that being scared was normal, that I was scared all the time too, of everything. But Nellie feared fear more than anything else. She was brave, and she was going to prove it—to me, to Kade, to herself. And because I didn't know how to stop her, I decided to help her.

I moved out of my dorm and together we found a cheap two-bedroom flat in the city and signed the lease. While I took classes in math and statistics, cooked our meals, washed our clothes, and cleaned our flat, Nellie sought out the best underground bare-knuckle fighting gym in London and struck a deal: full-time training and in exchange she'd mop the floors, scrub the toilets, and hand over any prize money she won from entering fights. For six straight months she trained, ten hours a day, six days a week. When she wasn't in the gym or pummeling strangers in the ring, she was working as a night-duty cashier at a twenty-four-hour grocer, and when she wasn't at the grocer, she was sprinting hills or lifting weights.

It was supposed to be an emancipation for her, a transformation from victim to aggressor. And, sure, it looked that way. People sidestepped her on the pavement. Boyfriends never stayed long enough to piss her off. She grew a reputation: hard-core, boss bitch, the girl no one messed with. But they didn't see her like I did: tossing in her sleep, nightmares that made her scream, scars that never healed.

PULLED FROM THE memory, I watched Sir Sebastian pace the floor in front of Nellie's suitcase, his fur raised, ears pinned back. For a moment it seemed like he was heading to the window, maybe in the hopes of escaping the grim atmosphere that had fallen like a black veil over our hotel suite. But then he froze, ears pricked, old yellow eyes looking dead straight at the hotel landline, which had just started ringing.

I lurched forward without hesitation, picked up the receiver. Somehow, I already knew.

"Hello?"

Crack, crackle, pause.

"Hello?" I repeated.

After a few seconds, a strained voice answered, barely audible. I pressed the receiver firm against my ear. No small talk, no preamble. "We have to run."

Words prickled at the back of my throat, but all I managed was a useless croak. "W-what? Where are you?"

"We have to leave," she repeated. "My favorite place. ASAP. I'm sorry. I love you."

And the line went dead.

I tried to redial the number, but it must've been blocked or set to private because all I got was a busy signal. Still, I tried again. Same thing. White-knuckling the receiver, I tried to focus, though the room was spinning. It might not have been the clearest line, but there was no doubt: I knew that voice; I'd know it anywhere. For one split second, I was elated. Nellie was alive and able to call me. That meant she must have escaped her kidnapper. Then I put two and two together and realized what I'd just heard her say.

Another one of our secret code phrases. *My favorite place.* MY. M plus Y equals Mong Yang, Myanmar.

Sir Sebastian yowled. He knew. Our Games were over.

6

I PACKED UP OUR SUITCASES IN A FRANTIC PANIC AND CALLED
the hotel front desk to tell them I was cutting short our stay because of a family emergency. Which was true, after all. Nellie
was the only real family I'd ever had.

Before I left the room, I checked Skyscanner for flights from
Heathrow to Yangon, Myanmar. The next one left at 10:05 that
night. Ten hours' flying time, plus a three-hour layover in New
Delhi. All right. No problem. It was 5:50 a.m., which gave me
just under seventeen hours to iron out some last-minute details
and get to the airport. It would be my last day in London, I
knew, because if I left like this, I was never coming back.

Don't think about it.

I picked up the landline and called Dax's cell phone.

"This is Daisy Duck speaking," said a sleepy voice on the
other end, "can I help you?"

"Umm, Sophia?"

"No, it's Daisy Duck."

"Sophia, listen: it's me, Janet."

"Have you seen the bad man yet?" she asked, her interest piqued.

"Not yet. But I'm sure I will soon," I lied. "Where's Dax?" *I need to tell him his life is going to change forever because he's about to adopt a homeless child and an ancient tabby cat.*

"He's in the shower. We're having chocolate chip pancakes for breakfast. I really like him because he's made me feel a bit less scared about everything. He's a good person, I think."

I scoffed at that; I couldn't help it. "Why are you answering the phone, anyway? The bad man's still out there and he's very dangerous. You said so yourself! You've got to be more careful."

"I know. That's why I'm using an alias."

I rolled my eyes. "Just give the phone to Dax! Tell him it's urgent."

I had to wait a total of three minutes and fifty-two seconds for Dax to get out of the shower and pick up the phone. During that time, I was subjected to an impromptu recital from *The Book of Good Advice*, covering everything from accepting unrequited love to how to be vulnerable, all of which just made me even more uncomfortable than I already was. And that's really saying something.

By the time Dax got to the phone, my voice was shaking with a combination of irritation and something else I couldn't name. "Dax, hi," I said stiltedly, momentarily forgetting the purpose of my call. "Where, umm, where are you at the moment? At your flat or the Laundromat?"

"My flat. We moved over here after you left. I didn't think the Laundromat was safe anymore considering—"

"No, that's right, yes, good thinking." I was gripping the receiver tighter than necessary and my mouth had suddenly gone so dry I wasn't sure I'd be able to get another word out. I reached for the opened bottle of Moët and chugged down a mouthful. It was warm and flat but it did the trick. "Listen, Dax, we've got a problem."

"Yeah, mate, you reckon?l Soph's really worried about her dad. She seems to think the kidnappers might've done something to him because she hasn't seen him since last week. I've been trying to dig up intel on him, but I've got exactly zip. Not even a photograph." He paused, then added, "I mean, I guess that makes sense since I don't think he's ever had any social media. Soph keeps saying he has this thing about the internet being evil or whatever. Or, I dunno, maybe I'm just not that good at looking."

I felt a fleeting stab of pity for the child, and even Dax—who was very clearly out of his depth. But, like always, Nellie was my priority. I looked at the looming pile of my belongings stacked near the hotel door. The sight reminded me of the day I walked out on Joel five years earlier. I had no money then, no job, no place to stay, and if it hadn't been for Nellie, I might never have survived what came next. It felt like that now too.

"Nellie and I have to leave town for a bit," I spat out.

"What? You've spoken to her?"

"Yes. She called just now."

"Oh, phew. That's good. So . . . where is she?"

"I don't know exactly, but we'll be meeting up soon."

This was true. I had no idea where Nellie was at that moment, only that she would be meeting me at the Costa in Heathrow International because that, too, was written down in the MY plan, code name *My favorite place*. Page one, paragraph three.

"So, wait, I don't understand," Dax said. "Why exactly do you have to leave town? And where are you going?"

I bit my lip in frustration, knowing I couldn't tell Dax anything about our plans, but also aware that I had to give him some reasonable excuse for why Nellie and I were about to "leave town for a bit," which in fact meant we were about to leave the country. And the continent. For good.

Nellie and I came up with the MY plan a few years ago in the South of France, while sitting on the boot of our MG eating crêpes suzette and sipping orange juice straight out of the bottle. At first it seemed more like one of the crazy childhood schemes we used to cook up whenever either of us got detention at school. My favorite was the one where we'd break into the principal's office, steal money from her safe, food from the cafeteria, buy a train ticket to Dover, and live out the rest of our days wandering the streets of Paris like a couple of French Oliver Twists. But what we discussed on the boot of our MG turned serious when we decided to store ten thousand pounds in a private vault in the center of London, secured with one set of biometrics from each of us—iris scanners and fingerprints. The money, we agreed, would be off-limits for anything other than the detailed escape ploy we'd concocted should there ever come a time when our true identities were uncovered and our lives were at risk. As it turned out, ten thousand pounds was precisely the amount of money needed for two last-minute one-way tickets to Yangon, Myanmar (plus visas), then a ride to the township of Mong Yang, where we had a shifty connection who'd promised to provide us with a pair of fake passports, a couple of cell phones and SIM cards, two wigs, and whatever else one needs to begin a new life in Southeast Asia. But why the township of Mong Yang in Myanmar? Well, can you point it out on a map? Do you know anybody who lives there? Have you heard about those three villagers who are wanted by the militia for dealing fake passports to expats on the run? No? I think that answers your question, then.

"The ransom's too high," I said to Dax, spitting out the only viable excuse I could think of on the spot. "The kidnapper wants money in exchange for Nellie. But it's way too much. Can't afford it. Anyway, none of that matters now because she managed to escape and we've got a chance to run." *Run run run into the hideout of some tiny village where I am told the mosquitoes are about the size of your hand.* "We'll just need to lay low for a few weeks, until this has died down."

"Jesus . . ." Dax murmured, sounding about as terrified as I was feeling.

"All right, so . . . I'm coming over to drop off some money. And the MG. And Sir Sebastian." A car, a cat, some cash, and a child. It really was his lucky day.

"WHAT?!"

"Just lock the doors and don't let anyone inside. Except me, obviously. Like I said, I'm coming over." I then added the phrase generally reserved for moments when all hope is entirely lost. "Don't worry. Everything's going to be fine."

7

I HUNG UP WITHOUT WAITING FOR A REPLY. WITH A SUITCASE
in each hand, my handbag slung over my neck, and Sir Sebastian, spitting like a creature possessed, I padded out into the corridor. It was just after seven in the morning, pouring with rain and gloomy outside. Above me, enormous crystal chandeliers glittered gently, sprinkling flaxen light onto the gilded columns on either side of the twisting staircase that led down to the lobby.

I'd always insisted on maintaining a sense of order and routine in the Games: planning every detail of every con, researching our marks until I knew them better than they knew themselves. And yet here I was, forced to leave all that order behind and step into a life I knew nothing about. It was terrifying, but as I paused at the top of the staircase, not quite sure if I could take the first step down, I remembered something.

It was the spring after Joel, close to Easter, and Nellie and I had just started planning out the details of our new lives as confidence tricksters. Having lost the court case with Joel (surprise, surprise), I was broke and basically unemployable. This new "career path" was, therefore, really and truly all I had left. But while Nellie had been a master pickpocket and grade A liar since the age of eight, I'd only ever watched her from the sidelines. A problem that had to be remedied. "If we're going to do this for a living," Nellie said, "it can't just be me dipping my fingers into pockets. You're going to have to learn too." And who better to teach me the tricks of the trade than the woman who'd taught Nellie, her great-aunt. We called her Gran.

While Gran was Gran to both of us, she wasn't really a gran to either of us. To Nellie she was her real gran's half sister, a brazen Scot who lived alone in a tiny cottage in Edinburgh and survived off the cash she made selling trinkets she'd swindled off people she despised. She swore like a sailor, smoked six packs of cigarettes a day, and had been arrested more times than anyone could recall. To me she was first an obscure legend, someone Nellie spoke about as if she were Robin Hood or a fairy godmother. After that spring in Edinburgh, though, Gran morphed into someone real, a person the new me could aspire to be.

Nellie and I stayed for three months in her cottage (the longest period of company she'd ever had), playing cards and dipper's chess, board games and mind games, doing our best to lighten each other's pockets and tell each other impossible fibs. I'm not sure I was any better at lying or stealing by the end of it, but when Gran got sick, really sick, we had no choice but to call it quits. Gran was dying. She was nearly ninety, her lungs jammed with tar, and her heart tired from a life lived entirely alone. Still, she dreamed of one last adventure before the end: a monthlong road trip across England. Taking the hint, Nellie and I replaced the long-dead battery in Gran's old cherry-red MG, pumped up the tires, rolled down the roof, and hit the road: Nellie at the wheel, me and Gran snuggled up together in the back. For the next thirty days, we hurtled along the Cornish coast, to Land's End, through the Midlands, into London, and back to Edinburgh. We lived on ice cream and beer and greasy fish and chips. We hardly slept, we visited every pub we came across, we flirted with the locals, cried until we laughed, laughed until we pissed ourselves. Gran died one week after we returned to her cottage, warm and cozy in her bed. Her heart, she said, was at last full. Nellie and I lost an irreplaceable piece of ourselves that day, but before Gran closed her eyes that final time, I asked her if she was afraid of death, the horrid uncertainty of it, of not knowing what came next. She flashed me a toothless grin and burst out in a throaty smoker's laugh. "Ah, but all life is uncertain, hen," she said, still giggling at the absurdity of my question, "and all control an illusion. You've just got to learn to be OK with that."

MAYBE SHE WAS right; maybe she wasn't. But what I knew for sure was that trying to control everything life was throwing at me now would be utterly impossible. All I could do was keep moving and hope that I ended up somewhere better. Surely it could only get better. I sucked in a shaky breath and made my way down the staircase.

Despite the early hour, the lobby was already packed with guests dressed in their morning best. I recognized some of the faces—celebrities and influencers, no doubt here for Saturday's Tiffany & Co. gala at the St. Jude gallery.

I pushed my way to the reception desk, handed over enough cash to cover our stay plus an enormous tip, then raced out and onto the street. I marched against the battering rain and icy wind, down Piccadilly, right onto Arlington, left onto Bennet. I paused as I saw her up ahead, our beloved MG, parked on the side of the street, one wheel propped up on the pavement. I stared at her cherry-red coat, dull and lackluster under the rumbling gray sky. I thought of Gran.

I opened the back door, threw in our suitcases, and popped Sir Sebastian into his ridiculously expensive custom-made cat seat. He meowed angrily. "Don't worry," I soothed. "You're going to stay with Dax for a bit. You like Dax, don't you?"

He hissed at that. Fair enough. I straightened, but as I closed the door, I felt something hard press against the small of my back.

I flinched, whipped round.

A tall man with bleached-blond hair, broad shoulders, and close-set eyes was standing in front of me, scowling.

"What?" I snapped, thinking he was just a street dweller trying to lighten my pockets (takes one to know one). Then I noticed the gun.

He raised it to my forehead. "Get in and give me the keys. Make it quick."

I stifled a gasp. "Who are you?" I asked, though I had a sinking feeling I already knew. *Bad man.*

He said nothing and brought the gun closer to my skull. Still, I held my ground while I frantically tried to work out what to do. If I let him take me away, I reckoned the odds of living to see my next sunrise sat at one in six. If, instead, I tried to grab the gun and turn it against him, the odds shot up to something closer to one in three.

But. *But.* Two problems.

One, I wasn't Nellie—a trained fighter capable of the kind of maneuvers necessary to grab anything from anyone. And two, what use was a gun to me anyway? Despite all my years as a professional criminal, I had never once touched a firearm. It just wasn't something Gran had thought to teach me.

"Get in and hand over your keys!" he repeated through gritted teeth while he fumbled to cock the gun.

"OK, all right, just . . . calm down," I said, handing over the keys and wondering if my kidnapper's apparent ineptitude with deadly weapons was something I could use against him. Always get to know them before they get to know you, Gran would say.

We stared at each other for a brief moment, but when my eyes flittered again to the pistol, he snapped back into action, opened the passenger door, and shoved me inside. Next thing I knew we were careering down Bennet Street, the MG screaming in protest. We turned right on Arlington, left onto the A4, back past the twinkling lights of the Ritz, right again and around Hyde Park. I tried to keep track of every turn, in case we ended up in some dingy back alley and I got the chance to leg it. But after we'd passed through Notting Hill, I lost my sense of direction, and when we finally came to a stop on a narrow street alongside a cemetery, I had absolutely no idea where we were.

"Who are you?" I asked again, turning in my seat to face him. He tilted his head, giving nothing away. "What *is* all this?" I asked next, realizing we'd just spent at least a minute studying each other, both apparently surprised by what we were seeing. "What do you want? Money? Surely all that stock you stole from us is enough."

"Nah." He paused a second. "That was just a deposit."

"Deposit for what? And how did you find us?"

"Long story."

"Well, go on. I don't have anywhere to be right now."

He pressed his lips together and scowled.

"You're a hacker or something, aren't you?" I squinted at

him, trying to decide if he looked like a hacker, then realized I'd never actually met a hacker—apart from Dax, I suppose—so how the hell would I know what one looked like?

"You want to know where she is or not?" the hacker asked, ignoring my question.

"Sorry?"

He pulled out a burner phone from his pocket. Our phone, I noted with a shudder.

"Your mate. You wanna know where she is or not?"

My chest tightened. I held my breath. I didn't understand what he meant by that. Nellie had escaped, hadn't she? She was on her way to Heathrow right this second.

"What . . . what have you done to her?" I asked, my voice shaking now.

"Nothing. She's fine, relax. I've no interest in killing either of you," he said flatly. "Not yet, anyway."

"Then, where is she? Tell me right now!"

"I will. But only after you do something for me, yeah?"

I nodded quickly, hoping he wasn't going to follow that up by asking about Sophia. What if he knew I'd let her escape? What if he told me to go back and find her, lock her up? Would I do it to save Nellie?

"Good," he said, grinning in a way that made me wonder if he'd just read my mind. "And by the way, I know who you really are, *Emma*."

I drew in a sharp breath and held it. *Emma.* No one in my new life, except Nellie and Dax, knew me as Emma. And in an instant I felt utterly exposed, as if I were in one of those horrific dreams where you find yourself strolling down a busy street stark naked.

"I also know exactly how you do it," he went on. "I know how you sell your products on Goods Exchange International, how you get your hands on them in the first place. Got to say, I'm impressed. You're the best that platform's ever seen."

It struck me then like a punch to the gut. The chink in our armor, the fatal flaw we'd overlooked: our reputation. We'd spent so much time worrying about being hunted down by the authorities that we'd forgotten to look closer to home. I had always been acutely aware of the risk of entrapment, of some slippery cop posing as a buyer in the hopes of nailing us when we handed over the product. It was why, whenever we sold an item on Goods Exchange, I made triple sure the buyer was legit, a longtime member who'd traded on the platform multiple times and was therefore as much a criminal as we were. But never had it occurred to me that it wasn't just enemies on the outside we had to hide from, but groupies on the inside too.

"You're on the platform." I said, voicing the theory. It wasn't a question, though. The only way he could possibly know what we did and how we did it was if he'd set us up just like a cop would've done. Maybe we'd sold him a Rolex, or a Chopard, or one of those custom Cartier Trinity rings we'd pilfered several weeks ago. Maybe we'd actually met him face-to-face at a handover. Could he have followed us from there, through Paris? Rome? Prague? Could he have been watching us for weeks, tracking us across Europe and back to London? I turned cold at the thought. And yet . . . even if all this were true, it left one question unanswered: How did he know my real name?

I frowned, waiting for him to say something else. Instead he pulled out a printed photograph, one of an expensive-looking bracelet displayed within a polished glass case, and threw it into my lap.

I stared at the bracelet a moment, the cogs of recognition

beginning to turn in the back of my mind. "The Heart of Envy . . ." I muttered, incredulous.

"You've heard of it? Good."

Heard of it! I looked again at the picture, sweat trailing down the back of my neck. For more than ten years, the Heart of Envy had reigned as one of the most coveted pieces in Europe's black-market jewelry trade. The reasons for this were numerous: its high-quality diamonds, painfully rare Colombian emeralds, a long list of famous wearers, and something about a nebulous reputation in bestowing good luck upon all who touched it. Also, I was pretty sure there'd been a pinned listing at the top of Goods Exchange International's buy-and-sell page for the past twelve months—basically a "preorder" for the bracelet. The listing had received something close to four thousand preliminary bids, the highest of which was in the region of sixteen million quid, a staggering price, even by Janet Robinson's standards. So yes, I'd heard of it.

"I assume you know there's a Tiffany exhibition this Saturday night," he went on, taking my silence as an affirmative. "The Heart of Envy will be one of the pieces on display." He paused to realign the gun, pressing it harder against my skull, just in case I'd some-how forgotten it was there. "And you're going to steal it for me."

"Umm, what? Sorry?"

He repeated slowly, "You are going to steal that bracelet from the St. Jude gallery on Saturday."

I let out a hysterical yelp, half laughing, almost crying. "Steal it! Are you *insane*?"

"Not really. Exhibition Month's the reason you're in London anyway, isn't it?"

"Yes, that's true, but we're not here because we're planning to break into the St. Jude gallery and steal one of the most famous bracelets in the world, for goodness' sake! We're here to con the attendees. At their hotels!" He had nothing to say to that, so I decided it was time for a more thorough explanation of the risks. "That exhibition will have impenetrable security. Impenetrable! I'm talking guards, plainclothes officers, high-tech alarm systems, the works. And there'll be press everywhere: journalists, influencers, photographers. The whole of London will be there, and anyone who's not there will be watching the live stream online. It'll be categorically impossible to steal anything from the gallery on that night, but *especially* the Heart of Envy."

It was as if he hadn't heard a word.

"After you've stolen it, you're going to set up a face-to-face street sale with the buyer, Mr. L. You know who that is, I hope."

My eyes widened with horror. In our world, this was much the same as asking if I knew who Beyoncé was (if Beyoncé were the most notorious black-market trader in Europe, with a reputation for murdering approximately fifty percent of her clients).

"Mr. L . . ." I stammered. "But . . . but . . . he's . . . I can't—"

"And when the sale's done, you'll give me the money. Sixteen million. In crypto, secured on a cold wallet. When and if I get my payment, and everything goes nice and smoothly, you'll get to see your mate again. Simple, yeah?"

I tried to take a deep breath but there was such a weight pressing down on my chest that it didn't seem able to expand.

"No," I eventually managed to say. "No no no! Whoever you think I am, whatever you think I do, it isn't *this*. I'm a swindler. I steal jewelry from rich idiots and sell it on the black market. I don't break into art galleries, especially not super-famous ones!"

He gave me a funny look and said the last thing in the world I expected him to say. "Emma, you have no idea what you're capable of. You *can* do this." Then he ruined it by adding, "And you will. Because if you don't, I'm going to kill your mate and then I'm going to kill you." *Tap-tap.* He wrapped his knuckles against the dashboard. "Bang, bang. One bullet each, got it, yeah?" I think I must have nodded or given him some indication that I was agreeing to what he was saying because he went on spiritedly, "So, this is how it's going to go." He dropped the burner phone onto my lap, followed by a piece of paper on which he'd scribbled a name and number: *James Reid +44 8827499270.* "You'll use that number and phone to contact me," he said. "But only if it's urgent. You've got twenty-four hours to come up with a plan to steal the bracelet. We'll be keeping an eye on you the whole time, so if you try to run away, or you try to bump me off, it won't be me you'll have to worry about." He nodded at the left-side mirror. I arched my neck, spotting a silver BMW parked just a few yards away, a burly figure in the driver's seat. "Oh, and by the way, the answer's no."

"W-what?"

"She didn't escape," he said flatly. "She only managed to untie her hands, steal my phone, and make those calls. One to you and one to the transport police, warning them of suspicious activity at Denmark Hill station. I'll be honest," he added with a shrug, "she almost ruined the whole thing. My idiot colleague hightailed it when he saw the police, leaving me to do the dirty work instead. She's a good friend, I guess. Pity you didn't run while you had the chance."

I shook my head, tears now streaming down my face, everything blurred, nothing making any sense at all.

"Twenty-four hours," he repeated coldly as he got out of the car. "That's nine a.m. tomorrow, yeah? I want to know exactly how you're going to pull it off. Convince me you and your mate are worth keeping alive."

8

AFTER JAMES REID HAD LEFT, I MADE SEVERAL PATHETIC AT-tempts to put the MG into gear and start the engine. But as it rumbled to life and I pulled off to nowhere in particular, a shiny silver car flashed its headlights in my rearview mirror—a painful reminder of the predicament I now found myself in.

I considered trying to lose the thuggish bastard, but somehow the idea seemed too ludicrous to pull off. I wasn't a very good driver at the best of times (Nellie was; *oh, Nellie*), and the MG didn't have the kind of acceleration I'd need to pull away and lose him in the London traffic. So instead I parked on the side of some deserted pavement and turned off the engine. As expected, my tail drew up alongside me and wound down his window. He was terrifyingly buff, with long black hair in a ponytail, several lip piercings, and a scar across his forehead.

"Where's the girl?" he asked in a low growl.

I gulped. This was exactly the question I'd been dreading. "I don't know," I said, trying to keep my voice steady. "She came to my room, gave me the note, and ran."

"I told you to lock her up!"

"You? But I thought it was Reid who—"

He whipped out a handgun and aimed it at my head, suggesting I should speak when spoken to. "Where's the damn girl?" he repeated.

"I . . . I said I don't know."

He watched me closely for a moment, as if trying to make up his mind about something. "All right, missy, how about this: you don't tell Reid she's escaped, I won't blow your brains out. We got a deal?"

I nodded dully as he moved off, only half-aware of what he'd just said, or what I'd agreed to. Outside, a group of women strolled along the pavement, chittering, arms linked. One of them looked at me, blinked, then turned away. Absently, I picked up the burner phone James Reid had returned to me and opened my contact list. There were only four numbers saved: Dax, Errol (our car mechanic), and our two emergency contact numbers. Nellie's was her brother, Jack, who now lived in Amsterdam. Mine, bizarrely, was my mother.

I didn't want to admit it, but the truth was . . . I needed to talk to someone, if not for advice, then just for comfort. But with Gran gone and Nellie out of the picture, my options were scant. It was in moments like this that I suffered the side effects of my guarded life most acutely and was forced to accept the vastness of my loneliness, how far it stretched out before me, a lifeless desert of rolling hills and endless sky, where the hope of finding solace seemed so small it was almost stupid trying.

Fighting the tightness in my chest, I scrolled through my contacts, crossing off options as I went: the thought of calling Dax *yet again* made me sick for a number of reasons I probably don't need to point out. Then there was Jack. But what was the point of involving him when he lived so far away? Also, Nellie was as protective of him as he was of her, and I knew she wouldn't want me to put him through the trauma of such a phone call unless absolutely necessary. So, in a daze of desperation and utter stupidity, I dialed my mum.

The call went unanswered, which I suppose was a good thing, because what in God's name would I have said if she'd picked up? My parents had no idea what I did for a living, that I was a con artist and went by a different name. I hadn't spoken to either of them in more than five years, not since my separation from Joel. I *had* tried, though—to call them, to reconnect, hopeful my childhood memories of their indifference toward me were a reflection of my own insecurities rather than reality. But I was wrong, and even in my darkest hour, when the police handed me that court summons, they'd looked the other way. It was abundantly clear then, as it had been my whole life: we were linked by coiled strands of DNA and nothing more.

I chucked the phone into the glove compartment and sank down in my seat, wondering what Reid must think of me now, the con artist extraordinaire, nothing more than a quivering mess.

IN THE DISTANCE, I heard the low rumble of the Overground. I pictured a train zipping from Kensal Green to Wembley Central, a route I knew all too well. And for one horrid split second, I felt like I was back in my old life, trudging off to work in my bright polo sweater and pencil skirt, a briefcase of costing documents under my arm and an almond milk latte in my hand.

After Nellie's stint at the boxing gym, she quit her job at the twenty-four-hour grocer and landed a position at Selfridges while I continued to battle endless lectures on statistics and mathematics. We lived together in our cramped two-bedroom flat in Kensal Green with its leaking toilet, cranky heating, and paint literally peeling from the walls. Still, we made it our own. I adorned the place with fairy lights and Nellie stuffed the shelves with smiling Buddhas, sticks of incense, miniature gongs and bells, and singing bowls. We ate dinner together nearly every night—sometimes Jamie Oliver concoctions we'd spend hours attempting to perfect, usually frozen ready-made meals from Tesco. After dinner we'd curl up on our tatty sofa, watch reruns of *Dawson's Creek*, or play games to keep each other sharp, flip through trashy magazines, drink cheap wine, and dream of a future where we'd travel the world and meet fascinating men who spoke a language we didn't understand. Deep down, though—like our childhood fantasy of living on the streets of Paris—I knew it wasn't ever going to happen. Not for me, anyway. Sure, I wanted us to stick together, like always. But the way I saw it, my fate was already sealed. I was a student, and soon I would become a working adult with a normal life and a nice house, a husband, and three beautiful children.

But for Nellie the dream never died, and on my last day of university, knowing I'd settled on the idea of staying in London, she told me she was leaving, anyway. Europe, Asia, South America. A solo backpacking trip with no set return date. I can still remember the day we said good-bye, sitting in our flat with a bottle of wine, boxes piled up all around us, fairy lights extinguished, Edward Sharpe's "Home" playing in the background. I cried at the words because they were so achingly true. Yes, I'd make friends at work like I'd made friends at university. Easy friends, drinking friends, friends who sort of knew me and sort of didn't, friends I'd try too hard to please. But no one would ever replace Nellie or fill the hole she'd left gaping. Nowhere would ever feel like home without her.

Still, I told myself things would be fine. Both of us needed a change, to follow our own paths and take from life what we most wanted. For Nellie that was freedom and a sense of independence. For me it was what everyone else my age seemed to want: a job to hate and a man to love. So, top achiever that I was, I nailed a double bullseye by landing an actuarial position at Green Fields Insurance Firm and getting engaged to Joel Beck, director of the company.

It was like a scene from a rom-com, the moment we met. I burst into the office on my first day, a box of things clamped under my arm, and walked straight into Joel's perfectly broad chest. As my box of things flew all over the floor, Joel placed a hand over mine, smiled, and introduced himself. Never had I seen eyes the color of his, burned gold flecked with green, or a smile as enigmatic as his. I couldn't speak, or think clearly, and yet I knew, right then, that this was the man I should marry. Whatever it took.

And even when the tedium of life took over, and the hours became long and meaningless—a blur of daily numbers, lunch, tea, train home, eat, sleep, repeat, all without Nellie—I surged ahead without complaint. Joel was the type of man who had no time for negativity or self-pity, or people who "dimmed his aura." He meditated daily, took two-hour Bikram yoga classes and cold showers, ate clean. All I had to do to get him to like me, I realized, was be happy, upbeat, and relentlessly positive. Even if it killed me. Namaste. And after a while it seemed I'd aced it. Things were going well on all fronts, even better than I'd hoped. I made friends at work, Joel professed his undying love for me, and on a balmy evening in July, sitting on the roof of our Chelsea apartment with a bottle of champagne and a plate of oysters, he proposed on bended knee. This seems tragically pitiful to say in hindsight, but at the time it really was the happiest moment of my life. No comparison. Everything I'd ever dreamed of was at last coming true: Prince Charming, the Ring, the White Dress, the Big Wedding, the Perfect Life. All mine. All real.

But of course, none of that was true. And so when Nellie came back and offered me the opportunity to change my life and start again, I jumped headfirst into her world, hoping I could belong there, a place where rules were made to be broken and freedom was a state of mind. I cast aside my old identity, along with my fears and insecurities. Rising from the ashes, I was reborn. And up until now, I'd been so sure that rebirth was a permanent one. I had changed: boarded up my windows, locked the door, and tossed the key. I wanted more than anything to be the person Reid thought me to be—the confident swindler, the brilliant con artist, the unflappable puppet master.

But now, with Nellie gone again, something snapped inside me. Accompanied with a flash of terror, I realized: the mask had slipped. And all the emotions I'd buried came rushing up, drowning me.

9

I FLINCHED AT THE SOUND OF A CAR DOOR OPENING, JOLTING me from my reverie. I peered in the rearview mirror to see Reid's thug shuffling around in the back seat of his BMW. A minute or two later, he moved to the boot to retrieve something that looked distinctly like a heavy-duty body bag, about my size.

I dropped my head into my hands and sobbed quietly while Sir Sebastian yowled from his cage in the back seat. Not only was the idea of escaping to Myanmar on my own unthinkable, but physically, practically, it was nearly impossible now. Reid's thug was monitoring my every move, making it highly unlikely I'd be able to get all the way to Heathrow and onto a plane without being shot. And even if I did manage to pull that off, Nellie wouldn't be coming along with me, so what was the point?

Whichever way I looked at it, running was no longer an option. I had to stay and do this, however dangerous or impossible that seemed. But as I glanced again in the rearview mirror, not entirely sure who I saw looking back—Emma or Janet or a person split cleanly in two—I wondered if, maybe, stealing the Heart of Envy was not just about saving Nellie's life, but about restoring the balance in mine. And if I was going to do both, I had to pull myself together and channel whatever remained of the coolheaded swindler I'd worked so hard to become.

I lifted my head, wriggled in my seat, the spark of an idea flickering in my mind. But before I did anything else, I had to make double sure Reid was telling me the truth about two things: Nellie was alive and she hadn't escaped.

I retrieved the scrap of paper he'd given me, along with my burner phone, and dialed his number.

"This better be urgent," he said through a crackling line.

"I'll do it," I said. "But I have one condition."

"Forget it."

"I need to see Nellie," I went on, ignoring his refusal.

"No."

I felt for a minute like caving, then remembered what was at stake if I did. "You can't expect me to believe she's alive just because you say so. I have to see for myself. I need proof."

"I'm not up for negotiations. You'll have to take my word for it."

I shook out my hands, chewed the inside of my cheek. If Reid had been a regular mark in a regular Game (and I hadn't been so unhinged), I would've known exactly what to say to get my way. I knew how to deal with men like him. I knew how to play them, how to control their thoughts and influence their decisions. At least Janet Robinson did. I closed my eyes and thought of Gran.

Fake it, hen, I heard her whisper in my mind. *He'll never know.*

I nodded to myself. "Proof," I repeated sternly into the phone. "Or the deal's off. Your choice."

Several seconds slipped by, neither of us saying a thing.

Doubt coiled in my stomach. Dread too. But I held my tongue, faking it as long as I dared. *For Nellie*, I told myself.

"All right, fine," he said at last, and I let out a silent breath. "My colleague will take you to see her in five. But remember: if you try anything heroic, she's dead. And so are you."

IT WAS A considerably long while later when Reid's thug threw me in the back seat of his BMW and started driving. During the high-speed journey to wherever we were going, I wondered if the spade and body bag lying on the seat next to me were about to be put to good use or if we really were going to see Nellie.

"Out!" the thug yapped as we pulled up at a converted warehouse in Wapping, East London, somewhere just off the main road.

Gingerly, I climbed from the car. It was still a dreary, cold day. Seagulls screeched overhead, and the stench of sewage hung in the air—matching my mood perfectly.

"You've got five minutes," he said. "No tricks. Understand?"

I nodded obediently as he shoved me along a short concrete track toward the looming warehouse, then paused outside a large reinforced iron door, sealed shut with several dead bolts. He knocked three times, and the door creaked open. A tall, slim figure appeared at the threshold, cast in shadow, his face mostly obscured. A second thug?

I stumbled inside, a light flickered on, revealing the cavernous grim interior of a vast warehouse filled with broken, rotting furniture and stacks of wooden crates. The entire place reeked of urine and drying sweat and some other horrid stench I couldn't name.

I forgot it all when I saw her.

Nellie was sitting—blindfolded—tied to a chair with several cords of thick gray rope. Duct tape had been strapped across her mouth and around her ankles, her hands bound in her lap. Her once sleek satin trouser suit was stained, frayed, and creased, her golden hair streaked with grease and muck. A sunbird in a rusted cage. All wrong.

"Keep your distance," the thug with the lip rings said as I took an automatic step forward, my eyes welling.

"I want to speak to her, at least," I demanded, nodding at Nellie's gag. "And take off her blindfold."

The thugs passed each other a look, smirking. The one with the lip rings ripped the duct tape from her mouth.

"Blindfold stays on," he said. "Don't push your luck."

"Nell!" I said as she doubled over, spluttering, wheezing. "It's me, I'm here." I noticed her hands then, bound together in her lap, her fingernails red and raw. Not since Kade had I seen her pick them to the quick like that. "I'm so sorry it took me this long to find you. I'm *so* sorry. Are you all right? Have they hurt you?"

She turned her head from side to side, trying to follow my voice. My chest tightened.

"What's going on?" she asked. "What are you—"

"I'll explain later, I promise." I took a tiny step forward. No one seemed to notice.

"What are you doing here?"

"I came to see if you were . . . well, to see if you're OK. I was so worried, Nell. I thought maybe—"

"I told you to *run*," she whispered angrily, cutting me off. "I called the hotel. I said our code. Why didn't you run? I even bought you time. The police, the station . . . You're an idiot for coming here!"

I couldn't help but smile at that. She looked broken, almost as bad as the night Kade had tried to kill her. But it was still there inside her, the fire, the fight. And, like always, her courage became mine.

"I'm very mad at you," she snapped.

I smiled again. "And I'm very mad at *you*."

She huffed. "Mad at me? For what?"

"For leaving the hotel without telling me," I said. "For leaving the shower running so I wouldn't follow you. For telling me to go to Myanmar without you. But mostly . . . for caring about my life more than your own."

"You'd have done the same," she said, her voice softer. "You're doing it right now by being here."

"So we're both fools, then."

She looked as if she wanted to smile but was too weak to do it. "I just . . . he threatened you when he called, said he knew where we were staying and that he'd kill you if I didn't come out to meet him straightaway. Alone. It was a trick, obviously, but at the time I thought I had no choice." She paused a moment. "He knows everything. *Everything.* Even our real names. I don't understand it. Bastard!" she hissed before I could reply. "If I'd been sure he was working alone, I would've knocked his lights out. I could've taken him if it were just the two of us, but he said he had someone who was watching you too."

"I know," I said. "He's using us against each other. We're no use to him as individuals. He needs us both. He needs leverage." I stared at the grim brick wall behind her, silent tears streaming down my face, coupled with an odd sense of comfort at the thought that—as ever—we were in this together. Because that's what best friends are, if you really think about it: strangers who decide to face life together, for better or worse.

"I heard them talking last night," Nellie went on, her voice so low now I could barely hear her. "I don't know what they've got going on here. Some kind of ransom exchange business, I think. But if they don't get what they want, they kill. Just like that. No questions asked. We're not their first either." She rotated her neck a fraction to the left. "Eight o'clock, I think. Under the sheet."

I glanced in the direction she'd indicated—a shadowy recess in the corner of the warehouse—and at first saw nothing. But as I focused harder, I noticed a lump, human-sized, covered by a large tarpaulin.

"W-what's that?" I asked, my voice a high whisper. It was a stupid question, though. I could *smell* it.

"You met the girl, I suppose," Nellie said. "The one that idiot sent to coax you out of the hotel."

"Yes . . ." I took a quick breath. "Her father works for Reid too. That's what she said."

"Works for him? No, I don't think he did. He was here be-fore me, held against his will. Kidnapped for ransom. That's what it sounded like anyway."

"And now he's . . ." I gulped, turning away from the tarpaulin–cum–body bag.

She nodded. "He wasn't covered when they brought me in. And you can smell it, I guess. Definitely dead."

Bile swirled around in my mouth. I gagged and swallowed it back down, trying very hard not to think about Sophia or how on earth I was going to tell her any of this.

Nellie moved in her seat, shifting her weight from left to right. "So? How much is it, *my* ransom?" she asked. "Now that you're here, we'll have to figure out a way to pay it."

"Reid and I have come to an agreement."

"What sort of agreement?"

"Long story," I said. "But first, I'm going to get you out of here. I promise."

Her lips parted, head cocked. Even with her eyes covered, she could tell I was omitting something.

And, of course, I was. Several things.

PART II

10

AS SOON AS THE THUGS DROVE ME BACK TO THE MG AND I BE-
gan to strategize, to puzzle out a solution to Reid's demands, I
felt the tiniest trickle of Janet Robinson seep back into my veins.
And while I felt as though I was walking through a haze, like I'd
just emerged from a horrible nightmare and was still trying to
sift through what was real and what was an illusion, I knew
there was no longer anywhere to go but forward. Impossible as
it seemed, I had to keep moving—albeit blindly—until I came
out the other side. *Embrace the uncertainty, hen,* Gran would say.

So, without giving myself a chance to change my mind, I
scratched around in the glove compartment for a pen and paper
and did what I did best: got organized.

First, I wrote down a list of questions that needed answers:

1) St. Jude Gallery. How to get in?

2) Payment. Crypto cold wallet?

3) How to get rid of bad men?

4) The sale. When/Where?

5) Mr. L?

I rolled my shoulders and started with question number one. How on God's green earth was I going to break into one of the most famous art galleries in the country on the night of one of the most prestigious invite-only events in the world? Nellie and I might've been admired for our confidence tricks and general criminal prowess, but that wasn't because we knew how to bypass security systems and pick locks. When we wanted to get in somewhere—a fancy-pants members-only clubhouse, for instance—we just walked in. Easy-peasy. No fuss. Gran called it tailgating, but all we really did was smile and follow someone legitimate through the entrance (you'd be surprised how many people even held the door for us). As a matter of fact, the only time we'd ever come close to breaking into anywhere was four years ago in Rome, when we conned a well-meaning security guard into allowing us access into the Colosseum after closing hours on Christmas Day. I can't remember exactly why we chose to spend the holiest of nights freezing our tits off in a crumbling amphitheater, but just one glance at the dazzling winter sky above Rome, an ancient galaxy illuminated by a million stars an impossible distance away, and I knew it was worth it. The security guard seemed to agree when we handed him our VIP tour tickets, complete with identification cards and QR codes, which of course he forgot to scan after we'd distracted him with a long story about the last time we'd done this tour and how much we'd loved it (we've done this before so we're obviously legit, get it?). After we'd passed through the gates, we cracked open a bottle of prosecco, laid out a cashmere blanket in the middle of the amphitheater, and spent the night counting stars, dancing and drinking and singing Taylor Swift at the top of our lungs, leaving only when the security guard finally got around to scanning our invites and realized they were, in fact, Canva fakes.

Something as simplistic as a fake invitation would never work for the *Serenity and Splendor* exhibition, given its tight security, but at the same time, I knew from experience that the more complicated you made the con, the higher your chance of getting caught.

"OK, so," I said out loud, eyeing Sir Sebastian through the rearview mirror, "what if, instead of using a fake invitation, I use a real invitation for a fake person?" He gave me a rare nod of approval. I scribbled down the idea on my notepad.

Satisfied, I moved on to question number two: payment.

James Reid had said in no uncertain terms that he needed the money from the bracelet sale paid to him in crypto. He'd also said he wanted it on a cold wallet. Going on what Dax had once told me, a cold wallet was a USB-like device with no internet connection used for storing crypto security keys. Cold wallets were supposedly safer than cloud-based "hot" wallets because they were nearly impossible to hack. You didn't have to be a genius to figure out that if Reid wanted his payment in this form, it meant he was super paranoid about the whole transfer process. This was great news for me because paranoid people make mistakes.

I ticked off the question and moved on to number three, the question that—without doubt—required the most careful consideration: *how to get rid of bad men.* In other words: How would I make sure Reid kept his side of the bargain and released Nellie once the heist was done? I'd been involved in the seedy criminal underworld for long enough to know that people who broke the law for a living were generally not the sort you could rely on to keep their word. Take me and Nellie, for example. But it wasn't just personal experience I was going on now. I thought back to the man lying stone-dead under the tarpaulin in Reid's warehouse— Chris Keeling, Sophia's dad. Something told me Nellie and I had a high probability of ending up the same way if I didn't put some measures in place to ensure our safety. Like, I don't know, load Reid and his friends into the back of a van and drive them off the edge of a cliff (that was a joke). But seriously, even if my heist plan went exactly the way I imagined, Reid and the thugs would still be a problem. I had to figure out a way to incapacitate them. But how do you incapacitate someone without killing them? I'd have to mull that one over.

Onto question number four: *the sale.*

Setting up a face-to-face sale with the notorious Mr. L, who was—as far as I knew—based in Europe's capital of black-market diamond trading, Antwerp—gave me the shivers right down to my bones. Could I really trust Mr. L to set up a cold wallet loaded with crypto keys to the value of sixteen million pounds? What if he just snatched the bracelet and shot me on the spot? The more I thought about it, the riskier the whole thing seemed to become.

For ten years, Mr. L had peddled deals all across the world— from Antwerp and Bangkok to Miami and Johannesburg— puppeteering an entire network of the darkest, foulest criminals you could ever imagine and becoming a multimillionaire in the process. He was considered the best in the business, and by that I mean he would rip out your guts if he so much as caught a whiff of betrayal or misdirection. In other words, he made Reid and the thugs look like a bunch of wimpish rabbits in comparison.

So I guess you could say I was terrified of having anything to do with him.

Unless . . .

I drummed my fingers against the steering wheel. A wild, dangerous theory floated across my mind, sparking terror and excitement in equal measure. Would it work? Was it worth the risk? I drew a line connecting question number three to question number five and turned in my seat. Sir Sebastian squinted at my notepad for a second, then stuck his nose in the air and let out an ear-splitting meow, which I wasn't too sure how to interpret. Possibly he thought I'd gone mad. Possibly he was right.

But as the minutes ticked by and the idea took shape, I really did start to believe I could make it work. There was just one *tiny* problem . . .

I chewed my thumb in frustration, trying to see a way around what I had to do next. Involving Dax, which I invariably had to do, made me squirm. I didn't want to bring danger down on anyone else's head. Also, if I involved Dax, I involved Sophia, and why was the idea of seeing her making me so uncomfortable? *Because she sees right through you*, a voice in my head whispered.

"Whatever," I snapped out loud. "If I can deal with Reid and his thugs, I can deal with Dax and his ten-year-old friend. Surely. OK, so, I'll first need to meet with Dax someplace close." I opened the glove compartment and pulled out an old London street map (my burner phone didn't have any GPS capabilities so it was back to the old-school ways). "It'll have to be somewhere I have a legitimate reason to visit alone or the thugs will get suspicious, won't they?" Sir Sebastian's left eye twitched. "Keep it simple, you're right! I'll just meet him at his flat in Warwick

Mansions. Right. OK. Warwick Mansions is on Cromwell Crescent, which is two miles from here. Too far to run. But what if I parked just a little closer, somewhere that wouldn't cause any suspicion . . . like"—I continued to scan the map—"YES!" I slammed the dashboard in jubilation. "Perfect. All right, Seb, we've got a plan. A good one." I reached over to the back seat, opened one of my suitcases, and pulled out the first outfit I could lay my hands on—a dull brown maxi-dress, large-brimmed sun hat, and blond wig. "Now, cover your ears, Seb," I said, "and hold tight."

I pressed my hands down on the MG's hooter and didn't relent until I heard a tap at my window.

"What the hell you doing?" snarled the main thug (the burly one with the lip rings).

"I wanted to ask you something," I answered with a weak smile, which he did not return. "What's your name, by the way?"

He stared at me, saying nothing. Fair enough. His beady eyes skimmed over my round, freckled face and settled on my generous bust.

Self-consciously, I pulled my coat closed across my chest and went on in a mumble, "I've got to take a drive to the shops in a minute," I said. "Just thought I'd let you know."

He pointed at the corner shop across the street. "Take a walk, rather."

"No. I need a proper shop."

He shot me a confused look. "Like?"

"Like a Tesco superstore. There's one two miles away near Earl's Court. It's the closest."

"Why do you need to go to a Tesco when—"

"Organic cotton super-plus tampons are the only ones I don't react to," I blurted out, the first thing that came to mind. It was definitely not the sort of thing Janet would've said (too personal, you understand), but I just didn't have the time or energy to come up with something better.

A strange look came over the thug's face—the same ill-disguised disgust I'd seen a few times on Joel's face whenever he was confronted with the realities of female anatomy. I figured I was onto something.

"And they're only sold at Tesco superstores," I went on, feeling encouraged. "Last time I used normal tampons I broke out in hives. Like, everywhere. I also need a pack of intimate wipes because I haven't had a shower in twenty-four hours and my vag—"

"OK. Fine!" the thug snapped, turning a worrying shade of green. "Jesus. You can go to the damn Tesco. But I'm coming with you."

I was about to wind up the window and drive off when I sensed an opportunity to gather some vital information. "Sorry, one more thing . . ."

He turned around, lips sucked in, eyes narrowed to slits.

"I was just thinking . . . won't Reid have a problem with this shopping trip?"

Wouldn't want to get anyone in trouble, would I? In order to plot out the finer details of how I'd outsmart Reid and his friends, I needed to understand the mechanics of this unholy alliance. Who were these two thugs following me around every second of the day, and what was their purpose in life? Judging by the "deal" this lip-ring thug and I had made earlier concerning Sophia's whereabouts, I got a feeling Reid was the head honcho and he'd have no problem killing anyone if they slipped up. But I had to make sure.

The thug rubbed a lip ring between his fingers and gave me an uninterested shrug. "Nah, he won't," he said blandly. "He doesn't care what you do, as long as you don't run away and as long as you get him that bracelet by Saturday."

"And what about your mate over there?" I nodded at the BMW and the shrinking figure in the passenger's seat.

He waved me off, then strolled back to the BMW, mumbling over his shoulder, "Just get on with it, woman."

Right. So. The hierarchy went something like this: Reid at the top of the pack, just as I had suspected. He was the one in charge of the grand ransom ploy and general mechanics of the whole thing, including whether or not Nellie and I were going to live to see the end of the week. Thug number one was second-in-command. Let's call him Boss Thug. He carried the gun. He drove the BMW. And he was probably in charge of making sure I didn't escape like Sophia had done. Finally, there was thug number two. The underling. The tagalong figure in the passenger's seat who looked like he'd rather be anywhere else.

Pity I didn't see it then, the two who were masquerading as someone else, just the same as I was.

11

ABOUT HALF AN HOUR LATER, I PULLED UP OUTSIDE THE TESCO superstore in Earl's Court.

"All right, Seb," I said, lowering him carefully into my handbag. He meowed and tried to claw his way free. "Just calm down, please," I urged, holding him still the best I could. "I need you to stay quiet for the next five minutes. Just five minutes!" He howled again, raised his gangly paw, and started swiping at the air but aiming for my eyes. "Look, I get it. You're tired and hungry and you miss Nellie. I know how you feel. *God*, do I know."

He lowered one paw, then the other. Taking a gamble, I stroked the grizzly fur between his ears until he relaxed, just like Nellie had done the day we'd found him wandering aimlessly along a highway in Budapest, soaked to the bone and as thin as a twig. He'd attached himself to Nellie right away, like everyone did when they met her, but had never really taken a liking to me. Was I trying too hard, or not hard enough? It was always so difficult to tell.

At last he began to purr, curled into a ball at the bottom of my bag, and nestled his head in my wig. I zipped the bag almost all the way shut and climbed out of the car.

I'd hardly taken a step when Boss Thug leaped out of the BMW and yanked me backward.

"Straight in and out," he growled. "Understand? Just remember what's at stake if you run."

As if I could forget. "I need to use the bathroom too," I said, "so I'll be a while."

"I said in and out. No funny business and no—"

Again, he left me no choice. "Have you ever tried to put a tampon in while sitting in a car? It can be done, don't get me wrong, but there's a chance I'll get blood all over—"

He cut me off with a revolted grunt. I nodded, ripped my arm free, and marched toward the Tesco entrance, my handbag clutched tightly to my chest and a small smile on my lips.

IT TOOK ME less than ten minutes to find the bathroom, change into the dull brown maxi-dress, large-brimmed sun hat, and blond wig, and march back through Tesco's swinging doors, around the block, and over to Warwick Mansions. Boss Thug and his friend actually looked me right in the eye as I left the store. I've said it before and I'll say it again: being unremarkable has its perks.

Reaching Dax's flat, I hesitated just a second, then rang the bell for 708 three times in rapid succession.

A muffled voice came through the intercom. "Who's there?"

"Dax, open up." I saw the miniature lens of the security camera flicker on, then remembered the wig and hat. I considered leaving them in place, comforted by the disguise they rendered. But who was I kidding? I ripped them off and repeated into the intercom, "It's me. Open up, quick."

The door buzzed and, after checking over my shoulder, I marched up the stairs and to his front door.

It opened on my first knock.

"About time!" Dax said, sounding vaguely angry, vaguely relieved. He was dressed in slacks and a loose-fitting white shirt. He smelled of soap and musk. I tried not to let it get to me. "Where've you been? We thought you'd—" His eyes popped as he looked down at the ridiculous wig and sun hat I still had clutched under my arm.

"Can't be long," I said, avoiding his eye. "Got to get back in five minutes."

"Back where?"

"Tesco. Long story."

He shook his head and groaned. "I thought you were coming straight here from the Ritz. It's been nearly five hours. What happened?"

"Sorry. Yes," I said as he guided me into the flat, both of us crab-walking through the door to avoid touching each other. "I, eh . . . ran into some trouble."

I'd only been inside this place—Dax's actual living quarters—on one other occasion, and I'm pleased to share that I did nothing remotely embarrassing that time. Not that I could remember, at least. The flat was sprinkled with mismatched secondhand furniture (including a well-worn gaming chair in faded red leather), the walls plastered with *The Matrix* movie posters, and every inch of available table space littered with how-to books (*Computer Hacking for Dummies*, *The Web Application Hacker's Handbook*, *Programming for Hackers*). It was like being inside a teenage boy's dream.

Dax noticed me staring at the array of texts and explained,

sheepishly, as if I'd caught him with a collection of porn magazines, "Just been trying to figure some stuff out, for the, you know . . ."

Before I could reply to that, Sophia burst into the room, dressed in a brand-new outfit—cream trousers and a beige shirt with an enormous dinosaur printed on the front. T. rex, at a guess.

"I'm so happy you're back!" she shrieked delightedly. "We thought you were lost. Or dead as a doornail!"

Dax nodded. "Yeah, we really did. Dead as a doornail."

"We even checked the book for advice," Sophia added seriously, glaring up at me like I'd caused her far too much worry for one day. "But it doesn't have anything about how to find a missing friend."

Did she just say "friend"? I risked a glance at Dax for confirmation. I think he might've given me a nod.

"I made something for you," she continued briskly, plucking a folded piece of paper from her pocket and handing it over. "It's a drawing of Daddy, just so you know what he looks like. I gave one to Dax, too, for when he goes out looking for him."

Dax rubbed his temples despondently.

"Ah . . . oh," I said, unfolding the paper to find a line of labeled stick figures holding hands: me, Dax, "The Friend" (who I assumed was Nellie), Sophia, and "Daddy" (who was more elaborately drawn than the rest of us and appeared to be wearing a cape and had what looked like a medal hanging around his neck). "Why am I twice as big as everyone else?" I asked, squinting at the oversized figure marked "Janet."

"Because you're the boss," Sophia answered simply.

"Huh . . ." I wasn't sure what to make of that. "And what's this in my hand?" It looked like a dinner plate with hair.

"That's your mask," she said humorlessly, turning her eyes to the ceiling in contemplation, which I hoped meant she didn't see the burn in my cheeks. "You've taken it off, but you still carry it around. Just in case."

I lapsed into a stunned silence for several seconds, then shoved Sophia's drawing into my purse and vowed to forget about it. "A-anyway," I stammered, clearing the lump from my throat. "I have something for you too." I shifted aside Dax's hacking books, lowered my handbag onto the dining table, and—like a magic trick—pulled out a purring Sir Sebastian.

Sophia yelped with glee, grabbed the cat from my arms, and kissed him all over his scrawny head. "Good day to you, sir," she said with a weird, deep voice. "How are you?"

Sebastian licked her hand cheerfully and rubbed his head against her chin.

"Can we keep him?" Sophia asked, looking up at Dax with pleading eyes.

"No," he said.

"Yes," I said. "For now, anyway. If you don't mind?"

Dax ran a hand through his hair, looking like he did mind quite a bit. "I've kinda got a lot to deal with here . . ."

"I can't wait to show Daddy!" Sophia beamed, lowering Sir Sebastian to the floor. "He loves cats!" She looked directly at me when she said it, her wide eyes like orbs, boring into my soul, seeing everything. "Now that you know what Daddy looks like," she added, "you'll be able to find him, won't you?"

"I, er, I don't . . . I'm not sure." I averted my eyes as I tried not to think about the lump under the tarpaulin. It didn't work, of course, because the facts were so terribly plain. Sophia's dad was dead, and now she had no one. No mother, no aunts, uncles, grandparents, siblings. Did that make me, Nellie, and Dax the only people in her circle? I really, *really* hoped not, for all our sakes.

Dax turned to Sophia and reassured her easily, "Of course we will, Soph, just give us a moment to talk now, OK?" But once she'd trotted off to the kitchen to pour herself a glass of juice, he lowered his voice, gestured to the books strewn around us, and said, "I've tried everything to find him and still got nothing. I called the shelter Sophia and her dad used to stay at but they wouldn't give me any info on past residents. I even tried to hack their files, but all I got was a record saying a Chris and Sophia Keeling had stayed there from August last year to February this year—" He broke off, frowning at the look on my face, sensing something. "What?"

I shook my head sadly. "You're not going to find him, Dax. Not even Edward Snowden could. He's gone."

"Gone? Like, left the country or something?"

"No, gone like . . . like dead."

Dax froze.

"His body was at the warehouse," I explained quickly. "I *saw* it."

"But . . . what, you mean—"

"They killed him. Yes. I don't know why. Something about him not doing what they asked. At least that's what Nellie thinks."

Dax puffed out his cheeks, put his hands on his head, and started pacing in front of me. "Ah, man. Shit, *shit*. That's rough. Poor kid!"

He stopped pacing, turned to me. "How are we supposed to tell her that? She's already had a mother walk out on her, and she's so convinced her dad's alive. She literally mentions him every five minutes."

"We lie," I said reflexively. "Say we don't know where he is."

"How's that a good idea?"

It was a good idea because it was the best we could offer her. If we lied, Sophia would be spared the pain of losing her father, which meant she'd get to live a little longer in that warm, comfy place where the people you loved most never left you and your heart was unbreakable.

"Just trust me. It is," I said shortly, as my nerves began to prick. *I need to get the hell out of here!* "Anyway, Sophia isn't the reason I needed to see you." I opened my handbag again and pulled out the photo Reid had given me in the MG. "I need you to forward this to Jen," I said, referring to the shiftiest and most corrupt jeweler this side of the Atlantic, Gran's longtime "colleague," whom she'd introduced us to back when we first started the Games.

His eyes traveled between me and the photograph. "This looks like the Heart of Envy."

"It is."

"*The* Heart of Envy?"

"Correct."

If his eyes had gotten any bigger, they would've popped out of his head. "But . . . it's part of the Tiffany exhibition, isn't it, that super famous one on Saturday?"

I didn't like the way he was looking at me, so I forced myself to stare at the family portrait he had pinned on the fridge door behind him. It had been taken a long time ago, judging by the photograph's grainy pixilation. The child in the center, who was clearly Dax (I'd know those eyes anywhere), was surrounded by four other kids of various ages and two adults, all of whom were standing on a tropical beach that I guessed was somewhere back home. "Umm, yes," I said, answering his question at last. "The *Serenity and Splendor* exhibition."

Dax marched over to the lounge, picked up a stack of magazines from under the coffee table—*OK!*, *Heat*, *Closer*—and began paging through. I saw flashes of well-known faces, glitzy dresses, splashy headlines: ALL THE LOOKS, ALL THE GOSSIP! MEET THE WHO'S WHO OF LONDON THIS SATURDAY! LONDON SOCIETY COMES OUT TO PLAY! At last he looked up, his expression a mix of disbelief and terror.

I rubbed my throat as if to force the words out. "So, anyway, I think Jen will have the design on hand. I'm sure I'm not the first criminal to ask her for a Heart of Envy replica."

"A replica?" he croaked, then faltered, something dawning on him. "Don't tell me that means you're planning on *stealing* it?"

I fiddled with my hands. "I'll need it by Friday, latest. The replica, I mean."

"But . . . what . . . I don't understand this." He squeezed the bridge of his nose, sucked in a breath. "Last time we spoke you said you and Nellie were leaving town. Now you're talking about stealing the Heart of Envy? What exactly is going on here?"

"We've had a change of plans," I said. "Nellie's kidnapper is James Reid. We don't know him, but he knows everything about us. And I do mean everything. The aliases we go by, our real names, how we operate. The works."

Dax swayed a little, righted himself. "How? I mean . . . I checked your laptop. I *really* don't think it's been hacked."

"James Reid is from Goods Exchange," I said quickly. I didn't have time to explain the entire theory, but I figured, at the very least, I owed Dax a basic explanation. "We must've sold him something once and he's been following us ever since."

"Do you recognize him?"

"Well, no. I don't think so. We've sold so many things to so many people . . ."

Dax nodded, then silently disappeared into his bedroom and returned several minutes later with what looked like a print-out of our delivery schedule—the list of products we'd sold over the past year, as well as the time and place of the handovers. He began paging through, his forehead creased with concentration.

"Anyway, the point is," I went on, "he won't let Nellie go unless I steal that bracelet for him."

Dax looked up. "Wait, no, wait, this is a *blackmail* deal?"

"Something like that."

"Which means Nellie's being held somewhere? Mate, there's got to be another way, surely! Can't we run or something? Leave London, come back when things have calmed down? That was your plan a few hours ago, wasn't it?"

"Yes, it was, back when I thought Nellie was safe and we could leave together. But she isn't, so we can't."

"Then tell me where they're keeping her and we can figure something out. We can break her out together."

"No. I just told you: these guys are nuts. And they're following me everywhere I go. If I try to break Nellie out and fail, they'll kill her. An escape plan is way too risky now."

"Yeah, dude, but so is this new plan of yours, by the sound of things."

I dug my nails into my palm as I noticed the time. I'd already been "in the bathroom" for twenty minutes, and there was no way Boss Thug hadn't caught on by now, even if he was a total idiot. And if he thought I'd bolted for good, he'd tell Reid and Nellie was toast. I *had* to hurry.

"Please, Dax, just forward the photo to Jen."

"But—"

"I also need another burner phone with a new SIM card. Just something simple. Can you get one for me?"

"A burner phone for what?"

"I'll explain everything as soon as I can. Just stay here and . . ." I looked at Sophia, still sitting on the kitchen floor with Sir Sebastian. She noticed me staring and smiled widely. "Keep an eye on the kid. We'll take her to social services when this is over."

"Come on, man! This is ridiculous! You can't just drop all this on me and ghost. Whatever you and Nellie have gotten yourselves into will end up involving me."

"Well, I'm sorry but—"

"And here it is, by the way," he interrupted, holding up the delivery schedule and jabbing a finger at the date: *Tuesday, January 29*, and the note written below it in red: *Cuff links (Cartier, canary diamond, two carats each. £11 987) Drop off at Denmark Hill Station, 2 p.m.* "Do you remember this handover from January? You went alone because Nell had the flu."

I nodded. How could I forget? It was the only sale on our books that had ever fallen through—an anomaly not just because no one ever stood us up, but because those Cartier cuff links had been such a hot ticket on Goods Exchange International that they'd gone through a fifteen-buyer, seventy-two-hour auction. But all for nothing. "The buyer ghosted," I said. "But hold on . . . maybe that was—"

"Seems likely. And look—" He dragged me over to his computer, opened up our profile on Goods Exchange, and scrolled through our seemingly endless list of past sales, pausing at the one marked *Cartier cuff links*. He clicked through to the buyer's profile. "He calls himself ENT00X, and guess what he's got pinned to his home page." He turned the screen toward me so I could see it clearly: the post I remembered from before, a pre-order listing for the Heart of Envy.

"Of course!" I said excitedly. "That's him, then, that's James Reid. For sure. It has to be. And you're sure he was the one we almost sold the cuff links to?"

"Yeah, very sure."

We high-fived and for a brief moment it felt as if we were going to hug too. I pulled back before it happened, thank God.

"Anyway," I said, scratching a nonexistent itch on my neck. "That clears that up, at least."

"Yeah, sort of," Dax muttered uneasily. "Except . . . you said this James Reid dude knows your real name, right? But you don't use your real name anywhere on Goods Exchange."

"I know, it's very strange. But we'll have to figure that out later. I've really got to go."

"I'll walk you out."

"No!" I said, panicky. "We can't be seen together." Dax looked down at his shoes, so I explained, "I don't think Reid or his men know about this flat, and they definitely don't know Sophia's here, but if they find out, well, there'll be big trouble. You've got to keep a very low profile. Don't let anyone see you. Or her. And don't go back to the Laundromat. In fact, don't go anywhere if you can help it."

"What about Theo?"

"Sorry?"

He raked his fingers through his hair, a faint glimmer of sweat on his brow. "My mate, the one I told you about. We meet up at the Costa down the road nearly every morning."

I was baffled. Was I supposed to read something more into that statement? Why did Dax insist on bringing up this Theo character whenever we were together?

His eyes moved to the family portrait pinned to the fridge door. "I think you two would really get along, actually. He's got a pretty shit family situation, so he knows all about that. And there's this older brother who's a super-successful Wall Street trader, with a beautiful wife, two kids, so it doesn't sit too well with the parents that Theo's jumping around from one low-paying job to the other, can't seem to settle. But, yeah, I'm just saying . . . he's a really nice guy."

Oh my God was he trying to set us up? Now? Really?

"Anyway, my point is, what am I supposed to tell him?"

I blinked, mute.

"You said I should keep a low profile," he elaborated, "not leave the flat unless I really have to. But if I just cancel my morning meet-ups, then he'll think . . . I don't know. It just won't be good for our . . . for work, you know?"

I was so flummoxed by this bizarre question and even more so by its pretext that I literally could not think of a single thing to say. Eventually, I landed on, "Well . . . just tell him you're sick." I eyed the door, eager to leave, then remembered something. "Hey, Dax . . . one more thing: How easy is it to hack an email account? Yahoo? Gmail?"

His eyes flashed with worry. "Oof, not easy at all. Unless the account is totally unsecured, which is unlikely these days."

"Great. Because I need you to hack the account of the St. Jude events manager. What do you need to make that happen?"

"Got to be kidding me," he mumbled. "All right, well, for starters I'll need the manager's email address."

"Easy. What else?"

"Their password?" he asked hopefully.

"Dax. If I knew their password I could hack it myself."

"Their cell number, then," he said. "I'll need to do a SIM swap to get their OTP and change the password."

I perked up. "Piece of cake! I'll have both for you by tomorrow, then all you have to do is search the email account for two de-clined RSVPs to *Serenity and Splendor* on Saturday and forward me the names and email addresses of the invitees. A picture, too, if you can find it. They'll need to be women, obviously, and non-celebrities. No influencers either, or politicians. No one anyone would recognize."

He let out a long breath. "Anything else you'd like? Maybe I could forge you an ID card while I'm at it."

"Is that possible?"

"Jesus, no. Who do you think I am?"

"Right. OK. Of course. Well then"—I hitched my handbag over my shoulder—"we'll chat soon." I turned to Sophia and Sir Sebastian. "You three look after each other, OK? Stay put, keep the doors locked and the curtains closed. I'll be back soon and then we'll—"

"Find Daddy?" Sophia suggested brightly.

"Sure," I mumbled, then gathered up my things and started for the door before I could make any more promises I couldn't keep.

12

IT WAS MONDAY, THE DAY I WAS SUPPOSED TO BE MEETING
Reid (alias ENT00X) at Dropkicks pub on Kensington High
Street to explain my plan to steal the bracelet from the exhibition. Instead, I was going there to explain my list of conditions
for the heist, which meant I now had a high probability of receiving a bullet to the brain within the next two hours.

The whole thing reminded me of the lead-up to a bad date,
which gave me an instant surge of anxiety because I'd had quite
a few of those. The first was many moons ago, back in the days
of dial-up internet and Britney Spears. His name was Brian and
to be entirely honest I can't remember what I liked about him.
Probably not his personality and definitely not his greasy hair or
cystic acne or the way he chewed with his mouth open. Still, I
was ecstatic. A real date with a real boy is not something you
pass up as a nerdy thirteen-year-old with braces and prescrip-
tion glasses.

Off I went to tell Mum and Dad the good news. "I've got a
date!" I squealed.

"A what?" Dad asked.

"A date. At the movies with Brian." I didn't bother explaining who Brian was because I knew they wouldn't care. "Can you take me? It's just down the road."

"We're busy, sweetheart," Mum said while she sipped her wine and Dad continued to read the newspaper.

"OK . . . but I really want to go," I said, glancing nervously at the time. "*Pleeeease*."

Mum and Dad looked at each other and rolled their eyes. They thought I didn't see, but I did. I saw everything. "Ask the boy's parents to fetch you," Mum suggested and went back to her wine. Dad put down the newspaper and turned on the TV.

But what if the boy's parents run a child-kidnapping ring? I almost said, then decided it wasn't worth another eye roll. So instead I did what I always did when in crisis. I picked up the landline and called Nellie.

"Code red," I said into the receiver. "Well, not yet, but it might be. Can you come with me to meet Brian?" I didn't bother explaining who Brian was because of course she already knew.

"Be there in fifteen," she said, and was there in ten, and together we tore off through London on our rusty bicycles, arriving at the cinema only to discover Brian had stood me up. I was OK, though, because I had Nellie.

But now, some twenty-odd years later, I didn't have the luxury of taking her along with me. I had to do this alone. I had to be brave.

THE MORNING OF the dreaded date, I woke in the back seat of the MG, stretched irritably, and blinked at the sun streaming across Kensington Park in great big shards of golden light. I would have preferred to spend the night at the Ritz, or any hotel or building for that matter, but thanks to my reckless exploits at the Tesco superstore the previous morning, Boss Thug was keen to make me suffer. And suffer I did.

After waiting a whole thirty-one minutes outside the store, Boss Thug finally smelled a rat. He marched inside, kicked down the loo door (only to discover an elderly lady with her trousers around her ankles), then raced back out of the shop (pursued by the shop's security team). Just as he tumbled through the swing doors, there I was, dressed in my dull brown maxi-dress, minus the hat and wig. I'll leave it up to your imagination as to what sort of tongue-lashing I was subjected to thereafter, but other than that there wasn't much the stupid lout could do to me. The security mob was hot on our heels and neither of us was too enthusiastic about spending the rest of the day explaining our peculiar behavior to the police. But after we managed to escape in our respective getaway cars, I was forced to pull up here, under an enormous oak tree on the border of Kensington Park, get down onto my hands and knees, and swear to the good Lord that I would never pull a stunt like that again. I also received a kick in the shins and was informed that, as punishment for my sins, I would be spending the night cramped up in the MG without food or water or a shred of sympathy. I didn't like the idea, but I didn't complain either. As livid as they were, I had a feeling the thugs were terrified of telling Reid they'd slipped up again. That meant Nellie wasn't going to suffer for it, which was all I really cared about.

I was reflecting on this horrid series of events when the BMW purred to life beside me, windows down.

"You go straight to Dropkicks or I'll put you to sleep, permanently," Boss Thug explained in his usual friendly tone. "I'm not in the mood for any more tricks."

Oh, but I was.

Shoulders back, chin up, I walked into Dropkicks pub—a traditional-looking wood-paneled watering hole in the center of London—my laptop under one arm and my handbag under the other. Reid was already there, sitting alone at the bar, slurping a coffee and scratching around at a plate of bangers and beans. He was wearing exactly the same outfit as yesterday but had shaved his bleached hair down to a buzz cut. I took the seat next to him while Boss Thug and thug number two slumped down at a cozy spot by the heater. It was the first time I'd actually gotten a good look at the underling. He was taller than Boss Thug, but slimmer too. His skin clear and bright, his hair a clean blond and his eyes a deep green.

"You got that plan ready?" Reid asked in lieu of a greeting as I ordered myself a cup of coffee and swallowed a Xanax. OK, two.

I wrapped my hands around my mug, briefly closed my eyes. I had expected to feel uneasy and unsure of myself—less Janet Robinson, more Emma Oxley. But in some sense I figured that was a good thing. In order to pull off this outrageously impossible heist, I would need to gain control over Reid's thoughts and decisions and to do that, I would first have to make myself innocuous by using one of Gran's favorite tricks. She called it "conditioning," and as with all her schemes and tactics, the principle evolved from her observations of human behavior. Gran was a loner, you see. "If you watch people for long enough," she used to say, "you'll see that we're all programmed the same way, *conditioned* to react to things without even knowing it."

"So," I said now, allowing my voice to waver. I dug in my handbag for a stack of papers, one of which I handed over. "This, eh, this is the to-do list for the next few days. It's not that comprehensive, but . . ."

He scanned the list for approximately three seconds, snapped his pale blue eyes up at me. "The only thing written down for today is 'Research,'" he grumbled.

"Uh-huh, yes. Correct." I placed my laptop on the bar counter, connected to the pub's Wi-Fi, and opened a tab for Google. I typed *St. Jude gallery security* into the search bar, then opened a second tab for *Serenity and Splendor Tiffany exhibition itinerary and guests* and a third for *St. Jude Events Manager*.

"But I asked you to fill me in on your plan for the actual heist," Reid said. "Not your preparation."

I ignored him and scrolled through the St. Jude gallery home page, taking notes as I went:

Serenity and Splendor by Tiffany and Co. in
collaboration with our curator, Wane McBride, will
bring in over 250 pieces from the House's archives.
On display will be everything from never-seen-before
state-of-the-art designs to historical favorites,
including the famed Heart of Envy. This piece was
originally designed for a member of the Spanish Royal
Family but has since been worn by a number of
celebrities, from Grace Kelly to Kim Kardashian . . .

Next, I clicked on the gallery's contact page and tapped out a quick phishing email to the listed events manager. With a touch of luck and some creative storytelling about needing to speak to the manager after hours, I would receive a reply containing their cell number and Dax could get started on his hacking business.

"Well?" Reid rapped his knuckles on the counter. "Let's hear it. Come on!"

"The heist plan, yes," I replied at last, closing the laptop. "I'll have that ready for you first thing Wednesday. Promise."

Reid slammed a beefy hand to the counter, his neck turning a dicey shade of red. "Wednesday! Are you kidding me? I said today! Twenty-four hours. That was the deal!"

I flinched. "Yes, I know, I know, I'm sorry . . . it's just that I had a crazy day yesterday." The veins in his neck started to pulse. "And quite honestly, James, if you wanted me to come up with a flawless heist plan so quickly, a plan that would require many hours of research, then maybe you should've told your friends to let me go somewhere with a plug point and internet access." I tapped my laptop, then splayed my trembling hands with the air of one who'd tried her best, but failed. "Also, the other reason I haven't got the plan ready yet is because there's just a teeny-tiny caveat I'd like to run by you first."

By this point, Reid's color had gone from red to something close to purple, his hands balled into fists and his mouth a tight line.

I offered him a Xanax, then drew back to a safe distance— out of striking range.

"I can't do this alone, James. No way," I said, Gran's words clear in my head: *It's easy to make them think you're incompetent when you're a woman. You hardly have to do a thing!* "Nellie and I work as a team, and if you want the heist to be successful, then you're just going to have to let her participate." No answer. Neck vein pulsing dangerously. Teeth grinding. "I know this is a big ask, but . . . well, surely you understand that I've never stolen or sold anything without Nellie. I can't. It's impossible. Just look at me! I haven't even been able to come up with a plan without her. Please, let her help me. It's the only way."

There was a loud clang as Reid slammed a fork down on his

plate and started to breathe—wheeze, more like—one, two, three times. Eventually, he rolled out his shoulders and answered, "I'll have to think about that."

I shook my head in desperation. "No, James. Please. There isn't time. The exhibition is in five days and we'll need hours and hours of practice and planning. It has to be this way. I can't pull off a heist of this caliber on my own. No chance. It's far too complex and I'll just end up getting caught and ruining everything."

Reid looked over at the thugs, then pulled out his phone and started typing a message. Five minutes went by as I sat there waiting for him to finish. I tried to get a glimpse at who he was talking to and what he was saying, but every time I looked at him, he angled the phone away from me.

"Fine," he said at last, placing his phone facedown on the table. "You can work together. But the boys will be watching your every move, got it?" I nodded dutifully. "And I'm not an idiot, I know you've been thinking about running. I know you reckon you could do it, get away once I let your mate out of that warehouse. But trust me, you don't want to do that."

I blinked, folded my arms across my chest.

"Leverage," he snapped. "If you think your mate is the only bargaining chip I've got, you're wrong. Don't forget I know everything about you, everything you've been trying to hide for the past five years. If you screw me over, I will ruin you."

I will ruin you. The same line Joel had used the day the police handed me the court summons. A coldness curled in my gut, a horrible sense of déjà vu. The truth, of course, was that despite Reid's thugs and their relentless threats, despite the plan I'd already set in motion, I *had* considered fleeing once Nellie was released from the warehouse. What sort of criminal would I be if a trick like that hadn't at least crossed my mind? It certainly would've been easier to follow through with the MY escape plan than steal the Heart of Envy. Any idiot could see that. But now Reid had made it abundantly clear that an escape—however well orchestrated—was out of the question. And I guess that was all the confirmation I needed. This was not something Nellie and I could run away from. This was a code red, and that meant: revenge.

Reid gulped down the last of his greasy breakfast and a fresh mug of coffee. "The boys will pick up Nellie tomorrow afternoon," he said, "then take you both to a hotel they've organized in Vauxhall. You'll be staying there together until after the heist. If you need to go anywhere else in between, you get my permission first. Clear?"

I nodded.

He considered me for a while, his fingers caressing the chunky silver chain that hung beneath his collar, an unfamiliar expression on his face. "You realize how dangerous this heist is going to be, yeah?"

I frowned at him.

"I'm just saying: you need to prepare yourself for the worst."

"Umm . . . OK, thanks?"

"You believe in God?" he asked.

"I'm sorry?"

"God."

I recoiled. *God?* The being who dropped me on this planet in the care of parents who would never love me the way they should have, who gifted me a tendency for hysteria, acne-prone skin, and nothing in the way of confidence? "No," I said. "No, I don't think I do."

"Unlucky," he said, and got to his feet.

13

NELLIE AND I CLAMBERED OUT OF THE BMW, WHICH HAD
taken us to the hotel in Vauxhall. Nellie, weak and exhausted,
had spent the trip from the warehouse curled up in a fetal position, her head resting in my lap. It was almost like we were teen-
agers again, passed out in the back of a cab on our way home
from a house party where the boys had been bad and the booze
good. And just like all those times back then, when the music
died, the alcohol wore off, and the boys vanished, the only thing
we had left was each other.

We linked arms as we walked slowly across the parking lot,
the two thugs trailing us like a bad smell, nobody saying a word.
Since I hadn't yet had a moment to enlighten her, I'd no idea
what Nellie thought was going on, or why she thought she was
being allowed out of the warehouse all of a sudden. But judging
from the blank look on her face, she was too tired to care.

We stepped inside the hotel—a gray-brick building with a
line of street-facing windows. Our room was on the first floor,
and presumably that was to prevent us from jumping to our
deaths because the place was as atrocious on the inside as it was

on the outside. It had a hob, a small fridge, an old armchair, and two single beds fitted with mattresses that were as thin as paper and as hard as concrete. The toilet was located directly under the shower, both of which looked as if they hadn't been cleaned in months. Oh, and the entire establishment smelled like piss.

"Guess it could be worse," I said as I threw our suitcases onto the bed and took off my coat. Unlike Nellie, who splashed out on vintage bottles of Dom Pérignon, fifteen-thousand-pound Hermès handbags, and crystal-embellished Louboutins, I'd never had a problem slumming it if need be. But even by my standards this place was the pits.

Nellie, staggering rather than walking, made her way to the other side of the room, where I'd piled up our luggage—three Bottega suitcases, handbags, and several boxes of shoes—mostly hers. She came to a halt, turning pale. I thought at first it was the sight of the place that had done it. Then she mumbled, "S . . . Seb? Where is he?"

"He's fine, I promise. I took him to Dax. Thought it would be safest for now."

She continued to stare at the pile of bags, like she expected her old cat to slink out from one of them. Her eyes glazed with tears but she turned away so I wouldn't see.

"I know," I said. "Everything's such a mess. But I've got a way to fix things. Trust me."

Nellie nodded, said nothing, ran a finger along the scar above her left eyebrow—the one Kade had given her years ago. I'd never seen her do that before and wondered what the gesture meant. Was she thinking of him? Had the hours she'd been locked up in that warehouse—isolated, constrained—brought long-buried demons to the surface? I looked at her fingernails, still raw and picked so low there was nothing left, and knew the answer was yes.

It had taken Nellie more than a year to gain the courage to report Kade's abuse to the authorities, and by that time, he'd caught wind of her bare-knuckle boxing prowess and relocated to Argentina under a false name. Like so many others before and after him, he suffered no consequences for what he'd done. His life went on as normal, while Nellie's crumbled in his wake. And so, to her, the Games became a way of righting wrongs in a world that had been brutal and unjust. Swindling a sleazy investment banker accused of sexual harassment wasn't ever going to undo the pain Kade had caused her, but if she couldn't balance the scales of justice for herself, at least she could do it for someone else. I'd never seen it that way myself. Except maybe this time.

She stared at me a moment now, her cracked lips parted as if she wanted to say something but couldn't. She peeled off her stained yellow trouser suit and silver block heels, extracted her diamond choker from inside one of her many secret pockets, and placed it on the side table. After taking a quick shower, she put on a pair of wide-legged chiffon trousers and a cream blouse and slumped down on the bed.

"We'll have to stay here a few nights," I explained. "It's not the best but I guess we're not really in a position to be making demands."

She waited for me to sit next to her, placed a cold, freakishly strong hand over mine. "What is this, though? I don't under-stand. Haven't you paid my ransom? Aren't we supposed to be free by this point?"

"Well, the thing is—"

"I really, *really* wanted you to run, you know that? I would've let them do whatever they wanted to me, as long as I knew you were safe." She hesitated, then added, "I wasn't scared of them."

I looked again at her fingernails. My chest throbbed. "I know. But I just couldn't do it, Nell. I couldn't face the thought of getting on that plane to Myanmar without you. Never without you."

She nodded slowly. "I suppose I should've known that. I just wanted to give you the chance." She shuffled closer to me and smiled weakly.

Sitting there on the bed together in that tiny, cluttered room, it was like we were kids again, mirroring each other's body language and moods, trading secrets we'd never share with anyone else: the boys we had crushes on, the things we were most afraid of or most excited for. Sometimes we didn't even have to say them out loud. It felt like that now.

"OK. I admit it," she whispered, straightening. "I'm sorta glad you didn't run. I hear they make *the best* rum in Myanmar and I'd be dead jealous if you got to taste it without me."

I laughed and glanced around the room, noting a bag of groceries in the kitchenette, which I supposed was Reid's way of informing us we wouldn't be going out for meals over the next few days.

"When was the last time you ate something?" I asked, pulling out a bag of pasta, Bolognese sauce, a small block of cheddar cheese, and some sad-looking vegetables.

Nellie staggered over, filled up a pot of water, and set it on the stove. "Can't remember. Last Christmas?"

"Spag Bol?" I asked.

She nodded, and I handed her the packet of spaghetti, which she threw into the pot. I diced an onion, tossed it into a pan, drizzled in a little oil. It popped and sizzled and started to brown.

"We haven't done this for ages," I said. "Always just hotel breakfasts and takeouts now."

Nellie smiled. "I know. And I miss it."

"My terrible cooking?"

"*Our* terrible cooking. But no, I mean living together in an actual home like we used to, not a hotel room." She surveyed the tiny space around us, as if seeing it for the first time. "Our flat in Kensal wasn't that much bigger than this." She stirred the spaghetti and chuckled softly. "Do you remember that god-awful sleeper couch in the lounge, the one with the metal rods in the middle that made it feel like you were sleeping on a fork?"

"Umm, yeah," I said, "the one you made all the boys crash on when you brought them home?"

"Only if they were dickheads." She mulled that over for a second. "Which they all were. Like, *every single one*. How is that possible?"

I laughed reflexively and, sensing her mood had lifted, decided the time had come. "Nell," I said cautiously, "there's something I need to run by you."

She tested a piece of spaghetti and, satisfied that it was ready, emptied the pot into a colander and turned off the hob. "Yeah?"

"You know when I said Reid and I had come to an agreement for your release?"

Her eyes narrowed. She set aside the colander, turned to me, and crossed her arms.

I twisted my hair into a low knot, pulled on a jumper, took it off. Not once did Nellie take her eyes off me. "Well, it wasn't so much an agreement as a . . . well, a job."

Her eyebrows went heavenward. "A *job*?"

"He wants to hire us."

"What!"

"I know, it's mad. But look, you've just got to trust me on this one, please. I've come up with a plan."

"What sort of plan?"

I checked the corridor outside our room. I was certain one of the thugs would be lingering nearby, but I couldn't see either of them. "I think there's a way we can do this that will get those thugs off our tail *and*—"

Our burner phone buzzed, cutting me off. I dived for it.

Nellie's eyes flashed dangerously as I plucked the phone from my handbag. "How'd you get that back? I thought Reid had it."

"He gave it to me. So we could keep in contact."

Her eyebrows shot up again as I opened the text, angling the phone away from her. It was from Dax:

Good news. Like you guessed, Jen's got the design for the bracelet all set so she should be able to knock up the "supplies" pretty quickly. She should have them ready by Wednesday latest. Also, Daisy Duck's still asking about her father nonstop. We really have to figure out what to say. Don't leave it all to me, please!

"Daisy Duck?" Nellie said, craning her neck over my shoulder. "Who on earth is Daisy Duck?"

Moving to the other side of the room, I tapped out a reply.

Perfect. Maybe you can drop off "the supplies" at our hotel when they're ready? We're staying at this address: 2A Meadow Rd, SW8. We're in room 5 on the first floor but definitely don't come by unannounced—things are bit complicated ATM. And about Daisy Duck . . . I know it's a sticky situation but just stall her for a bit longer. There's nothing else we can do now.

"Didn't know you and Dax were back to texting," Nellie said suspiciously. "I thought you were dead set on avoiding him."

"I am," I said. "It's just—"

My phone buzzed again with Dax's reply, and once again, I left Nellie hanging.

So this is really happening, then? You are actually going to steal THOE? Dude . . .

A second later, another message came through, this one a reply to the text I'd sent earlier that day containing the email address and cell number of St. Jude's events manager.

By the way, finally managed to get you the details of a declined invitee who isn't famous. Her name's Sheryl Yardley and since the invite had a plus-one (apparently for her sister, Deborah Stern), you should be good to go. Email Address: she.yard77@gmail.com. Couldn't find a photo but apparently Yardley's the wife of some investment banker who frequently makes donations to the gallery.

"Who the hell is Daisy Duck!" Nellie repeated with a snap.

I groaned, having run out of distractions. "You remember the man under the tarpaulin? In the warehouse?"

"Of course I remember."

"Daisy Duck is his daughter. Her name's Sophia."

"The girl who was in the car with that idiot thug when I was kidnapped?"

I nodded hastily. "Yes. Correct. And as it happens, she's staying at Dax's until after the heist. To be honest, I've no idea what we're going to do with her because her mother's vanished and now her dad's dead and it's all so awful but—"

"Wait, *what?*"

"Chris Keeling's daughter, Sophia. She's an orphan now and staying with Dax because—"

She held up a hand, silencing me. There was a certain look Nellie had that scared me a little bit sometimes, and she was using that look right now—a sort of oh-no-you-didn't vibe. "No-no," she said coolly, licking her lips. "I heard that part. You said 'heist.' What heist?"

"Oh, right, yes, that." I chuckled but knew she wasn't fooled. "I mean it's not exactly a—" But before I could finish, she whipped the phone from my grip, so fast there was nothing I could do about it.

As her sharp blue eyes scanned the chain of messages, her jaw tightened. I tried to judge her mood. She looked angry, sure, confused and exhausted too. But there was something else just visible beneath. Curiosity.

"As I was saying," I went on carefully, aware that if I wanted Nellie on my side, all in, I'd need to convince her this wasn't just something we were doing because we had no other choice. "It's not exactly a heist in the truest sense of the word."

Nellie gave me the phone, put her hands on her hips.

"You remember what we came to London for in the first place?" I went on. "The *Serenity and Splendor* exhibition at St. Jude?"

She picked up her diamond choker, threaded it through her fingers. "You mean the most prestigious event in Exhibition Month?" she said tonelessly. "Go on."

"Did you know that one of the pieces on display is the Heart of Envy?"

"I don't like where this is going . . ."

"Reid has asked us to steal it for him," I said before she could continue. "And if we don't, he said he'll 'ruin us.'" I paused for effect. "Those were his exact words." She recoiled, the diamond choker slipped a little in her grip. "But, of course, like I said, this isn't a real-deal jewelry heist. We don't do that kind of thing. Not ever. I mean, it really would be total madness to *steal* the Heart of Envy. Total raving madness."

Nellie's eyes darkened. I knew she could see it, the wild and crazy idea forming in my mind, the Game I was plotting. "Madness . . ." she repeated slowly. "Yes, it would be. Unless—"

"—you're Janet Robinson and Annie Leeds?" I suggested. "And you've just been threatened?"

"That sounds a bit like a code red to me," she said, a small smile playing on her lips.

"Possibly."

She strolled across the room to the window, the diamond choker swinging from her fingers like a pendulum. "But it's not going to be easy, you know that, right? Those boys are smarter than they look. We'll need to keep our minds sharp."

"Of course."

"And we'll need to be careful."

"Absolutely."

She turned to face me, her expression serious now. "You think Reid and his thugs will fall for it?"

"With a little luck, sure."

14

THE THING ABOUT LUCK IS THAT IT RUNS OUT. YOU START OFF
at birth with a certain amount, like a cat with nine lives or a con
artist with several chances to evade the police, but as you grow
up and make mistakes, your luck begins to trickle through the
hourglass, bit by bit, until there's nothing left at all. And while
Nellie and I were going to need all the luck we could get for the
next stage of the Game, considering what happened to us in
February last year, I had a terrible feeling our luck gauge was
already hovering just above empty.

We were in Vienna for the Opera Ball, arguably the city's
most dazzling annual event. Think *Bridgerton* in the twenty-first
century—gentlemen in tuxedos, debutantes in white, champagne in crystal flutes, a world-famous philharmonic orchestra,
ticket prices to make your eyes water. Of course, Nellie and I
weren't there to enjoy a special rendition of Mozart's Requiem
or mingle with the who's who of Europe's high society. And after
we'd collected the Audemars Piguet fifteen-carat white-gold
watch we'd come for, Nellie hitched up her evening gown, I
brushed off my usher's uniform, and we made for the exit, happy

as clams. "We really are the luckiest bitches alive," Nellie said, exactly one second before we spotted a wall of Bundespolizei blocking our way. We knew right away the worst had happened: that the owner of the Audemars Piguet had realized his watch was missing and that at least one of the women who'd offered to fix his broken cuff link was a pickpocket. We were done. Finished. It was over. But then Nellie patted the secret pocket of her bright-blue Balmain gown and used up the last scrap of luck remaining in our arsenal. Her pocket was empty, she realized, the inner lining ripped open at the perfect moment, allowing the two-hundred-thousand-euro watch to slip to the floor just a few minutes before the police decided to body search us. It was the closest we'd ever come to being arrested and yet it felt like nicking a sandwich at a kids' picnic compared to what we'd gotten ourselves wrapped up in now.

IT WAS THE following day, and Nellie and I were back at that god-awful converted warehouse for our first official get-together with Reid and his men. Bearing in mind that the last time I'd been inside the place I'd seen a dead body, I would've definitely preferred to set up our headquarters at the hotel. But Reid was adamant. Maybe because he was worried a hotel guest might eavesdrop on our dark plans and report us to the police. Or maybe because he wanted to remind us what happened to the last person he'd kidnapped. Either way, as we stepped inside the warehouse that afternoon, I scanned the dark corner where I'd seen the body under the tarpaulin. It was gone. Reid noticed me looking, but I didn't dare ask any stupid questions—like what had happened to it. My luck, as I said, was running thin.

I SET UP my laptop on a table I'd pushed in front of a line of three chairs, connected it to a projector I'd borrowed from Reid, and adjusted the lighting just so. While I was at it, Nellie sat watching me, dressed in a spotless all-white Alexander McQueen suit, Dior scarf, and bright-orange Louboutins. The look was so outrageously impractical that only Nellie could've pulled it off.

She looked up at me, running a thumb along the ridges of her diamond choker. I noticed Reid's eyes follow the movement, his pupils wide. He was different around her, I realized. Something close to scared. Lucky he didn't know she was too.

"OK, so . . . I'll j-just . . ." I tapped my pointer against the wall to get my audience's attention—Reid, Nellie, Boss Thug, but not the underling, who'd apparently caught some nasty stomach bug and was on bed rest for the day. "I, eh, I know we all have a lot to get done today so I won't keep you long. I just want to give you a basic outline of the plan and . . . well, hopefully everything should be set and ready by Friday night."

I opened the presentation Nellie and I had been working on all night. The first slide showed an enormous close-up of a sparkly emerald-and-diamond bracelet resting on a cream silk pillow.

Reid straightened in his seat. Boss Thug gasped.

"The Heart of Envy by Tiffany & Co.," I said, gesturing at the slide while I recited what I'd managed to dig up on the famed piece. "Fifty-five-carat high-clarity round-cut diamonds and thirteen pristine Colombian emeralds sitting on several inches of solid white gold. At first glance, not the most valuable piece of jewelry you've ever seen. But the Heart of Envy isn't *just* a string of diamonds and emeralds; it's a symbol: of honor, of prestige, of glory, and—most importantly—it's a talisman. The bracelet was designed and crafted in New York City in the late twenties. I believe it was originally made as an engagement gift for a member of the Spanish royal family but was later auctioned to some big-name Hollywood producer and has since been loaned out to several A-listers. According to some, the bracelet is said to bring its wearer so much good fortune that they will become an object of envy and desire, hence the name." I clicked over to the next slide, a vintage photograph of a blonde dressed in a champagne-blue French silk gown, clutching an Academy Award, the Heart of Envy just visible dangling from her pale, bird-boned wrist. "Grace Kelly at the 1955 Oscars. Just two months after this picture was taken, Kelly met Prince Rainier III of Monaco, and one year after that, she was married to him."

"How long were they married for?" Boss Thug asked, rubbing his nose on the back of his hand.

"Twenty-six years."

"Don't know if I'd call that lucky," he supplied with a stupid grin.

I ignored him, clicked over to the following slide—one of Brigitte Bardot on the red carpet, cameras flashing in the background and the Heart of Envy sparkling in the light. "One year later, Bardot was loaned the bracelet to wear at the premiere of *And God Created Woman*, which turned out to be the biggest success of her career."

"Never heard of it," Boss Thug said. "Sounds like some feminist crap."

Nellie sucked in a silent breath and I backed her up with a stern look.

I clicked on to the next three slides, which I presented in

silence: Julia Roberts, Meryl Streep, Kim Kardashian—all embellished by the strip of diamonds and emeralds.

"Every one of these A-listers hit some sort of major jackpot within six months of wearing the bracelet," I explained. "Most within weeks. So as you can imagine, the bracelet now has a pretty solid reputation as a talisman."

"You believe in luck, James?" Nellie asked in a dangerous drawl while turning in her seat to face him. "Is that why you picked the Heart of Envy for us to steal? Things haven't been going your way lately and you're in need of a little good fortune?"

Subtly, he shook his head, though his eyes remained fixed on the projector as he stroked the chunky silver chain hanging around his neck. His own talisman, maybe?

"*I* do," Boss Thug piped up. "Believe in luck, I mean. My pops won fifty thousand quid on a scratch card once, and Mum won a trip to Paris for her thirtieth."

"Oh really?" Nellie said. "So how do the luck gods work? Enlighten me."

"Simple. Luck is luck. You believe in it, you get it. Pops always said he was one of the lucky ones, and look what happened to him."

Nellie licked her lips. "Cool. So it's like karma, then?"

"Karma?"

"Yes. Karma," Nellie snapped. "You know, bad things happen to bad people. Good things happen to good people. So on, so forth. Here's an example: a bastard who likes to beat women half his size ends up with a broken—"

"Karma is just energy," I cut in before Nellie could finish. She blinked up at me. I smiled gently because I knew she knew what I was going to say next, the thing Gran said whenever she brought up Kade, and the sort of life she thought he deserved. "And energy can neither be created nor destroyed—"

"—because all that is spent must be returned," she added, finishing my sentence as she slowly unballed her fists and her gaze grew distant.

I gave her a short nod because I felt it too—Gran was with us in this. Always. Nellie inclined her head in reply while the two men exchanged a confused glance, right on cue.

I looked at my watch, then back at Nellie, giving her the signal. Now that we'd done just enough to disorient our audience, it was time to get into the weeds of what we'd come here to do.

While everything I'd presented so far was true, the same could not be said for what was coming next. Because in order for me and Nellie to pull off the heist without getting arrested, or, better yet, chopped up by Mr. L, we had no choice but to keep some elements of the plan concealed. In other words, from this point onward, my presentation would be peppered with half-truths and straightforward lies. Or, as Gran preferred to call it: "misleading information."

Because lying, you see, is serious business. Anyone's capable of doing it, but as with all Games, some people play like amateurs, some like professionals. The first step toward becoming a professional liar is realizing that the best lies aren't lies at all. The truth, told in a misleading way, is far more powerful than even the most well-constructed fib. For instance, when Joel proposed to me all those years ago claiming, "I'll never love anyone the way I love you." This piece of highly misleading information got me good because, while it was true, it didn't mean what I thought it meant. In my head, *the way I love you* equaled *perfectly and loyally*, when what it really meant was *like shit*.

"So, anyway," I went on, shaking the memory away, "as you know, the *Serenity and Splendor* exhibition will take place at the St. Jude gallery of modern art this Saturday. The event is a huge deal in London's society calendar and will draw politicians, celebrities, and influencers from all over the world. In fact, some are even comparing it to New York's Met Gala."

I could see Reid's eyes glaze over. He'd obviously never heard of the Met Gala. Figured.

I clicked a few slides on. "The evening will kick off with a cocktail hour in the gallery's main foyer and some form of entertainment. *The Daily Mail* says it'll be John Legend. *OK!* magazine says Billie Eilish. But as far as our plan goes, it doesn't matter."

Again, all I got from Reid was a blank stare of incomprehension. Boss Thug frowned.

"Following this, the guests will be asked to relocate to the exhibition hall, where the Heart of Envy, along with the rest of the collection, will be on display. Now, there's no way we could steal the bracelet at this point. It will be locked up in a glass display case that's fitted with countless alarms and weight-detecting technology."

At least this got Reid fired up. He blinked, frowned, then cracked his neck from side to side. "So what's the plan, then?"

I twirled the pointer through my fingers and brought up the next slide on my presentation. "OK. Let's say it's eight p.m. The guests have had their cocktails, finger snacks, and entertainment; they've mingled and gossiped and seen the Tiffany collection glittering in its glass case. Now the fun begins. Some of the pieces, including the Heart of Envy, will be handed over to specially selected guests to 'model' inside the gallery. And by that I mean: walk around sipping bubbly and chewing on caviar. This," I added, tapping my pointer against the desk in front of me, "is when Nellie and I will strike."

I looked left, past Reid. Boss Thug was sitting motionless at the end of the row, hands balled into fists and resting in his lap, his eyes staring at the wall ahead of him.

"The general idea is pretty simple," I went on carefully. "The heist will take place in three stages. Stage one: Nellie and I arrive at the gallery at around five forty-five, just as cocktail hour is ending and the entertainment is starting. This means we'll avoid as much mingling as possible, lowering the odds of any unnerving interactions with people who might wonder who we are. We'll hang around the foyer until the entertainment is over, then move into the exhibition hall for the display. We'll use this time to survey the gallery setup, security, check for CCTV, that sort of thing. Then, at about eight p.m., the Heart of Envy will be given to a guest to wear." I flashed Nellie a knowing glance. She smiled coyly. "And us to steal. Now, the actual stealing part will be done by a classic switch," I went on. "Something Nellie and I have done several times before." *Although not with such an expensive piece*, I didn't add. "We're going to take the real bracelet from whoever is wearing it and replace it with the replica we've commissioned from our jeweler friend. She's an expert in the rare-gem business, so I'm pretty sure the counterfeit will be more or less indistinguishable from the real thing."

"And who is this wearer going to be?" Reid asked.

"I don't know. But I'm sure they've already been picked and vetted and made to sign a thousand documents."

"Cool. So you're just gonna wing it, then?"

I never winged anything, obviously. It went completely against my nature. Still, I figured it was probably better if he thought I did. I ignored his question and went on. "Next, stage two: we'll leave the gallery as quickly as possible but without raising suspicions, then shift the bracelet onto the buyer, who will hopefully be waiting for us in a street nearby. Finally, stage three: we'll give the buyer the bracelet, and in exchange he'll hand over a USB worth approximately sixteen million pounds in Bitcoin, calculated at the time of agreement. Now, bear in mind that we'll have to have a laptop with us to check the Bitcoin is actually in the wallet, but other than that, it'll be a piece of cake." I paused, looked dead straight into Reid's eye, and asked, "Just to be one hundred percent clear on this, you *definitely* want us to sell the bracelet to Mr. L?"

Reid's Adam's apple bobbed in his throat. "Yeah, I do. It has to be him."

I had an urge to ask him why, of all the buyers in the criminal underworld, he wanted to do a deal with one of the most ruthless and inflexible. But I stopped myself because the truth was: selling the Heart of Envy to Mr. L suited our plans just fine.

I nodded. "All right, then. Mr. L it is. So we'll need to confirm with him the exact time and location of the handover. We'll also need to tell him we want the Bitcoin keys stored on a hardware wallet." I shifted my weight from one foot to the other, my gaze still fixed on Reid. "I presume you'll handle that communication yourself? Or would you like us to?"

"I'll do it," he snapped suspiciously, "but thanks for asking."

"My pleasure."

Reid moved in his seat. "So how exactly are you planning to get inside the gallery for this 'classic switch' operation? You said the event's a huge deal, yeah? Biggest night in London's social calendar, packed with celebs and politicians. So how you gonna get in if you don't have any invitations?"

"Good question," Boss Thug said.

I pouted. "Who said we didn't have invitations?"

Yesterday evening, after some hard-core research on Sheryl Yardley and her plus-one, sister Deborah Stern, I'd discovered that Dax was right. Yardley was the forty-five-year-old wife of an investment banker who frequently made donations to the gallery but had declined her invitation because she and her husband were currently away on vacation in Bora Bora. And because she wasn't going, Stern's invite had fallen through the cracks. Satisfied with this information, I set up a fake Yahoo account under Yardley's name, which I then used to contact the gallery's event manager and explain that my invitation to the exhibition had been sent to an old Gmail account and was thus declined incorrectly. The event manager was quick to accept the story and resend the invitation to my brand-new Yahoo account. And I, of course, RSVP'd *yes*.

I was just about to explain this brilliant piece of news to Reid and Boss Thug when the warehouse door flew open and the underling dashed inside, his long, weedy legs shaking, his blond hair plastered to his forehead, and a raincoat hanging halfway down his arms like he'd been trying to take it off mid-sprint.

"Well, well, look who's back from the dead," Nellie droned. "How's the stomach feeling?"

The underling ignored her, gave Reid a sheepish grin, then turned to Boss Thug. Boss Thug leaped up, and the pair of them began a whispered conversation while Reid looked on, obviously furious.

A minute or two later, the underling and Boss Thug wrapped up their conversation and Reid turned to face me. "I want to see that replica when it's ready."

"OK, but—"

He cut me off mid-sentence. "We're done here."

15

BACK AT THE HOTEL, NELLIE LIT A STICK OF INCENSE (SAGE, TO "cleanse the bad vibes"), kicked off her Louboutins, and laid a dazzling array of designer jewelry on the bedside table—three enormous Tiffany rings fitted with various gemstones—onyx, rubies, tanzanites—a rose-gold Omega watch, a pair of platinum Chopard earrings, and, of course, her diamond knuckleduster. Even after everything she'd been through—a kidnapping, tied up in a grimy warehouse, three nights of no sleep—she somehow managed to look like she was on her way to dinner at Buckingham Palace. And me? I guess I just wasn't as good as Nellie at concealing the tension flowing through my veins.

"Sooo . . . that was weird," I said, pouring out two cups of instant coffee and kicking off my Topshop ballet flats.

Nellie wasn't listening. "*Hmm?*"

I looked down at my to-do list for the day:

—Present plan

—Confirm location and time of sale

—Collect replica

—Rehearse the Switch

"Reid's been dead set on hearing my plan for the heist," I said, ticking off the first item on the list. "Then he cuts me off right in the middle of it. What's more important to him than knowing how we're going to steal the Heart of Envy?" I slipped the list back into my handbag, then checked the corridor outside our room. Boss Thug was nowhere to be seen. Which was also weird, since he'd escorted us back to the hovel and was—surely—supposed to be keeping an eye on us.

I dropped precisely one and a half packets of sugar and a teaspoon of powdered milk into Nellie's coffee—exactly as she liked it—and handed over the mug. She drank the whole thing with a big smile, even though I knew it was the worst coffee she'd ever had in her life. Another reason I loved her.

"Looked to me like the underling had something important to share," she said, placing her mug on the side table with an expression of relief. "But he didn't want to say it in front of Reid."

"Yes, I know. And I've got a feeling—"

"I like the change," Nellie interrupted. "By the way."

"Change?"

She yanked open her suitcase and started rummaging through her vast collection of designer dresses—satin, silk, and chiffon flying everywhere in a rainbow of colors. "Something happened to you while I was locked up in that warehouse, didn't it?"

"If you mean, was I confused and terrified and did I have the worst breakdown of my life? Yes, I suppose that's *something*."

"*Hmm.* But you feel better now, right? Which means it was less a breakdown, more a metamorphosis."

"I wouldn't say that—" I stopped mid-sentence. I definitely felt better. More in control of things. More assured. But "metamorphosis" was a strong word. And if I had changed, what had I changed into, exactly? I looked past Nellie to the mirror hanging on the wall behind her. Were my shoulders less hunched, the muscles in my neck less tense? Maybe.

"*Dreams and Desires,*" Nellie muttered to herself, as if the previous conversation had never happened.

"Sorry?"

"The theme for Saturday's exhibition," she said. "*Dreams and Desires.* So I'm thinking we'll need to wear lots of sparkle, yes? Blacks, midnight blues." She paused to look up at me, frowning with concentration, her fingers steepled. "All right, now think of a card."

"What? Now? Nell . . . I'm not in the mood."

"We promised each other we'd keep our minds sharp! So, come on, do it. Think of one. And don't let me get it right this time!"

I knew she'd already slotted the number and suit into my brain without me realizing it, so I recited our most recent conversation, trying to remember what it was. Something about dreams and desires, then blacks and midnight blues. Pairs of things, always. So was it the number two?

As for the suit . . .

She'd steepled her fingers, hadn't she? The two of diamonds?

"All right," I said triumphantly. "I'm ready. Let's go. On three. One, two—"

"Five of hearts," I said at the same time she called out, "Two of diamonds."

She laughed and patted me on the shoulder. "Well done, babe. You win."

I shrugged. "For once."

"But seriously," she said. "I do really want to know what you're going to wear."

"Umm . . ."

While I'd planned out every last step of heist day, every detail, every word we'd need to utter, I hadn't once considered that if we were going to mingle with London's upper-*upper* crust, we had better look the part. I noted my collection of dresses folded in my suitcase, which still lay open and unpacked on the floor. Everything was either black or gray or camel, discreet colors I always preferred to go with, colors that allowed me to be who I was meant to be. Nobody.

"My black backless number?" I suggested. "The one I wore to the Savoy a while back. It's the fanciest I've got."

Nellie raised an immaculately plucked eyebrow. "That's a cocktail dress."

"I know. And I'll top it off with a smart blazer. How's that?"

She winced.

"And some fancy heels?"

"Oh my God. OK, just hold on." She leaned over her suitcase and picked out a shimmering gold fishtail with a sweetheart neckline and sheer lace sleeves. "How about this?" She rubbed the material between her fingers. "Calvin Klein, obviously, so it'll feel like you're wearing nothing."

"Is that supposed to be a good thing?"

"And it'll go perfectly with those beige Jimmy Choos you never wear."

"OK. But what size is it?"

She pressed the dress to my chest and beamed. "My size. And we're basically the same, so . . ."

"God, I love you. But I'm not so sure about the gold." I

squinted at the pile of frocks, a flash of pink catching my eye. "That dress over there"—I pointed at the flamingo V-neck I'd seen the other day at the Ritz—"that's mine, isn't it? From my uni graduation. I thought I tossed it."

"You did. Straight in the bin the day we opened the Games. Along with all your other colorful things."

"So why's it in your suitcase?"

She watched me for a second, a small smile on her lips. "Just thought you'd want it back one day."

I wandered over to the hotel window, picturing myself alongside Nellie on the red carpet on Saturday night, one of us the diversion, one of us the thief in shadow. Naturally, Nellie had always been the diversion. Was it time to shake things up?

I lost myself in this thought for several minutes, but it was soon eclipsed by another, more unsettling reflection. We'd been back at the hotel for several hours now. Unaccompanied. Something strange was definitely going on with Reid and the thugs, and, like I'd been trying to tell Nellie before she changed the subject, I had a bad feeling it involved Sophia. As far as I knew, the only thing Boss Thug and the underling were keeping from Reid was the slightly inconvenient fact that Sophia had escaped and was now MIA. So . . . had the underling really been off sick with a stomach bug, or was that some kind of excuse, an alibi maybe? Had he actually been out looking for Sophia? Had he found her?

Suddenly dizzy with nerves, I turned my focus to the parking lot outside, now completely devoid of cars, save the BMW and our MG—which Boss Thug had fetched from outside Kensington Park earlier that day. It was a clear afternoon, and the setting sun cast a blanket of salmon pink across the horizon. In another world, in another lifetime, it would've been beautiful.

But as I stood there, the light fading swiftly and the streetlamps flickering to life, I noticed something that made my nerves twitch all over again.

"Nell," I muttered, "Nell . . . come here. Quick." Squinting out of the window, I pointed in the general direction of our car, which was parked under the light of the nearest lamp. "You see that? Over there, behind the MG?"

She dashed to my side, craned her neck, then drew back, frowning. "Looks like a shoe to me. Is someone hiding behind our car?"

"Can't be Reid, can it? Or the underling?"

"Spying on us from the parking lot? Bit weird, but I wouldn't put it past them." She strolled back over to the bed and slumped down, dresses, shoes, and sparkly accessories everywhere.

I was about to say I agreed when the crouching figure emerged from its hiding spot and darted across the parking lot toward our window. I backed away instinctively, then realized who the figure was. And that he wasn't alone.

"Dax! Sophia!" I breathed nervously, ripping open the window while Nellie dived across the room and locked the door.

Dax got onto his knees and made a stirrup with interlaced fingers, allowing Sophia to hop onto the sill. I pulled her inside.

"Janet!" she said, throwing her arms around me in a tight hug. "I've missed you so much!"

"Oh, I . . . I've missed you too." I staggered backward as Dax leaped in after her. I scanned the parking lot. Seeing nothing, I drew the curtains.

"We've been out looking for Daddy," Sophia explained excitedly. I shot Dax a wide-eyed look of horror. He shrugged in return. "At our old shelter," Sophia went on. "And . . . some other places. We haven't found him yet but Dax says we will soon."

I turned again to Dax.

"Had to do something," he mouthed.

For reasons I couldn't understand, seeing Sophia standing there, slightly out of breath but grinning like this was all some great adventure, made my chest squeeze so hard I had to look away. How was she so trusting and hopeful when all she'd ever known was rejection and disappointment? Had she discovered some great big life secret I'd missed? Nellie always said the greatest lessons come from the most unlikely teachers. I thought about Gran, the lonely spinster who'd taught me how to pick pockets and lie. I guess Nellie had a point.

"Dax Frederick . . ." Nellie said, snapping me back to the present. "To what do we owe the pleasure?"

"Hey, Nell. You look"—his eyes traced her shoulders, neck, chin, as if scanning for injuries—"OK, actually. Are you?"

She shrugged coolly.

"Hello," Sophia said next, addressing Nellie. "Do you remember me? From the car? I was there with the bad man when he took you. I'm sorry about that, by the way."

"The famous Daisy Duck," Nellie said with a nod, taking Sophia's hand in hers and offering a quick smile, which Sophia mirrored instantly. "Of course I remember you." I could see the unease behind Nellie's expression, which no doubt came as she remembered Sophia was now an orphan and no one had bothered to tell her.

"So, yeah," Dax said as he wiped a trail of window muck from his arm, "we've been out on a wild-goose chase. But also . . . went to fetch *the supplies* from Jen this morning." He opened the haversack he had slung over his shoulder and handed me a plastic bag.

Inside was a burner phone, much the same as the one Nellie and I used for business.

"Thanks," I said. "Has it got a SIM card?"

"Yeah. And I loaded airtime too." He crossed his arms and attempted to throw me a tough look. "So? You gonna tell me what you need it for?"

"Yes, of course. In a bit." I reached again inside the plastic bag and pulled out a small black box. There, curled up on a cream velvet bed, was a coil of green and glittering white: the Heart of Envy replica. I examined the masterpiece, for a moment transfixed, then snapped the box shut and dropped it back into the plastic bag.

"This is . . . brilliant," I said, a hint of uncertainty in my voice as I looked at the door, an indistinct shuffling sound coming from the corridor. My heart beat unsteadily. "But, Dax, I told you to text before you came. You really can't just drop by like this. We're being watched twenty-four-seven."

He lumbered over to the bed and sat down. Sophia followed, hopped onto his lap, and slung an arm around his shoulders. I peeped through the keyhole but the corridor was empty.

"Yeah, that makes four of us," Dax said. "I think the Warwick flats are being watched too."

My heart leaped into my throat. "What?! Since when?"

"Don't know, but Sophia saw one of the bad men hanging around outside this morning. He was looking up at the window with binoculars."

"And when he saw me looking at him, he ran off," she chipped in, then added after a thoughtful pause, "Never trust a man who can't look you in the eye."

Dax pulled Sophia closer to his chest, his arms wrapped around her waist protectively. "So we slipped out the fire escape just to be sure. We went to fetch the replica from Jen right away, but it took forever because, as you know, she lives in Norwich.

Then we came here. I didn't want to risk leaving Sophia behind or even going back to the flat until things had chilled out."

"*I* wasn't scared of being left alone," Sophia declared, setting the record straight. "Not since Dax showed me where he keeps his golf clubs."

Nellie turned her eyes on Sophia and smiled proudly.

"So wait, hold on," I said, thinking out loud. "When exactly did you see this bad man outside your building?"

Dax looked at his watch. "Can't say exactly. Sometime late morning. Eleven thirty?"

"We were on our way to the warehouse then," Nellie said. "So . . ."

"The underling," I provided.

"Underling?" Dax repeated. "Who's that?"

Nellie turned to him. "Good thing you got away. Nick of time too."

"This isn't good," I said. "If the thugs know Dax has been hiding Sophia . . ." I trailed off in a mumble, still nagged by the feeling we were missing something.

I was going to mention this to the others when a loud *ping* came from my laptop. A message from ENT00X was waiting in my Goods Exchange International inbox.

"It's Reid," I said, mostly to myself. "He's just confirmed the price with Mr. L."

"Mr. L?" Dax yelped. "*The* Mr. L? No, wait, you didn't tell me we were involving him!"

"And?" Nellie prompted me, ignoring Dax.

I read the message under my breath. "He's all in. Offering six hundred and fifty Bitcoin. That's equivalent to about sixteen mil at the current exchange."

Dax put his hands behind his head. "Jesus."

"Reid says we'll do the exchange at nine thirty," I went on, typing out my reply as I spoke. "Opposite the Royal Hospital Chelsea. That's just two blocks behind St. Jude on the border of Burton Court." Another DM came through almost immediately, and I read it out loud. "He says Mr. L will be driving a Mercedes-Benz Maybach with blank number plates."

"Got it," Nellie said. "And what about the appraisal? Has Reid asked Mr. L about that?"

I nodded, reading out Reid's last message: "'Mr. L says he wants to personally assess the bracelet before he hands over the Bitcoin.'"

"Brilliant," Nellie confirmed.

Dax, however, looked as if he was about to be sick. "Hold on, just hold on a second!" He took a minute to collect himself. "Let me get this straight: You're going to waltz into the St. Jude gallery under a false name, steal *the* Heart of Envy, and sell it to Mr. L, the most dangerous buyer any of us have ever heard of?"

Dead silence on all fronts.

"And then what?" he asked. "We're done? Criminals on the run for life? Stealing the Heart of Envy will definitely bring us infamy, if that's what we're going for. Or it might get you killed. Actually, get *us* killed. Ah, man, seriously! You've roped me into this mess, now the least you could do is tell me exactly how it's going to work. I want to know everything. And I really mean *everything*. If you can't trust me, then I'm out. Simple as that."

"'Trust,'" Sophia declared, staring down at *The Book of Good Advice*, which she'd promptly drawn from Dax's haversack, "'is like chicken pox: easily spread between friends and family, but once gone, it's gone for life.'"

Dax nodded in agreement, Nellie rolled her eyes, Sophia closed her book, and I got to explaining.

SOMETIME LATER, DAX gathered up his things—haversack, car and house keys, jumper—and padded to the window as if to leave. His mood had taken a definite turn since my long-winded explanation of the Game, though I wasn't entirely sure in which direction and for what reason. I'd expected him to be content, now that he'd been filled in. Or at the very least . . . grateful. Instead, he looked unsettled, maybe even irritable. Sure, the Game was ludicrous and dangerous and likely to get us all shot or thrown behind bars. But still, have a little faith!

"There's just . . . just one more thing," he said, turning back round to face me as Sophia trotted off to interrogate Nellie on the glittering objects lying on her side table. "What happened the other night between us—"

No, my God! Was *I* the reason for his mood shift? Had spending the past hour and a half cramped up in this dingy rat-filled hotel room brought back memories of *that* night? Had I done something—touched him, looked at him—to make him think another overture was imminent? Was he about to remind me he wasn't interested in a relationship? I simply could not bear the thought of it.

I grabbed the nearest object—my phone—and started pressing buttons at random, my cheeks hot. "Sorry, just, eh, I have to organize some things—"

He shoved his hands into his pockets and started speaking while I did everything possible to block out his words.

". . . the way things go sometimes."

Not listening.

". . . love but not *in* love, you know?"

Not listening.

". . . just didn't want to make you feel that way."

Still not listening.

Giving up on the phone idea, I turned my attention to the rustling curtains behind Dax's head. Had I left the window open? That was a mistake. What if Reid or the thugs were standing in the parking lot listening in?

"I'm gay," he finished.

I blinked, looked up. "Sorry, wh-what?"

The room fell silent. I was pretty sure Nellie and Sophia had heard it too.

"I'm gay," he repeated. "I didn't realize you didn't know or I would have said something sooner."

My mouth was hanging open. I snapped it shut.

"And Theo, that's the guy I've been seeing," he went on to explain, stunning me a second time. "I was hoping you'd catch on after all the hints I dropped, but then I figured you were pretty upset and I guess you felt rejected by me, which made me feel bad because it wasn't really like that. I mean . . . not in *that* way."

I risked a glance over my shoulder and caught Nellie's eye. She shook her head in a well-there-you-go fashion. It hit me then with exquisite force: Dax hadn't rejected me because I'd opened up to him emotionally or because I'd been vulnerable or because I'd let him see the real me. In fact, Dax hadn't really rejected me romantically at all.

"So, anyway," he said, "I really wanted to clear that up." He reached out and, before I could stop him, touched me on the arm. Something clicked back into place inside me. I didn't know what, but it felt good. "I'm happy. And I want you to be too. I like you. A lot. I especially like getting to know who you are under all this"—he waved his hand around in front of me—"and I don't want that night to change things."

I laughed as my mood brightened. "Ah, OK. Well, thanks for letting me know."

He laughed back. "So we're good? Promise? One hundred percent good?"

I nodded. "One hundred percent."

An easy silence fell between us. I didn't blink or look away, nor did I feel the need to fidget or say something just for the sake of it. Behind me, Nellie and Sophia let out a sigh of relief.

Dax looked at his watch. "Anyway, I really better get going now."

The muscles in my arms twitched. Just five seconds ago, I couldn't bear to look him in the eye. Now I wasn't sure I could bear to watch him leave. Him, Sophia, Nellie, any of them. It was like a bubble had formed around us, a place where, for once, I felt safe and at ease. Where I felt like, well . . . *me*. Couldn't we just stay like this forever?

"I've booked into an Airbnb in Central," he explained, "just until things clear up. But I need to head back to the flat first." He turned to Sophia with a look of concern. "Soph, listen. You're gonna stay here with the girls until I come back and fetch you, OK? Then we'll go to the new place together."

"No, wait, no," I said stiltedly. Dax paused. "It's just . . . that seems like a really bad idea. What if Reid or the thugs are hanging around at the flat again, waiting for you to come back? I mean, they almost certainly are."

"No choice. I have to fetch Sir Sebastian. I left him there when we went to Jen."

"OK, but you don't have to leave *now*, at least. It's too dangerous. Reid and the thugs could be anywhere," I added, thinking out loud. "But the one place we know they're not is right here at this hotel. Stay until they come back, then you'll have a clear run to the flat and wherever else you decide to go, knowing they haven't followed." It was irrefutable logic and we all knew it. But just to solidify my case, I retrieved my to-do list and held it up for everyone to see. "And anyway, I need your help with something. You and Sophia."

Sophia squinted at the list, reading out loud the only item left unticked for the day. "'Rehearse the Switch'?"

I reached inside the plastic bag Dax had given me, pulled out the small black box and, from inside, the counterfeit Heart of Envy. I held it to the light, smiling. "That's right."

16

THE VERY FIRST TIME I SAW NELLIE PERFORM THE SWITCH WAS on a bitterly cold Christmas Eve in Prague, five years ago. Six months had passed since she'd picked me up in a black cab outside my Chelsea apartment and convinced me to pack up my things, close my bank accounts, get off social media, and join her on our long-awaited childhood adventure across Europe. And while I'd completed my three-month "training course" at Gran's and knew the basic mechanics of purse-picking and mind control, I was still very much an amateur. If we were going to do this for a living, Nellie wanted me to have real-world experience.

The decision to start our exploits in Prague was based on Nellie's go-to logic of "why not?" Prague was famous for its Christmas markets and general December cheer, which meant the streets would be filled with awestruck and exhausted tourists; in other words, just the sort of people who were easy to swindle. Not that we were planning to actually steal anything. This was just a training exercise (or so I thought).

Keen to set the bar high for the years to come, we used what was left of Nellie's fight-club money to check into the Don

Giovanni—a luxury five-star hotel—and spent the next six days chatting wistfully about our future plans and how we'd go about building our empire. We drifted through the bright, crisp mornings and icy nights in the hazy bliss of our rekindled friendship. For the first time in my life I actually felt free, careless, *alive*. I had no responsibilities, nothing to work toward, no milestones to reach. No one to please but myself.

Every morning we strolled arm in arm along the banks of the Vltava River, people watching, daydreaming. We walked through the historic Jewish Quarter and across Charles Bridge, snacking on chimneys of crisp, sugary pastry brushed in butter, or tins of artisan chocolate. In the evenings we rode the tram up to the monastery and Gothic cathedrals, patrolled the eerie forests that bordered the city, then moseyed back down to the town center for a hearty dinner of beef goulash and a pint of pilsner. On the evening of the twenty-fourth, after an early boozy dinner, we headed to the Christmas market in the Old Town Square.

"OK, Game time," Nellie said, flashing her famous megawatt smile.

"What? You mean . . . ? Gosh, I'm not sure I'm ready, Nell. What if I get caught? I'm not spending Christmas Eve in prison!"

"Confidence, Em. Remember what Gran always said: it's the storyteller that counts, not the story. It doesn't matter what you do or say; as long as you're confident, you can get away with anything." She squeezed my shoulder. "She taught you everything you need to know. You've got this."

I looked up; the prismatic lights of the square's enormous Christmas tree flickered and danced. The falling snow glittered like sheets of white gold. Carols drifted out from speakers hidden among the food stalls. The air smelled of mulled wine and hot chocolate. "Gran would've loved it here," I said, my heart twisting at the thought. Oh, how I missed her then, and always.

Nellie chuckled softly. "Yep, true. But you know what she would've loved even more than the Christmas lights and hot chocolate?" She gestured at a passing tourist and the large ring on their finger. "Now, come on. I'll go first. All you have to is copy me."

Without further ado, she untangled herself from my side, marched across the square, and disappeared into the crowd. I paused under the Christmas tree, shivering, bemused. After a moment, I heard what sounded like an argument, voices growing louder and more furious. I followed the sound, weaving through the stalls, dodging tourists and vendors until I came out the other side. I emerged in a dark, narrow street that threaded off into a maze of baroque-style buildings. A little way ahead, a group of women were huddled together, admiring what I realized was some sort of street play—two actors arguing with each other in a Charlie Chaplin–style performance. Just in time, I caught sight of Nellie striding toward the throng. As she passed a young gentleman who was hovering nearby, she tripped on the cobblestones. Instinctively, the man reached out to steady her. She curled her fingers around his wrist, and *poof!* just like that, his watch was gone. I only knew it because she dangled the thing up in the air behind his back just to show me what she'd snagged. I can't say I felt good watching her steal from someone just for the hell of it, but this was back before we'd agreed on the rules and ethics of the Games. In any case, I needn't have worried, because she slipped the watch back onto her mark's wrist, thanked him for his chivalry, and walked on. The whole thing took less than five seconds.

I stared at her, awestruck, as she reappeared at my side. Of course I'd seen her pick pockets before, more times than I could count. But this was different in a way I couldn't have recognized back then. All I knew was that it didn't look like petty street crime. It looked like magic.

"Gran called it the Switch," she explained with a wistful smile, ordering us each a steaming mug of hot chocolate and two sugar-encrusted chimney cakes, *trdelníks.* "It was her favorite trick. Much more advanced than simple pickpocketing. And much more useful."

I frowned. "Useful? How? You took his watch and then you gave it back."

She winked, then drew back her coat sleeve to reveal a watch that looked very much like the one she'd just given back to her mark. "Or did I?"

I got it then, the reason Gran called it the Switch.

"OK," NELLIE SAID now, standing between me and Dax in the middle of our hotel room. "Game time. Let's imagine it's heist night—and Dax, you're the wearer of the bracelet." She fastened the glittering replica to his right wrist, then nodded at me. "We're obviously Sheryl Yardley and . . . whoever—"

"Deborah Stern," I provided.

"Right. So, Dax, we're going to try and take the Heart of Envy off your wrist without you noticing. Do whatever you can to make sure that doesn't happen."

"Easy enough, I guess?" Dax said, making it sound like a question.

Sophia, who'd been observing us from the bed with a pen and paper (taking notes?), held up her hand and squeaked, "And me? Can I play too? Please!"

Nellie thought for a moment. "Sure. You can play the security guard."

Her mouth fell open. "Security guard? But I don't know how to—"

Nellie cut in, "Your job is to keep an eye on the Heart of Envy at all times. No one who isn't Dax should touch it. Not even for a single second. Got that?"

She seemed to turn the task over in her mind, as if trying to decide whether she was up to it. She gave Nellie a quick salute, put down her pen and paper, and marched to Dax's side.

Hiding a grin, Nellie turned her attention to me and, when no one else was looking, slipped a small black box into my palm. "You remember the golden rule?"

"Focus," I said easily, dropping the box into my pocket and at the same time extracting the MG keys.

"Bingo," Nellie said proudly.

I twirled the keys between my fingers, a flash of adrenaline rising inside my belly. Although Nellie and I had gone over the Game a hundred times already, this was our first opportunity to see how it played out in real time. We had fifteen variations of the Switch in our arsenal and could use whichever one most suited the circumstances on heist night. We wouldn't know that until the last minute, though, which meant we'd have to practice every single variation beforehand.

Subtly, Nellie raised an index finger on one hand, then five fingers on the other. Variation number six. I grinned as she turned to Dax and said, "Everyone thinks a pickpocket uses distraction as their main tool. But actually, we use the opposite. *Focus.*" She closed the distance between them while I shuffled to the left, so slow that Dax didn't even flinch. Sophia frowned at Nellie, ignoring me. "So, yes, I could distract you with a loud noise," Nellie continued, just as I let the MG's keys slip from my grasp. They clanged loudly against the tiled floor, causing Dax to recoil and Sophia to yelp softly. "Or maybe some meaningless chitchat." She winked at me. I smiled back as she placed her right hand on Dax's shoulder. "But that's risky, isn't it? Because you're not really focusing on anything specific. You're just *distracted*."

Dax cocked his head, obviously confused. I took another step left, then forward. Sophia saw me this time and scowled. I smiled innocently, hands in my pockets.

"So, no. We never try to distract our marks," Nellie said, absently tugging at her Dior scarf. "Instead, we try to refocus their attention on something else, force them to concentrate so hard on one thing that they don't see, feel, or hear anything else."

She slipped her hand down Dax's left arm. He smiled warily and recoiled.

"Hey!" Sophia snapped, pointing at Nellie. "I see what you're doing there, miss. Stand back!"

Nellie laughed, bowed gracefully, backed away. "Good one. You got me, Daisy Duck: head of security."

Meanwhile, I shuffled one foot in front of the other until I was less than a yard away from Dax's right side. Sophia would've noticed if she hadn't been so focused on what Nellie was doing. *Focus*, you remember?

"Is it just me or is it hot in here?" I piped up out of nowhere. Everyone turned to look at me with a frown. I fanned my face with both hands, though I wasn't really feeling hot at all.

"Is that a trick?" Sophia asked suspiciously.

"Ha, I wish." I surveyed the room. "It's a hormone thing."

"*Hormones*," Sophia echoed. "I've heard of those. They make people do crazy things."

"Yep," Nellie said. "Like fall in love with the wrong people."

"We've all been there," Dax added, flashing me a knowing glance.

"Umm, so, I need a glass of water. Like now," I said.

Nellie marched over to the bathroom sink and got me one.

I dipped my fingers in and splashed the cool liquid over my face while Nellie fanned me dry with *The Book of Good Advice*. When the whole fiasco was over, I held the empty water glass limp at my side, like I didn't know what to do with it. This was Nellie's cue to shift into a new position.

Gentleman that he was, Dax took the glass from my hand, and as he did so, I slipped my fingers under the strap of the replica bracelet and loosened the clasp.

"Thanks," I said.

"No worries." He flashed me an easy smile that suggested he was happy we were able to do this at last—stand around and stare at each other without feeling awkward.

"All right," Nellie said, tapping Dax on the elbow (I don't think he noticed). "Where were we?"

"Focus," Sophia provided. "You said the trick is to always make sure—" She broke off and gasped. "Hey! The bracelet!"

Dax lifted his right arm, eyes wide with confusion. "What the . . . It's gone. When? How?"

"Gone? You sure about that?" Nellie said.

And while Dax continued to fumble around looking for the bracelet, I dipped my fingers in and out of the back pocket of his jeans.

"Check your pockets," Nellie suggested.

He faltered, and a tiny blotch of red touched his cheeks. "It . . . How?" he mumbled, stupefied, extracting the replica from his back pocket.

Sophia slapped a hand to her mouth and started giggling.

ABOUT TWO HOURS later, after we'd practiced all fourteen other variations of the Switch, I said with a pant, "OK, well, I think we've got this waxed."

Dax and Sophia collapsed into the armchair while Nellie flopped down on the bed, threw her arms out behind her, and let out a long groan.

"Let's hope so!" she said. "I think if I practice one more minute, my fingers will fall off."

Sophia, looking deeply concerned, consulted her book. "Nothing in here about loose fingers, sorry."

We all burst out in a sort of frazzled, hysterical laugher, a little louder than we should've. And for a tiny fraction of time—I'm talking less than a split second—I actually felt OK about things, maybe even bordering on happy. Not a flicker of concern crossed my mind: not about Saturday's heist or the million things that could go wrong on the night. Not about the fact that we still hadn't heard from Reid, which meant he and the thugs were still out there doing whatever was more important than keeping an eye on us. My to-do list for the day was all ticked off and everything was going to be fine. Actually, better than fine. It was going to be great.

And then Sophia trotted over to the window, tears of delight still streaming down her cheeks, breath catching, and said, "Oh no! He's found us! The bad man's found us!"

Dax got to his feet, posture rigid. *"Theo?"*

17

NELLIE AND I FROZE, NEITHER OF US QUITE SURE WHAT WE'D just heard. Or what it meant.

Theo? As in Dax's boyfriend? Here?

Sophia was still pointing out the window, Dax still just behind her, looking over her shoulder. There was a racket in the corridor—footsteps, maybe, someone at the door.

I blocked out these sounds and focused on what was happening in front of me.

Dax's smile, like mine, had vanished. The streetlight outside cast a dim, sick light onto his face. He took a step backward, groping at the thin air, muttering, "I . . . No . . . What?"

I stumbled closer to the window and nudged Sophia to the side. Something that tasted distinctly like bile rose in my throat.

"Theo?" Nellie asked, looking at Dax. "Your *boyfriend*?"

I peered through the grimy, oil-stained glass. The horizon outside was dark and menacing, the clouds swelling, the wind swirling. A storm was coming. A big one. And right in the middle of it, there he was—the underling—marching across the parking lot, hands in his pockets, his gaunt, thin frame somehow more menacing than I remembered.

"Who's Theo?" Sophia asked, frowning. "That's the bad man, the one who was watching our flat!"

It was all the confirmation I needed. Theo and the underling were the same person.

It was enough to make me feel like throwing up. Instead, I whipped Sophia away from the window and pulled the curtains closed. I turned to look at Dax—and surely my face showed an expression of horror. There had been a time—not so long ago—when I hadn't trusted him. But things were different now. I really wanted to believe that. Dax wouldn't have lied to us while all this was happening. Not possible.

A brief, throbbing silence followed as we all began to figure out what this meant. We stared at Dax—Nellie, Sophia, and I—expecting some explanation, but he appeared to have slipped into a hypnotic trance, unable to speak.

"Dax," Nellie said, her voice dead calm. "One of the men who kidnapped me is your *boyfriend*? Explain. Now."

He shook his head, backing away. "I didn't . . . I didn't know. He's not Theo, or I mean he's not . . . there's got to be some other—"

Sophia shrieked as the door rattled on its hinges. Someone was yelling for us to open, and *oh God*, it sounded very much like Boss Thug. Or maybe Reid.

The door rattled again, harder this time, like someone was actually trying to kick it in.

Sophia crouched near the bed, eyes the size of saucepans, her whole body trembling.

"Boss Thug . . ." I mumbled nervously. "We can't let him see Sophia!"

Nellie, as if noticing the noise in the corridor for the first time, dragged the armchair over to the door. It wouldn't hold anyone off for long, but it would at least give us a moment to strategize.

"I don't believe this!" Dax said, his hands clasped over his head. "This whole time?" He turned to me and Nellie, his gaze searching and desperate, as if urging us to believe him. "I swear I didn't know he was involved! I swear it! *Fuck!*"

Nellie and I shared a look. I wanted her to confirm what I wanted to believe: that Dax hadn't betrayed us, that he'd been hoodwinked just the same as we had. My heart seemed to think he was innocent, but my head—still cluttered with the memories of all the times I'd been let down and betrayed before—wasn't so convinced.

Nellie, though, seemed certain. She gave me a small nod of assurance and turned to Dax. "We know," she said flatly. "But you've still got some explaining to do."

He opened his mouth to speak, but I cut him off swiftly. "Not now. We have to get Sophia out of here!" I opened the curtains and examined the parking lot. It was empty, which had to mean Theo was already inside the hotel.

"Quick, sweetheart," Nellie said to Sophia, reading my mind. "Through there."

Sophia stalled. "But . . . but it's dark. And I want to stay!"

"You can't," Nellie insisted, her voice stern but kind. "It's too dangerous. The bad men are looking for you, remember?"

"But—"

Nellie was insistent. "As soon as you're out, run. You understand? There's a big post office just off the main road and a quiet street behind it. You might've seen it on your way in."

Sophia nodded, her lip trembling. "Think so."

Nellie smiled comfortingly, squeezed her hand. "You run straight there, sweetheart. No stopping. No looking over your shoulder. And when you get there, find a safe place to hide. You know how to hide, don't you?"

Sophia turned her big brown dinner-plate eyes on me, Nellie, Dax. "And you'll come and find me, won't you," she said with surprising certainty. Less a question, more a statement.

"Of course we will," Nellie answered. "Just stay put and we'll be right there. Be brave, all right?"

"And remember what the book says about courage," I chipped in.

She sniffed and nodded. "'Sometimes it takes the scary things to show us how brave we are.'"

I kissed her forehead and, with Nellie's help, lifted her onto the windowsill. After double-checking the parking lot was empty, we grabbed a hand each and lowered her gently to the ground.

She turned to face the darkness, alone. She was scared, of course, but I could see the courage spark behind her eyes. She straightened her spine, took a breath, and was gone.

I looked back at the door, slats breaking, dust flying, Boss Thug roaring. A second later, there was an ear-splitting crash, and wood splinters flew across the room as Boss Thug kicked the door in.

Gun in hand, he looked at Dax.

Dax raised his hands in surrender. "I need to speak to Theo. Where is he?"

Ignoring him, Boss Thug cocked the gun, then barked over his shoulder to someone in the corridor. "She's not here. Must've gone through the window. Check the parking lot. Quick."

Footsteps beat down the corridor. Theo? Reid? I guessed it didn't matter. We didn't have time to wait and find out.

I looked at Nellie, the diamond choker dangling from her

fingers. Was she close enough to Boss Thug to incapacitate him, knock the gun from his grip? Was Dax? Was I? As if reading my mind, Nellie launched herself—arms outreached—at Boss Thug's throat, while I swung left, aiming for the hand holding the gun.

The footsteps in the corridor came to a sudden halt as Theo tumbled into the room, pale, panting.

Boss Thug staggered backward, still holding the gun. He turned round, gun raised.

Theo dived forward, pulled the weapon from his grip, and aimed it at Dax.

I couldn't track everything that happened next, but I saw Dax taking a step toward Theo, as if trying to talk him out of whatever he was about to do. While he was at it, Boss Thug reached again for the gun. There was a loud, horrible bang. Someone screamed. It might have been me.

And then blood. Lots and lots of blood.

I BLINKED, TURNED. Boss Thug staggered across the room, his left leg bleeding profusely.

"No . . . No. I . . . I'm sorry," Theo stammered, looking at Boss Thug, his hands shaking. "I didn't . . . I didn't mean to pull the trigger. Just . . . happened."

Boss thug threw him a furious glare, then collapsed to the floor, out like a light.

"Well, this is great!" I said, my voice high-pitched and panicked. "Now what?"

Dax, whose face was blank with shock, said, "We can't leave him here. He'll bleed out."

"And we can't hang around either," Nellie said. "That gunshot was loud as hell. Someone's probably already called the police."

All three of us looked up at Theo, whom—for a brief moment—we'd forgotten about. He was standing there, as if frozen, the gun held limply at his side.

"Hand it over, underling," Nellie said, untying her Dior scarf from around her neck. "Before you do something else you'll regret."

"But . . . I . . . I can't," he mumbled.

Despite the gun, Nellie closed in on him. Her voice was slick, persuasive, almost hypnotic. "You can't shoot us all, honey. Either you wait around for the police to arrest you, or you hand over the gun and we help you get out of here. What's it going to be?"

He slowly raised the weapon. I held my breath while Nellie held out her hand. I bet I was the only one who saw the tremble in her fingers.

Theo faltered, then passed over the gun.

"I'll call an ambulance once we're out of here," Nellie said, wrapping the gun in her scarf and placing it in her bag.

"But what about Reid?" Theo asked. "I'll have to tell him what's happened."

"So call him," Nellie suggested.

"What?"

"Call Reid and tell him Boss Thug's shot himself in the leg and is now in hospital. Say he was drunk and fell down the stairs."

Theo was delirious. "He'll never believe that!"

"Why not? Who's going to tell him otherwise? Now, let's get moving! Dax—go get Daisy Duck and we'll meet you at Peckham Rye station. I know an Airbnb nearby we can use to regroup." She pointed at the window. "Everyone ready?"

Dax and I nodded. Theo threw up all over his shoes.

18

AS PLANNED, NELLIE, THEO, AND I MET DAX AND SOPHIA AT
the Airbnb in Peckham in the early hours of the following morning. We took our seats around the dining room table, staring at
one another in strained silence.

Theo's iPhone buzzed. "It's Reid." He gulped. "Fourth time
in under an hour. I've got to answer!"

"Dream on," Nellie said.

"But he'll be wondering where I am! I've already fed him that
stupid lie about Nico shooting himself, and now I'm ignoring his
calls. What if Nico tells him the truth?"

Nellie and I shared a satisfied glance, happy we finally knew
Boss Thug's name.

"Just relax!" Nellie snapped. "Nico's in hospital and probably
out cold. We'll worry about Reid later."

Theo opened his mouth to argue, but Dax got in first.

"So I'm guessing the night we met at Opium was a setup,
then?" he asked furiously, the muscles in his forearms twitching
like he was ready to throw a fist in the underling's direction.

Opium was the fancy-pants dim-sum bar in Leicester Square

Dax had told me about, where he and Theo had bonded over their love of vegetarian potstickers, astronomy, and computers. It was also where the pair had been the night of the Laundromat break-in and Nellie's kidnapping, which suggested Theo's primary role in this heinous setup had been to keep Dax uninformed and out of the way (and possibly lovestruck).

Theo slumped in his seat, tendrils of golden hair sticking to his forehead, his face ashen. Although I wasn't sure how necessary this was, considering we had the gun, Nellie insisted we bind his hands and feet with duct tape *and* strap him into the chair. She wasn't taking any chances, apparently.

"No. I mean . . . yes. Yes," Theo confessed miserably. "It was a setup, but not by me. Not my idea."

"So what, then? You were forced into it somehow?" Dax barked. "Pretended to like all the things I liked? Pretended to like *me*? Is your name really Theo Fletcher? Are you even gay, or did you lie about that too?"

"No! It is. I . . . am; that's why he . . . that's why this all—" He took a ragged breath and started again. "Meeting you at Opium *was* a setup, yes. *Reid's* setup. And yes, I was forced into it. He knew you went there a lot because he'd been following you for a while by then."

"Wait, what?" I said. "Reid has been following Dax too?"

"Obviously," Theo grunted. "He knew about Dax because he'd followed you to the Laundromat the night of the cuff link sale in January."

Of course. I remembered it now, going back to the Laundromat to see Dax on the pretext of needing to do a stock count but really because Dax was alone and so was I and, well, you get the gist.

"But the rest," Theo went on, speaking only to Dax, "everything else that happened between us, all those nights together, everything we talked about, our families, our lives, our dreams . . . all that was genuine, I swear. I like you, Dax. You have to believe me. None of that was a lie. In the beginning, yes, but not . . . not . . ." He groaned. "The thing is, the more I got to know you, and the more I realized we had in common, the deeper my feelings became and the worse I felt about everything. I didn't want any of this. I just got sucked in, and by the time I knew what was really going on, what Reid had planned, it was too late to get out."

"Bullshit!" Dax leaped up from his seat, then slumped back down, defeated. "You just tried to kill me, for Christ's sake!"

"Kill you?" Theo shrieked. "Are you serious? Really? I saved your life in that hotel room! I knocked the gun away!"

"No, you aimed it at me and pulled the trigger!"

"Well, if that's the case, then why aren't you dead?"

"Calm down, both of you!" Nellie cut in. "We don't have time for a lovers' tiff." She placed her knuckle-duster on the table in front of her—as a reminder of who was in charge—and added, "You can scream and shout at each other all you want, just not before I get some answers." She looked at Theo, though it was more like a glare and caused everyone in the room to stiffen. Except Sophia, who was leaning back in her seat, arms crossed, her eyes narrowed and fixed on Theo. If looks could kill, he'd be dead in ten.

"I want to know where Daddy is," she said abruptly, her tone etched with a deep, hollow sadness that shot like a lightning bolt through my chest. "I know you know. You've been keeping him from me, haven't you?"

Theo stammered, "H-he's, I, well—"

Nellie silenced him with a look, then curled her fingers

around Sophia's small hand. "We'll get to that later, honey. I'll make sure of it."

I gulped. Sophia grumbled something but soon fell silent.

Nellie turned back to Theo. "All right, now, start from the beginning. I want to know every. Single. Thing. How did you and your friends do this and how did you get tangled up with Dax?"

It took a while for Theo to come to the decision that he had no choice but to get talking. And fast. He tried to shift in his seat, hands still bound, then shot a quick, nervous glance at each of us in turn.

"James Reid is, well, you could say he was a friend of mine. And a colleague. We both worked for that online gaming company I told you about." He nodded at Dax, who glared back. "Reid was just a paper pusher, really, an intern for the marketing team, while I worked with the actual game design stuff. We were there for three years together, got to know each other a bit, hung out. Then, a few months ago, Reid told me he had this vintage signet ring he wanted to sell but was struggling to find a buyer. That's when I made the huge mistake of telling him about the dark web trading group I'd joined a while back to sell—"

"Stolen goods?" Nellie provided.

He hesitated for a second, then scowled. "Like you lot, yes. But unlike you, I didn't do it for an ego trip. I really needed to make money. To survive."

"Drop the act, babe," Nellie said. "If you were trading on Goods Exchange, you're as much a criminal as the rest of us. Might as well admit it."

Theo knocked his head back in frustration. "No, you don't understand. I was desperate, *really* desperate. The gaming company was about to retrench half its employees and I knew I'd be one of them. I didn't know what to do. I'd already lost my house to the banks, and my car. I was bankrupt and it was all thanks to my idiot brother, the golden boy Wall Street investor genius who basically conned me into investing in this shitty start-up he and my parents had dreamed up, which flatlined before any of us could take our cash out."

Dax looked surprised. This was news to him too. "What start-up?"

"Some buy-and-sell app that was supposed to screen users and prevent fraud," Theo said. "Ironic, huh? Anyway, the point is, if it had happened the other way round, and I'd been the one to lose all the golden boy's money and put the family name to shame, he and my parents would've disowned me without a second thought. Instead it was all just a little 'mistake' we could brush under the carpet. Technically, I'd put less money in than Mum, Dad, or Michael, so no one seemed to think it was a big deal. 'Oh, just a few thousand quid,' they said. Only everything I had to my name. In fact, I think in some ways they thought I deserved it." His voice softened and slowed, the anger now replaced with a lingering sadness. "My parents hadn't ever really accepted me, you know, not *all* of me. They'd raised me and my brother to be buttoned-up, traditional, all that white-picket-perfect-wife-perfect-life shit. Michael nailed it, obviously, but I failed at every turn. No interest in marriage or kids, low-paying job with a company that sells cheap entertainment to layabouts. Couldn't have been worse, really, unless I ended up homeless and unemployed, which was where I was heading."

Dax looked almost like he understood where Theo was coming from but didn't want to admit it. Maybe I did too.

"Anyway," he went on, clearing the hitch in his voice, "Reid sold his stupid ring on Goods Exchange for way more than it was worth, and I guess that's when he got his grand idea. He started monitoring the group more closely and soon realized there was basically only one profile everyone on there followed, one profile that had all the biggest sales, all the best listings." He inclined his head at me and Nellie. "Next thing I knew, Reid came by my house, said he had a proposition for me. 'Exhibition Month is coming up,' he said, like I knew what that was. He didn't tell me anything about the bracelet at the time, just that he was going to 'coordinate a sale' for some expensive piece of jewelry and he needed my help. See, Reid didn't really know much about the tech side of things. He needed my help to set up an anonymous platform for him, one he'd later use to track and research the profile he'd become obsessed with. Yours.

"So I signed up to Reid's gig," he explained. "Worst decision I've ever made, I realize that now. But at the time . . . I dunno . . . Reid lured me in, saying how we'd make millions. It was a no-brainer. Like I said, I *really* needed the cash, and it struck me as pretty brilliant that I might get back the money Michael had lost for me by trading on an illegal buy-and-sell forum . . . the exact opposite of the one he'd failed to get started. But of course," he added with a grunt, "it didn't turn out to be so easy. For starters, it wasn't just me Reid had roped into his grand plan."

"Nico?" I guessed.

"It was only when Nico joined the deal that Reid told us he was actually planning to steal something. And not just any old piece of jewelry, but an iconic bracelet from one of the world's most famous exhibitions. I thought he was joking at first. Either that or he'd lost his mind. But then he explained the whole plan, how he was going to use the two of you to do all the dirty work . . . and, I dunno, by the end of it I actually thought it might work."

He stared blankly at the space in front of him and continued. "As you know, it started when Reid set up the cuff link sale. He tailed you back to the Laundromat, saw Dax, decided he was an easier phishing target, and started tailing him as well. A few weeks in, when he saw Dax out at Opium with some guys, he sent me in to get close to him, siphon whatever I could from him. When he thought he had enough, he broke into the Laundromat and sent Nico to kidnap Nellie." He moved his bound feet farther under his chair, dropped his shoulders. "And, yeah, the rest you know, I guess."

An edgy silence followed, punctuated only by the occasional creak as Theo shifted uncomfortably in his seat.

"OK," Nellie said at last, glancing at Sophia. "Now tell us about Chris Keeling. How does he fit into all this?"

Sophia straightened in her seat. A lump rose in my throat. I knew Nellie had to ask this question, but the fact that Theo's answer would inevitably lead us to the horrid reality of Chris Keeling's fate made my stomach twist into knots.

Theo made a point of avoiding Sophia's eye when he answered. "I only met Keeling a few weeks ago when Reid recruited him, but—" He broke off, cleared his throat. "I don't know what Reid needed him for, but whatever it was, Keeling had more to lose than the rest of us if things went south."

"*Hmm.*" Sophia mused. "And what does this James Reid man look like?"

Theo thought for a moment. "You heard of Eminem?"

Sophia was confused. "The sweets?"

Theo groaned impatiently. "All I know is that when things started getting serious and Keeling realized what we were going to steal and how dicey it was, he said he wanted to back out. He said he had a kid and it wasn't worth the risk of getting locked up."

Sophia nodded proudly. "Sounds like Daddy. *Sensible*."

"Problem was," Theo went on, ignoring her, "Reid didn't want us ratting him out. Any of us. But Keeling was adamant, and so, eh, yeah . . . that's when Reid decided to kidnap Sophia as an insurance policy. In case Keeling made good on his threats about going to the police." He waited a minute, then added, "But I don't know what happened after that. I haven't seen Keeling since last week."

Sophia placed *The Book of Good Advice* on the table and drummed her fingers against the cover. Still, *still*, it looked as if she had hope. "I don't believe you!" she burst out. "You know where Daddy is. I know you do!"

Theo rocked nervously in his chair, a film of sweat gathering above his lip.

"Hey, Soph," Nellie said gently, "why don't you go get yourself a glass of juice? There's some in the fridge, I think."

She hesitated but eventually nodded and scampered off into the kitchen.

Nellie rounded on Theo. "*We know*," she said in a whisper. "Chis Keeling is dead. We saw the body in the warehouse. The least you can do is tell us exactly how he died."

Theo dropped his head, shook it slowly. "Reid got into an argument with him at the warehouse last Friday. Like I said, Keeling wanted the girl released but Reid wasn't going to let that happen. I don't know how he . . . I was there when they got into the argument but I left before, you know. I didn't want to see it."

"And the body?" Nellie asked next, her voice—for the first time—breaking. "Where did he move it to?"

"I'm sorry . . . I don't know that either. Reid told Nico to get rid of it."

I looked across the room. Sophia was staring at me, sitting

on the floor with her glass of juice, too far away to hear anything, and yet I was so sure she could see the truth on my face.

"But listen . . ." Theo went on, now in a frantic whisper. He leaned forward, eyes darting this way and that. "If you keep the girl out of Reid's sight, he'll think Nico's still got her tied up. Like he's supposed to. And she'll be safe. For now, at least."

"Yeah, thanks," Dax snapped. "We had it under control until you started spying on me outside my flat."

"It wasn't like that!" Theo said. "I was trying to find her before Nico did! He knows Reid will be fuming if he discovers she's escaped so he's been trying to track her down. He was supposed to move her somewhere the night of Nellie's kidnapping, but instead he used her to get to you"—he nodded at me—"and then she disappeared. He always suspected Dax was hiding her and kept asking me to check. I squashed his suspicions for as long as I could, even though I was sure he was right. But yesterday morning he put a gun to my head and told me that if I didn't find her, he'd tell Reid I'd been hiding her myself."

"So you came to my flat to kidnap her?" Dax asked, his voice a growl.

"No! I came to warn you. To tell you to run before Reid or Nico got to the girl. Or . . . maybe we could've run together." He closed his eyes and mumbled something I couldn't make out. "After I saw her through the window, I waited outside for you to come down. But I guess you slipped out the back, because I lost you. It was only later, when I arrived at the hotel, that I realized Nico had you all locked up in that room. And, well, yeah, that's why I pulled the gun from him like I did. He would've killed you if I hadn't, or at least maimed you badly enough to get you to tell him where Sophia was."

I almost didn't want to look at Dax. I suppose it's a stretch to say I knew what he was feeling, but I did at least know what it was like to be betrayed and manipulated by someone you loved.

Dax muttered something, his gaze turning distant, blank.

Sophia returned to the table, slumped in her seat, her eyes wet. I looked from Dax to her and back again, my heart tight with a sadness that wasn't my own. What was I supposed to say to either of them? I turned to Nellie in desperation.

She mouthed, *"I got this,"* and said briskly, "Soph, I need your help. Quick."

Sophia continued to look at her hands. "With what?"

"A lot of things. Bring that book of yours and come with me. We'll need you as well," she said to me. "And Dax—how about some coffee?"

"OK," he said, equally miserably. "I'll put the kettle on."

"WE HAVE TO figure out what to do next," Nellie said, as soon as we were gathered together in the kitchen and out of Theo's earshot. "But first things first: Sophia, what does that book of yours say about family?"

Sophia held the book limply at her side. "Don't know," she said gloomily while Dax laid out the cups, milk, and sugar and turned on the kettle.

"Well, let's have a look." Nellie held out her hand. Sophia relinquished the book and Nellie began paging through in silence. After a moment, she said, "Right. Here we are. Listen up: 'Families stick together, no matter what. Even when they're mad at each other. And even when their hearts are breaking.'" She snapped the book shut and passed it back to Sophia. "So, if that's what the book says, then who are we to argue? We stick together. In good times *and* bad times, like it or lump it."

"The book is stupid," Sophia grumbled. "I don't care what it says anymore."

"Families stick together," Nellie repeated, lowering herself to Sophia's level.

Sophia shook her head. "Not all families . . ."

"But," Nellie went on, unfazed, "the thing is, not everyone gets a family when they're born. Some of us have to wait a bit longer to meet our families and some of us get new families when our old ones leave. Like Emma here. Right, Emma?"

"Who's Emma?" Sophia said, then looked at me, her eyes widening with interest. "Emma!"

"Correct," I said, lifting my chin. "And no, I definitely didn't have a family when I was born."

Sophia looked deeply concerned. "You didn't have a mummy or daddy? But that's impossible."

"No, I did, sort of. They just weren't, well, they didn't really want to be my mummy or daddy so—"

"The point is," Nellie cut in, "Emma's found her real family now. And here we are. Together."

"But what about Dax?" Sophia asked. "Did he have a family when he was born, or is he part of ours too?"

Dax looked off into the distance, as if deep in thought. "I did have a family once. But they live a long way away now. I don't get to see them too often, and"—he twisted his hands together, eyes downcast—"some of them don't really understand me either. So yeah, I'd like to be part of this one. If that's OK?"

I gulped.

"And what about Theo?" Sophia pressed. "Is he part of the family?"

"No!" we all answered together.

"More like a distant cousin," I suggested.

"Twice removed," Nellie chipped in.

"Ousted," Dax confirmed.

"Anyway," Nellie went on, "what I'm saying is, the four of us are a family now. Which means we have to look after each other and we have to stick together. Always. No excuses. Got that, everyone?"

We nodded silently. Sophia brought the book back to her chest and I wiped my eyes on my sleeve when no one was looking.

"And as for your daddy," Nellie added more carefully, "once this is over, Emma and I will find out exactly what happened to him, OK?"

Sophia beamed. For the hundredth time, I tried not to think about how we were going to break the news that he was dead.

AFTER A QUICK time-out in the bathroom, blowing my nose and patting the redness from my eyes, I returned to the kitchen to find the conversation had taken a darker turn.

". . . just wish I'd figured it out before," Dax was saying. "I even caught him once, you know, going through my phone. He gave some excuse about checking the time, but it didn't sit right. I had a feeling he was reading my texts, though I thought it was because he suspected I was cheating on him or something." He paused, then something seemed to dawn on him. "Shit! That's it, then, isn't it?"

"What?" I asked.

"How he knew your names. Your *real* names." He drew out his phone and showed me his contact list. "I've got you saved as Emma and Nellie, not Janet and Annie. Mate, I'm sorry. I should've been more careful."

I waved off his apology. "If anyone's been making the mistakes here, it's me. I should've known that cuff link sale was fishy from the get-go."

"Everyone makes mistakes," Sophia declared spiritedly, perusing her book. "And they're good for you. It says so in here, look: 'Each day, aim to make at least five mistakes by lunchtime.'"

I smiled at her and poured myself a second cup of coffee, then padded to the door to check on Theo. He was right where we'd left him: sitting at the table, his hands bound, head bowed. "So what do we do now?"

"Nothing's changed," Nellie said. "We go ahead, full throttle. Reid doesn't have to know we know who Theo really is. Or where Sophia and Dax have run off to. If we pretend everything is as it was before, then we can go ahead with the heist as planned. With Boss Thug out of the way, all we have to do is make sure Reid thinks Theo's still on his side and we're good."

"Which reminds me," Dax said. "There's just one thing I want to check up on. Nell, is there any chance you can get Theo to tell you Nico's surname?"

"Easy," Nellie said.

"No, I mean, like, *subtly*. Without him thinking anything of it. He's smarter than you think."

Nellie rolled her eyes. "Spare me. Wait here."

She was gone for thirty seconds. I am not kidding. Thirty seconds.

"Nico Kappas," she said dryly, strolling back into the kitchen. "So? How does this help us?"

Dax stared at her, clearly filled with admiration. "I, ah, I don't know yet. Just thought I'd do some cyberdigging and see what comes up. On him and Theo. Also Reid. Just in case."

"Good idea," I said encouragingly.

"In the meantime"—Nellie turned to me—"we better figure out what we're going to do with idiot number two over there."

I thought for a moment. "You still got Boss Thug's gun?"

She nodded at her Gucci bag lying on the counter behind us.

"Give it to him."

Nellie blinked. Even Sophia looked up in shock.

"That sounds like a great idea," Nellie said sarcastically.

"Because it is. Think about it. You said we have to make sure Reid believes everything's fine and well and going according to plan. We also have to make sure he doesn't think Theo's on our side. But how is he going to buy any of that if the underling's moping around with his tail between his legs? So we give Theo the gun and tell him to act like he's got us under control. Boss Thug–style."

"And you reckon he'll play along?" Nellie asked.

"We're just going to have to hope so."

"All right," Nellie said. "I'm in."

"Me too," said Dax.

"Me three," said Sophia.

19

NONBELIEVER THOUGH I WAS, I SAID A SILENT PRAYER AND performed three signs of the cross as Nellie, Theo, and I arrived at our "headquarters" the following day—the warehouse in Wapping. *Please, good Lord, if you're up there, let this be the very last time we ever set foot inside this dingy hole.* For her part, Nellie lit three sticks of incense (sage for cleansing bad vibes, vanilla masala for luck, lavender for stress relief), lined up her stone Buddhas, and mumbled something about revenge.

I wasn't entirely convinced any of it would help us. Would Reid believe the story about Nico's tumble down the stairs? Would he sense something had changed with Theo? And if he did, then what? Would he drag Theo through some grisly interrogation until he had no choice but to spill the beans? Not just about where Sophia and Dax were hiding, but about us, the Game, everything. Still, amid the doubt, I couldn't help but feel a bit excited. I imagined the look on Reid's face when he finally realized what we had in store for him, and let out a bark of laughter.

"**WE HAVE THE** replica at last," I said to Reid, finding him alone in the warehouse, pacing in front of the boarded window and looking even more peeved than the last time I'd seen him. He was wearing a blue drawstring hoodie, baggy black jeans, a gray beanie.

He surveyed me, then Theo, who was aiming Boss Thug's gun in my general direction like the brilliant actor he was.

"What have you been doing all this time?" Reid asked, addressing me.

"Practicing the Switch, of course," I said sweetly. "With the replica, like you asked." I pushed my shoulders back and smiled evenly. "I think we've got it waxed."

"You think?"

"I know."

He narrowed his eyes. "I tried to call Nico's mobile. But he's not answering."

"H-he was in surgery," Theo answered a little too easily while waving the gun around a little too carelessly. "Don't think he's come round yet. Probably lost his phone too."

Reid slipped a finger under his chunky silver chain. "So he shot himself in the leg, yeah?"

"Er, yes," Theo said.

"Because he was drunk?"

"As a lord," Nellie said. "Pitched down those stairs like a sack of rice. Lucky he didn't end up shooting himself in the head."

Reid rubbed the stubble on his chin and once again cast his beady eyes from me to Nellie and on to Theo. "If this is a last-ditch escape effort," he said, directing the statement at me, "and you're not planning to show up at the gallery tomorrow—"

"It's not," I assured him.

"Definitely not," Nellie confirmed.

"Don't worry," Theo piped up. "I'll keep an eye on them. We can't go back to the hotel after the . . . well, because of the, you know . . . but I've got us an Airbnb in Peckham. We'll stay there tonight. Together."

Reid still looked uncertain, so I, keen to demonstrate just how serious we were about the whole thing, extracted a small black box from my handbag and passed it over to him. He flicked it open, revealing a glittering green-and-silver bracelet. The chain had been made from carefully crafted and weight-adjusted nickel and embellished with a reflective silver paint that resembled the Heart of Envy's striking white-gold links. Fifty crystal cut-glass studs had been stained a deep sea green to mimic the bracelet's Colombian emeralds, and, of course, twelve cubic zirconia had been dotted in between in the place of diamonds.

"Our jeweler has done everything in her power to make it look and feel as real as she can," I explained. "But because she's never seen the Heart of Envy in the flesh, she's had to do a bit of guesswork. We won't know for sure how accurate the replica is until we're in the gallery and can compare the two."

Reid examined the bracelet, dangling it from his index finger. I could tell he was impressed. I could also tell he was trying not to show it.

"So," I said sharply, "as you know, the heist will be completed in three stages. Stage one: Nellie and I get inside St. Jude, survey the setup, find out who's modeling the Heart of Envy, perform the Switch. Stage two: we shift the bracelet on to our buyer. Stage three: we receive the payment. Now, stage one starts at the end of cocktail hour, so just before six p.m." I opened my purse, drew out a folded sheet of paper—our invitations. "I will enter first, claiming to be Sheryl Yardley. Nellie will follow shortly behind as my 'sister.'"

"What if someone knows who they are?" Reid asked. "This Sheryl Yardley and her sister are real people, yeah? So what if you bump into someone at the gallery who knows what they look like?"

"It's just a risk we have to take," I said. "But as long as the usher and security team checking the invites at the door don't know what they look like, we should be good. As soon as we're inside, we'll remove our name tags." A slightly more complex version of Gran's good old-fashioned tailgating.

"Hah . . ." Reid mumbled. He thought this idea was either brilliant or brazen or just outright ludicrous.

It was all those things, as far as I was concerned. I went on regardless. "When the main event has started and the bracelet has been fitted to its wearer, we move forward. Once we have the bracelet, we're on to stage two. Nellie and I will excuse ourselves from the gallery for a cigarette break, make our way around the block, and prepare for the handover." I paused a beat, then added, "James, you said Mr. L has agreed to meet us opposite the Royal Hospital Chelsea at exactly nine thirty, correct?"

He nodded.

"Great. That's about a three-minute walk from the gallery so we shouldn't have a problem getting there on foot. But just a warning, under no circumstances can we be late. Mr. L won't like that."

"Agreed," Nellie said. "Better never than late in this scenario, trust us."

I noticed Theo's knees shake. Reid, too, appeared to flinch at any mention of Mr. L. His posture shifted, and a blood vessel in his neck fluttered wildly. If he'd done his research on Mr. L, he'd have come across that infamous *Guardian* article from several years back. I could probably recite it word for word because it had been published around the time Nellie and I were gearing up to start our careers in the conning business. If you must know, the article detailed a grisly incident in Bristol involving some poor sucker (*could've been me*, I kept thinking) who'd apparently gotten roped into some messy trading deal with "the New Al Capone" and was, as a result, shot twice in every limb before being thrown over a bridge. The article never gave a motive for the crime, but I had a feeling Reid's imagination might've filled in the gaps. As had mine.

But on the off chance that Reid still thought Mr. L was someone he could screw over, I felt it necessary to say, "Now, James, I know you said Mr. L told you he'll be running some checks on the bracelet before he hands over the cash, but did he say what sort of checks these would be?"

Reid worked his jaw. "No, he didn't. And why the hell does it matter?"

"It doesn't. Just asking."

Reid watched me watch him, my expression deadpan. It was imperative that—while he feared Mr. L like a kid fears the monster under the bed—he felt assured that I'd thought everything through and that our plan was foolproof. Because of course I had, and it was.

"So," I went on, "once Mr. L is happy with the product, he'll lead us into stage three, where he'll hand over the Bitcoin on a USB hardware wallet, which of course we'll have to verify on a laptop with the accompanying pin code and recovery phrase." I slipped my hands into my pockets, passed Nellie a look. She gave me a quick nod. "So . . . while Nellie and Mr. L are completing these checks, the rest of us will wait just out of sight."

"You fucking mad?" Reid said suddenly. "Nah, nice try, missy, but there's no way I'm letting either of you go off with that bracelet on your own. I'm not a fucking idiot."

"Listen, James," I said in my most reasonable voice, "I understand your concerns, but if we show up to the rendezvous with two or three people, Mr. L will either shoot us all or he'll leg it. Trust us, we've dealt with him enough times to know what he's like."

"Always expects a double cross," Nellie confirmed with a solemn nod.

I splayed my hands and let out a long sigh. Reid almost certainly knew I was putting on an act, which was exactly what I was hoping for. "If we want to make sure we don't spook him," I said, "only one of us should be present at the handover."

"Fine," he snapped, pushing back his shoulders. "But if it's going to be only one of us, then it's going to be me."

Bingo.

PART III

BACK AT THE AIRBNB, STANDING IN FRONT OF THE MIRROR, I pulled on my old flamingo-pink V-neck frock. The last time I'd worn it, at my university graduation ball, I'd been dewy-eyed with excitement for my future, filled with hope and romantic ideals, ready for the perfect, well-ordered life I was so sure lay ahead of me. But I was also naïve then, thin-skinned. I wanted to be seen and heard and loved, whatever the cost. And maybe that person, the old Emma I'd worked so hard to bury, had been just as much a fraud as the string of alter egos that had come after her. Maybe I'd been wearing a mask my whole life and it was only now that I'd finally allowed myself to drop the disguise and look in the mirror. To *really* look. Maybe it wasn't so much a transformation that was required but an acceptance. Because wasn't I already who I was meant to be?

Sophia barreled into the room. Her face lit up. "Wow! Wow! You look like a princess! I *love* the pink! It really suits you."

Dax followed right behind. His mouth fell open. "You look . . . yeah, *wow!*"

Sir Sebastian, whom we'd managed to collect from Dax's flat

after our meeting with Reid, trotted in next, chin up, then screeched to a halt in front of the mirror. His eye whiskers shot upward. Like Sophia and Dax, he'd never seen me in anything other than grays or blacks. I got a feeling he liked the change.

Nellie was last, dressed in effortless sheer white lace, her blond hair loose about her shoulders, her tanned skin literally glowing. She swished across the room, her megawatt smile turned up to full power. "I knew it!" she said, eyeing the dress. "You look perfect."

She dipped her head onto my shoulder and I smiled at our reflections. I used to think Nellie would always outshine me, no matter what I wore or what role I played. Now, though, I wondered if perhaps we reflected off each other instead. The Light and the Sun.

"I hope you can see it at last," Nellie said.

Dax and Sophia nodded, as if they knew exactly what she was talking about.

I stole a glance at the people in the mirror behind me, beaming with genuine happiness. We were certainly an odd, seemingly incompatible bunch, and I wondered how whoever had thrown us together—the universe or God or fate or some other abstract, unprovable force—had known how well we'd fit. Or had we sought one another out instead, like how rivers find the ocean?

Sir Sebastian weaved through my legs, purring, while Dax fixed a string of silvery pearls around my neck. Warm, fuzzy happiness pulsed through me at the thought of returning here at the end of the night, free of James Reid and his idiot thugs. We were so close to that reality now. I could taste it.

"Where's Theo?" I asked, turning to the bedroom door.

"Waiting in the car," Dax said. "You got the phones?"

I opened my bag to check I had our old burner phone, the

one Reid had stolen from Nellie, then given back to me a few days ago. "I've got mine. You've got the spare, Nell?"

She showed me the second burner phone, which Dax had bought for us. "Yep."

"Right. OK. Then I guess this is it?"

"You better get going," Dax said, checking the time. "Theo will need to pick up Reid before you head to the gallery."

"And just remember," Nellie said, threading her fingers through mine, "whatever happens tonight, I'll be right there with you the whole time. Like always."

"And we'll be waiting back here with a bottle of fizz to celebrate." Dax raised an imaginary glass.

Sir Sebastian licked his lips.

Sophia nodded. "Family celebrations."

"Swear it?" I croaked to all of them.

They answered in chorus. "Pinky swear."

After one final wardrobe check, Nellie and I left Dax and Sophia at the Airbnb, jumped into the MG with Theo, and drove three miles across town to a sketchy sports pub where Reid was waiting to be picked up. For the sake of appearances, we let Theo climb into the driver's seat before Reid caught sight of us.

Less than half an hour later, we pulled up outside a twenty-four-hour kebab shop five blocks from the gallery. We couldn't get any closer because the surrounding streets had been closed off by police barricades and security checks, making parking impossible.

"Right. OK," I said as everyone got out. "We'll just have to walk from here. I'll go first."

Nellie hitched up her dress, squinted into the blackness. "How far away are we?"

"You'll be fine," Reid snapped, shutting her down. "It's less than a mile. Get a move on."

She fixed him with a deadly glare. "When last did you walk a mile in six-inch heels, James? Just wondering."

Reid cursed, Nellie cursed back, and they were off. The racket was fine by me, though, because during their dustup, my phone *pinged*. A text from Dax. I checked to make sure Theo wasn't watching, then read the message.

Any chance you can take a pic of Reid and send it to me?
Just need to check something.

I reread the message, something cold and slippery turning in my stomach. A picture of Reid? Now? Just as I was about to walk into St. Jude? Why hadn't he told me about this earlier, at the Airbnb? The last thing I needed at this stage was another complication.

I looked up. Nellie was caressing her diamond choker while Reid caressed his gun and Theo continued to stare wistfully into the distance in a way that suggested he wanted this whole ordeal to be over just as much as I did.

My eyes fixed on Reid, my phone in hand—camera app open—my thumb hovered over the OK button.

"You all good?" Nellie asked, perhaps noticing my stiffened shoulders and tight jaw.

I smiled thinly. "I'll see you in a few. Wish me luck."

Nellie squeezed my arm encouragingly. "You don't need it."

Reid grunted, "Luck or no luck, don't come back without that bracelet."

As he turned to glare at me, I lifted the phone as inconspicuously as I could and snapped a covert picture, praying to the universe, the Virgin Mary, Baby Jesus, and whoever else would listen that he didn't see me do it.

21

THE SCREAMING STARTED LONG BEFORE I APPROACHED THE grand Georgian building that housed the St. Jude gallery. I couldn't hear words, just shrill, overzealous shrieks from the hundreds of fans queuing en masse behind the barricades on either side of the red carpet (not to see me, obviously). Scattered among them were knots of paparazzi, journalists, camera crews, security personnel, and policemen with batons and neon vests.

It should've terrified me: the attention, the dazzling lights, the all-too-familiar feeling of being at a party I hadn't been invited to, a voyeur to the lives of the beautiful and popular. But as I slipped through the crowds, moved closer to the entrance, I felt an unexpected sense of calm and realized . . . I had shed all that.

I passed several checkpoints and eventually made it to the main barricade, where a suited usher was guiding guests onto the red carpet.

"Good evening, ma'am."

The usher stood directly in front of me, a man in his late fifties with a kind, plump face and bushy eyebrows.

"Evening," I said.

This was it. Either the usher had no idea what Sheryl Yardley looked like, or I was about to be arrested for identity fraud in front of hundreds of onlookers and paparazzi. I reckoned the odds stood at one to one.

"Are you here as a guest or member of staff?" the usher asked.

"A guest," I answered smoothly.

He smiled. "Wonderful. May I see your invite, please?"

I handed over the invitation in Yardley's name, complete with the gallery's logo in silver script and a QR code in the bottom left-hand corner. It wasn't so unlike the time Nellie and I had handed over our fake invitations for the Colosseum's private night tour. This time, though, the invitation was real but the invitee fake.

The usher scanned the code with his phone while his colleague to the left guided Emily Blunt and that guy from *The Office* through the checkpoint without so much as a peek at their invitations.

"Ah, yes, Mrs. Yardley," he said at last, looking up with the slightest frown. Was he confused? Suspicious?

I held perfectly still, my chin raised, a small smile on my face. Surprisingly, I found being someone else was even easier now that I knew who I was.

He nodded at last, grinning. "So glad you could make it after all." He handed me a name badge—an ugly laminated card attached to a blue lanyard that I was pretty sure would only be given out to non-celebrities. "I take it your sister, Miss Stern, will be joining you tonight?"

"Yes," I said confidently. "She's on her way."

He faltered again, though just for a second. "Wonderful.

Now, just to say, we discourage the use of phones inside. Photos and social media especially. However, a select number of influencers have been invited to cover the event, and, of course, there will be several official photographers present. May I ask that you turn off your device for the remainder of the evening?" I nodded happily. "Well then, Mrs. Yardley, I do hope you enjoy the event."

WHILE THE GALLERY'S exterior was majestic, regal, and immoderate, inside it was the opposite. A vast ocean of flawless white extended out in front of me—two hundred feet of empty space, double-height ceilings embellished with exposed trusses and contemporary light boxes that stretched from one end of the foyer to the other. Three photographers hovered in the entranceway, but I slipped past them behind a couple of long-limbed fashionistas who were all too eager to get their pictures taken by London's finest shutterbugs.

After receiving a complimentary glass of Moët in a crystal flute, I glided across the sleek white floor, a trail of sweat dripping down the furrow of my spine, causing the silk and chiffon of my dress to stick uncomfortably to my skin. Though my mind was cool and calm, my body still registered danger.

Everywhere I saw faces I recognized: actresses, supermodels, politicians. Even one or two low-ranking members of the royal family. But—I noticed with some relief—scattered among them, looking bewildered and out of place, there were those like Sheryl Yardley: people who'd been invited out of necessity. Ordinary people.

Keen to get a glimpse at our prize as soon as I could, I dodged the crowds in the foyer and shuffled across to the main exhibition hall, where, below a large arched window and in front of a line of security guards dressed all in black, stood a row of spotless, shimmering glass cases. *Those* glass cases. I gave my empty champagne flute to a passing waiter, then strolled casually down the row of display cases, peering at their glittering contents, my hands behind my back, my posture clean and upright. Each item was as extravagant as the next—the Marie Antoinette choker, the Pink Rose ring, the Star of Atlanta earrings, the Napoleon breast pin, the Sun Drop tiara. Diamonds and sapphires and emeralds. Gold and silver and platinum—more than I'd ever seen in one display in my life. My entire body tingled as I imagined the cool touch of each around my neck, my wrist. I was bewitched, almost salivating at the sight of them.

And then . . .

I paused briefly as I saw it, glinting at me beneath its glass shield: the Heart of Envy. Even though I'd seen it a thousand times in print—pictures posted on Goods Exchange International, in the newspapers, in magazines, on social media—nothing could've prepared me for the sheer wonder of seeing it in the flesh. It glimmered more than I thought it should, the emeralds and diamonds polished to an impossible shine. And maybe it was just my imagination, but it really did seem to hold a sort of magnetism, a force that drew you in. Not exactly the most desirable quality for something I was hoping to nick without anyone noticing.

"Can I offer you a drink, ma'am?"

I tore my eyes away from the bracelet as a waiter appeared at my side, holding a silver serving tray bearing ten slim, gold-rimmed flutes.

"More champagne?" he asked. "This one's a Bollinger special selection, a blend made exclusively for the exhibition. Or I can get you some wine if you'd prefer? Or a cocktail of your choice?"

"Champagne's fine, thanks." I grabbed a flute and took a sip. The liquid was perfectly crisp and warmed me instantly. I tried to resist turning back to the bracelet, but just as I'd had this thought, I realized I was staring right at the thing—gawking at it, actually.

"Really is something, isn't it?" the waiter said with a knowing grin. "Almost seems . . . unreal."

"Ha, yes, it kind of does." I blinked and handed him my half-empty flute, just as an announcement rang out from the foyer: the entertainment had arrived.

Rita Ora burst through the crowd. The music started. Everyone cheered, except me. I had work to do.

I WAITED UNTIL the performance was in full swing before I turned left, to where the exhibition hall ended and a short marble corridor began. I followed the corridor to the guest toilets, stepped inside a cubicle, and locked the door behind me. Thanks to Rita's sterling performance, there was no one else about.

I got out my phone—still turned on—and forwarded Dax the photograph I'd taken of Reid outside the gallery. It wasn't the best shot—grainy, dark, and slightly blurred—but there was no way I'd risk going back outside to take another. It would just have to do.

I waited impatiently for a reply, hoping Dax would text back to tell me why he'd wanted the photo in the first place. But after five minutes, I gave up and decided to call. It rang for ages before being picked up, but I couldn't hear who answered.

"Dax. Did you get the picture? Hello?"

The line scrambled.

I cut the call and scrolled through my list of recent texts, but the message with Reid's photo attached was marked by the alert *Sending Failed*. I checked the reception bars at the top of the phone's screen. There was only one. I paced around the cubicle, phone held aloft, watching the bars appear, then disappear. One, two, one, none.

"Dammit!"

Then a call came through.

"Hello?" I answered breathlessly. "Dax? Can you hear me?"

The line crackled for several seconds, then a small voice replied. "Hello. This is Daisy Duck speaking."

I smiled, briefly pacified by the sound of her voice. "Sophia, hi, it's me. Put Dax on, please, honey."

"He's busy on the computer doing research. Are you all right?"

I lowered the phone to check the reception bars. One had appeared, but I doubted it was enough to send a message with a photo attached. "Sophia, listen," I said hurriedly, ignoring her question. "Tell Dax I'm not supposed to use my phone inside the gallery and the reception's really bad in here. I don't know if the photo will come through until I'm outside again. Ask him if that's OK, or if this photo thing is urgent."

No answer.

"Sophia? Are you there?"

White noise filled my ears, then the sound of . . . what? Pages turning?

"Hello?" she said. "I can't hear you very well. What did you say? What's wrong? It sounds like you're very far away."

"The reception's really bad in here," I repeated. "Just tell Dax I've taken the photo and it'll hopefully come through soon."

". . . some advice?" Sophia asked, her voice crackling, barely audible.

"No, sorry, not now. I'm in a bit of a rush—"

"'When someone says you can't do something,'" she went on anyway, "'just think about how great it will feel to prove them wrong.'"

"OK," I said on a laugh, "I'll keep that in mind. Thank you."

The call cut and I slipped my phone into my bag, wondering again why Dax had asked for the photo and if I should wait around to find out. But after checking the time I realized I couldn't. I had to get moving.

I removed the Heart of Envy replica from my purse and fastened it as loosely as I dared around my wrist. Then, dropping my arm to my side, I checked that, with just a little movement, the bracelet could glide easily over my hand. Satisfied, I pulled the sleeve of my dress over the replica, took three deep breaths, and made my way back to the exhibition hall.

Let the Games begin.

BY THE TIME I got there, Rita was on to her next song. The foyer was packed to capacity and everyone was bobbing around to "Ritual," glasses held above their heads, A-listers and influencers rubbing up against one another, mouthing the words and pouting for the barrage of pictures that would invariably pop up all over Instagram by this time tomorrow.

But where was Nellie?

I'd been inside the gallery for more than forty minutes now and she was supposed to have followed me in ten.

I did a perimeter lap of the exhibition hall (which was basically empty), then the main foyer (where everyone was congregated), then another of both.

No blonde in sheer lace and diamonds anywhere.

I checked the restrooms, thinking that maybe she'd slipped past me and was waiting in a cubicle.

Nothing.

I looked up at the grand arched window above the display cases to see the rain pelting down, dark clouds swirling dangerously. In the distance, beyond the boom of the music, I heard the shriek of a lashing gale, a crack of thunder, and the repetitive drone of King's Road traffic. What on earth could be keeping her? Had Reid done or said something to delay things? Had Theo?

Or . . .

I marched across the foyer, dodging photographers and swaying hips. I grabbed an umbrella from the entrance and slipped outside. Back down the red carpet, which was completely deserted, the screaming crowds having moved off long ago.

"Excuse me, hi," I panted, approaching the main barricade.

But the usher who turned around to face me was not the same as the one who'd been at the barricade earlier, a fact that made my insides clench with fear.

"Hello, ma'am," the mousy-haired woman said, unsmiling. "Can I help you?"

I opened my mouth to answer, but as I did, I saw a flash of blond hair in the walled garden beyond. Nellie caught my eye— soaked to the bone, her hair limp against her shoulders, her sheer lace dress clinging to her skin. Her expression was a mix of panic and shame. Subtly, she shook her head.

"Ma'am?" the usher prompted. "Are you looking for someone?"

One of the many things you get from knowing someone all

your life is the ability to read their thoughts from a simple look, which is why I understood exactly what had happened: Nellie's invitation had been declined by the mousy-haired usher standing in front of me. That meant the mousy-haired usher actually knew Deborah Stern (and possibly Sheryl Yardley), and *that* meant, if I said another word, I'd get booted out like the dirty fraudster I was.

"Ma'am?"

"Oh, no, sorry," I said, forcing a smile and a steady breath. "It's nothing."

22
6:55 P.M.

I WANDERED BACK ACROSS THE FOYER. RITA WAS GONE, HER performance over. The crowds were now gathered in the exhibition hall and I joined them robotically, my eyesight blurred, limbs heavy.

Noise and people were all around me, but I couldn't take in a single thing. How could this be happening? One of the only completely true things I'd told Reid was that I couldn't steal the Heart of Envy alone. It was why I'd begged him to release Nellie from the warehouse in the first place. For five years we'd played the Games side by side. The perfect double act. Good cop, bad cop. The diversion and the kill shot. The liar and the thief. Those who knew us knew us only as a pair. Janet Robinson and Annie Leeds. Never one without the other. We'd always had the comfort of knowing we'd be there to fix each other's mistakes, to cover each other's tracks—in life and in the Games. If one of us fell or failed, the other was always there to pick up the pieces. But now . . .

I rubbed the throb from my chest, looked up. I don't know

what I expected to see. Maybe a solution to my problems. Hopefully Nellie.

Instead, I saw Joel.

"EMMA." HIS VOICE was saccharine, his expression bright and unfazed, like it was no surprise at all to see me standing in front of him after so many years.

I tried for several seconds to speak, but nothing came. Was I imagining this? Was Joel Beck really here? *Right here in front of me?* I'd often imagined how I'd feel if I bumped into him after the heartbreak of our split-up. Embarrassed? Nostalgic? Sad? But here he was and I felt . . . what? Shock, and not much else. I couldn't even tell you what he was wearing. A suit, I think. Tailored, designer.

I snapped myself out of my stupor, took him in. Yes, it was definitely him. His chestnut hair was as sleek as I remembered, no grays in sight. Of course not.

"Joel . . ." I trailed off, gathered myself, and started again. "Joel. What . . . what are you doing here?"

He laughed softly, rubbed a thumb against the stem of his wineglass, a habit I remembered with a sudden prickle of irritation because he only did it when he was feeling confident and in charge. "I asked myself that same question a minute ago," he said. "I get to rub shoulders with the rich and famous now? What is this life!"

I almost laughed—an old reflex, one that had been etched into me like muscle memory. If I laughed he would feel heard, seen, loved, cherished—all the things I used to want for him as much as for myself. But then I slipped my hand into my purse.

Maybe it was subconscious; maybe I remembered. My fingers touched paper, the folded drawing Sophia had given me and which I'd vowed to throw away but never had. In my mind's eye I saw the figure labeled "Janet" and the mask she held in her hand. Sophia had said I still carried the disguise around, just in case. She was right then, but not anymore.

Joel took a sip of wine while he waited for my reply. The dimple in his left cheek showed as his eyes traced my dress. He was impressed, I could tell, and probably a little surprised that I was just standing there in silence, not fidgeting, comfortable in the awkwardness of it all. It certainly would be out of character for the Emma he knew. "And what about you?" he asked with a tone bordering on impatient. "Here for work or . . ."

"Yes. I work for the gallery, actually," I lied smoothly, though some part of me felt like telling him the truth: that I was a con artist, the best in Europe, that I made millions of pounds every year, that I was here to steal the most famous bracelet at this collection. I wanted him to watch me do it.

"Oh, nice." He paused for a minute, his eyes moving away from mine. "Crazy that you're here, though," he said, refocusing with a frown. "In London, I mean. Like, you just disappeared after the . . . you know. Everyone was so shocked. We thought you moved to Paris or something."

I could've said so many things to that: *Yes, Joel, I disappeared because you ruined my life. I disappeared because you took away everything I knew and loved and left me hollow. I disappeared because if I had stayed I would've walked back onto that busy street and closed my eyes.*

Instead I felt no need to explain anything, or apologize—if that was what he'd been hoping for. I raised a shoulder and said with a smile, "Yeah, crazy, huh?"

He didn't seem to know how to take that. His eyes flickered left and right, like he was trying to find an excuse to leave. I had to admit it was fun to watch him squirm a little. But soon his excuse arrived.

A tall platinum blonde sashayed to his side, carrying an iPhone attached to a selfie stick. Her hair was fixed in a faux-messy bun; her skin glowed like it had been dabbed with actual gold dust. Her eyes were the brightest, clearest green I'd ever seen.

"Darling, hi," Joel said with a note of relief, drawing the blonde into him and planting a kiss on her cheek. "We were just talking about you."

She eyed me curiously, smiled, extended a hand.

"Rachel, this is Emma," Joel said, his voice wavering slightly. *He's terrified*, I thought. *Good.* "She's my . . . ex-colleague from the firm."

I considered correcting him. I considered embarrassing him. I even considered spitting in his face and stomping on his feet. But what a bunch of wasted energy that would be, bad karma that would one day come back to me.

All that is spent must be returned.

"Rachel's one of the influencers covering the event," he went on to explain, talking to me but looking at her.

"Oh, nice," I said.

Rachel frowned. She was clearly uncomfortable, like she could smell the history between us and knew Joel was omitting something. It dawned on me in that moment that I didn't hate her, even though I'd once been so sure I did, or should. She was me and I was her, connected in a way the man between us could never understand.

And so I smiled at her, warmly, knowingly, and walked away.

23

FEELING LIGHTER THAN I HAD IN YEARS, I MARCHED INTO THE glitzy crowd, my hands clasped behind my back, careful to keep the replica bracelet from slipping over my wrist. It was as if my encounter with Joel had flicked a switch in my head, and a new feeling bubbled up within me: I *could* do this alone. Not because Nellie was inconsequential but because I was strong enough— and always had been—to fill in the gaps her absence exposed. It reminded me of something Gran had said.

"You and Nellie are soulmates and everyone can see it. But do you know what a soulmate really is?"

"A person you can't live without?" I suggested.

"No," she said. "A person who teaches you there's no such thing."

I SWISHED ACROSS the gallery foyer, transforming easily into the role I'd come to play. When anyone asked who I was or— in a very subtle, upper-class way—why I'd been invited to the exhibition, I gave vague, ambiguous answers that I altered as required: the wife of a parliamentarian, a gallery sponsor, an architect. No one pressed me for details, of course, but only because they were trying to be tactful.

At eight, I sneaked back to the toilets, took my phone out of my bag. I tapped *send* on the unsent photo in my drafts folder, but the reception bars were still hovering around one or nothing. I waited, tapping my thumb against the screen while the message prepared to send, started sending . . .

Cubicle doors opened and closed; heels clipped on the marble floor; hushed voices rose and fell, laughter, gossip.

Sending . . .

Failed.

All reception bars vanished from the screen. *No Service.*

Dax would have to wait. I dropped the phone into my bag and headed back toward the exhibition hall.

THE ATMOSPHERE HAD heightened by the time I returned, the vast ocean of white now rippling with a kind of contained anticipation. Glasses clinked; dresses rustled; voices murmured. A woman in a slim black dress and red kitten heels had positioned herself in front of a microphone just to the left of the display cases. She clinked a fork against her champagne glass, and after the third try, the room gathered in several disordered lines and went still.

"Good evening, ladies and gentlemen, esteemed guests. My name's Jessica, head of the St. Jude events committee, and it is my great pleasure to welcome you to this special evening, Tiffany & Co.'s iconic and long-standing *Serenity and Splendor* exhibition."

There was a round of soft, polite applause and several people raised their glasses in acknowledgment. I followed suit, just for the sake of appearances.

"We're so delighted to have you with us tonight, and to share with you this awe-inspiring display of some of the world's most illustrious pieces of jewelry. From Hollywood to Buckingham Palace, these pieces have been worn by the rich and famous and regal . . ."

After the speech and some milling about, a group of seven guests was quietly escorted to the back of the gallery by a gang of very large and serious-looking security guards while the rest of us were distracted by another round of drinks, canapés, and a performance by some famous Italian pianist.

With a glass of wine in one hand and a spoon of caviar in the other, I kept my eyes fixed on the far end of the hall, where the fittings were taking place. It wasn't long before I spotted her—an elderly woman in steel-rimmed Bulgari glasses, a faux-fur coat, and a long black velvet dress, the Heart of Envy glittering on her wrist.

My limbs tingled and my heart thumped unsteadily in my chest as I began to analyze the situation, taking mental notes. The wearer wasn't a celebrity, as far as I knew, so she was likely a politician or the wife of one. I noted her posture, build, the way she moved, the expression on her face. I studied her interactions with the guard trailing her and the guests around her. Judging by the way she kept lifting the bracelet to her eyeline, twisting it in the light, she was enamored with the piece. A bad sign. But judging by the three-second pause between a waiter offering her a glass of Moët and her accepting it, she was distracted. A good sign. Her reflexes were slow, too, I noticed—by counting the time it took for her to adjust the flute of fizz that had tipped dangerously in her grip. Safe to say it wasn't her first glass of the evening.

An easy target, if only she'd been alone.

The security guard standing behind her was more than six foot tall and as wide as a bus. His keen eyes traced every guest that came within five feet of the woman wearing the Heart of Envy, the muscles in his arms twitching at every movement. Taking all this into account, I realized that without Nellie to create a diversion, there was no chance I was going to be able to get anywhere near the bracelet without him noticing me. And if I couldn't get close, I couldn't perform the Switch. That meant I had only one other option, and it went against everything I knew, everything I'd relied on up until that point: divert his attention *toward* me. Become the center of his focus. *Force* him to notice me. *Force* him to watch me. Because if he was watching me move and fumble, he wasn't watching me dip.

Ignoring the twist of nerves in my stomach, I handed my glass and uneaten caviar to the nearest waiter, nodded at the security guard, and, without hesitation, sauntered over to the woman in the faux-fur coat.

"Gorgeous," I said when I reached her side. "Isn't it?"

She smiled politely and lifted the bracelet into the light, admiring it. The security guard's eyes tracked my movements closely, and the bracelet's. He had his hands pressed together at his waist, his back stiff and straight. The curly white cord of an earpiece was peeking out from under his shirt collar.

"Indeed," the woman said. "It's absolutely magnificent. What a treasure. I was so thrilled when they invited me to be the wearer. From Grace Kelly to me, can you imagine!"

I chuckled. "Yes, the bracelet's stunning. But I was talking about that chandelier, actually." I watched her wrist lower, her gaze travel upward, settling her attention to where I needed it to be—on the large avant-garde chandelier hanging above our heads. The security guard, however, kept his eyes on me. "Catellani & Smith," I said. "Custom-made for this exhibition. Ten-carat gold leaf and three hundred and seventy hand-fitted Swarovski crystals. Incredible that it's actually able to hang there like that. Must weigh a ton, if you think about it."

"Oh yes, I suppose so," the woman agreed halfheartedly, blinking at the light.

"My husband's in lighting," I explained. "He was on the team that fitted this one, actually. Total nightmare. Took up so much of his time I was tempted to use it as an excuse for divorce." I laughed again, then droned on some more about the chandelier, all of it made up, Rumpelstiltskin at her finest. Gran would've been so proud. Nellie too.

"Hmm, fascinating," the woman mumbled, nodding respectfully as I finished up.

I smiled again, fell into a short silence. This was the part where Nellie—who should've been standing just three feet in front of me—would've shifted off to the left, her sheer lace gown and megawatt smile as dazzling as the famed jewels on display. She would've waited no more than thirty seconds before creating her diversion, shrieking with delight as she spotted an old friend in the crowd, then letting her glass of champagne slip from her fingers.

"Well," I said, "I better hunt down the hubby before he drinks himself into oblivion. Enjoy the rest of evening. It was lovely to meet you."

She looked relieved to see me go. "And you."

I tensed, eyed the security guard. His attention was still

shifting between me and the bracelet. Back and forth, back and forth, like he was watching a tennis match.

I felt a surge of pure white-hot adrenaline shoot from my chest to my gut, down my limbs. I knew this was it. Maybe a better opportunity would present itself in time, but probably not. I had to take a punt right now or I might never get another shot.

Deep breath in. Long breath out.

I took one perfectly measured step sideways and pressed the heel of my left shoe onto the poor old bat's big toe. She inhaled sharply, stifling a yelp of pain.

"Oh my God! I'm so, *so* sorry!" I said, reaching forward to steady her as she lifted her foot and swayed dangerously. "I'm such a klutz. You all right?"

She mumbled something noncommittal and crouched to examine her foot. Out of the corner of my eye, I saw Joel and Rachel turn to see what all the commotion was about. Joel rolled his eyes and whispered something to Rachel, who frowned.

I looked up at the security guard with pleading eyes, my right hand now blocking his view of the bracelet.

"Excuse me, ma'am," he said urgently as he lurched toward me. "Please step back."

I ignored him. "Take her hand!" I demanded, then grasped the woman's left wrist and, as I did, slid the nail of my pinky finger under the Heart of Envy's clasp, tilted it up and back.

"Ma'am!" the guard repeated, gripping my forearm. "Please step back! Right now!"

The clasp released with a click I didn't hear but could feel.

The guard tried to pull me back, but the old woman, still swaying on her injured foot, reached out for me in an attempt to steady herself. She could've grabbed the security guard's arm, if only he hadn't been so fixated on yanking me out of the way.

"Easy, there we go," I said, holding her steady while I guided the Heart of Envy off her wrist. Thanks to the throb in her foot, I was sure she didn't feel a thing. I wriggled my hand, allowing the replica to slip over my knuckles and over her fingers, onto her wrist. I let the bracelets slide over each other. And when the replica was in place, I tightened the clasp and dropped the real deal into my purse.

I looked Joel dead in the eye as I did it. And smiled.

I WOULD'VE GIVEN ANYTHING TO LEAVE THE GALLERY THE minute I dropped the Heart of Envy into my purse, but the security guard was still flashing me the side-eye and I didn't want to give him any reason to doubt my intentions or—heaven forbid—examine the (now fake) bracelet on the old woman's arm. At the same time, I couldn't delay things too long. One of the many details I hadn't told Reid was that the bracelet, along with all the other pieces at the exhibition, was going back into its high-tech glass case at ten thirty on the dot. And we were screwed the second our replica touched that lovely white satin cushion with its weighted alarm system. Or, more precisely, *I* was screwed.

So, after giving the security guard a quick, innocent smile, I edged my way across the hall, mingled with a few guests in the foyer, downed another glass of champagne, and made for the exit. I told the usher at the barricade—the same mousy-haired one—I was popping out for a cigarette break and would be back soon, then I bolted through the walled garden and pretty courtyard onto King's Road and around the block.

THEO WAS SITTING alone in the back seat of the MG while Nellie and Reid waited for me in the street opposite.

Nellie pulled me into a hug the moment she saw me, her drenched hair sticking to her pallid face, her limbs ice-cold and trembling.

"I'm so sorry," she mumbled into my shoulder. "I broke my promise and I'm so, *so* sorry. The usher called my bluff. I could've pushed it, maybe I should've, but I was worried about taking you down with me. She knew Stern, like, *really* knew her. I couldn't believe it." She drew back, hands on my shoulders, examining me, her sharp blue eyes catching the truth I was so sure I'd hidden—from everyone else, at least. "How did it go? Did you . . ."

Nellie's declined invitation was definitely *not* part of my grand heist plan. And yet, now that I thought about it, it provided me with an unquestionable justification for the bomb I was about to drop on my good friend James Reid.

I gave Nellie a tight nod, then twisted out of her grip to face Reid.

"Well? Where is it?" he snapped, catching me by the elbow. He pulled up my dress sleeve, stared at my wrist, bare. The color drained from his face.

I shook my head, gulped. "The security guard . . . he . . . I don't know why . . . I think . . ."

Reid repositioned himself to seize me by the shoulders and tried to shake some sense into me. "Slow down, woman. What happened? Where's the bracelet?"

"I'm sorry," I sobbed, tears streaming down my face, my nose running, my hands shaking—the works. "I couldn't do it . . . I tried but I couldn't."

"Just breathe," Nellie soothed, playing along. "*Breathe* and tell us everything."

"I couldn't do it," I repeated. "I couldn't get it. The security was too tight and I was afraid I'd be caught."

"Are you fucking kidding me!" Reid bellowed, rocking me back and forth with such force I nearly toppled over. "You're standing here crying like a little baby, wasting my time? Get the fuck back in there and try again! I told you not to come out until you had the bracelet!"

I sobbed hysterically for several minutes, only stopping when Reid threatened to get his gun out.

"There isn't time," I said, steadying my voice at last. "Even if I could go back, which I can't, there isn't time. Mr. L is meeting us at nine thirty, remember?" I looked at the time on my cell phone, my hand trembling more than ever, not with fear now but with something closer to excitement. "That's twenty minutes from now! There's no way I can get the bracelet in twenty minutes. Not even with Nellie by my side."

Reid began to pace, muttering to himself. Eventually he turned to face me and said, "I'll call and tell Mr. L there's been a delay. We'll need more time. Simple."

I wiped the tears from my face and looked over at Nellie, inviting her to chip in.

"Call him?" she said with a smirk. "You have him on speed dial or something? You chums now?"

Reid curled in his lips. There was no way he had Mr. L's personal mobile number and we all knew it. "Fine. Then I'll message him on Goods Exchange."

"Won't work," I said hastily. Reid glowered at me, so I went on to explain. "He won't be sitting in front of his computer now, will he? He'll already be outside the Royal Hospital Chelsea, waiting for us. And anyway, he doesn't work like that. He gives you one chance and no opportunity to change plans. If we're not at the meeting spot in twenty minutes, he'll think the deal's off, which means he flew to London for nothing; and if that's the case, he'll be so livid he'll, well . . ." I left it at that. Sometimes, the less said the better.

Nellie and I stared at Reid, who was scowling. If I had to guess, I'd say he was trying to decide if it might just be easier to cut his losses and put a bullet between our eyes. I was pretty sure he was itching to, and at the same time, I knew he wouldn't. We really were no use to him dead. He just had to accept that.

He looked past me at something in the distance that I realized might've been Theo in the MG. He stared for a while, lips moving silently, then turned his focus back on me.

"You got another plan, then?"

"The old plan," I said breathlessly. "We stick to it. It's our only option now."

"The old plan?" Reid echoed.

I nodded gravely. "We have to give Mr. L the replica bracelet instead and hope for the best."

"How the fuck are we gonna get away with that?"

"We're going to get away with it because we're that good," Nellie said, confident.

"Oh yeah? So we'll just hope the buyer doesn't notice it's a fake? That's the plan? What about all those checks he said he's going to do?"

"Not a problem," I said. "No one can tell a diamond from a cubic zirconia with the naked eye. He'll have to look at it under a loupe, and for that he'd have to take it to a professional, and by then you'll be long gone and sixteen million pounds richer."

I can't even call that one misleading information. It was a

straight-up lie. There was no doubt in my mind that Mr. L—
having been in the business for more than a decade—could spot
a cubic zirconia from a mile off (just ask that poor sucker from
the *Guardian* article who tried to con him with a fake diamond
ring). Also, I was pretty certain he'd be able to take one look at
our replica's green glass beads and tell they weren't Colombian
emeralds. Hell, I bet he could even spot the fake just by its altered weight. And the chance of him having a loupe and several
other professional appraisal tools in the back of his Mercedes-
Benz? Ninety-nine percent, I reckoned. In other words, the only
way Reid was walking away from this sale with a fraction of a
Bitcoin in his pocket and his head still attached to his body
was if he *did* actually hand Mr. L the Heart of Envy, the *real*
bracelet curled up in my purse. Which was, of course, the plan
all along.

So why had I told Reid he was going to hand Mr. L a replica
when in fact he was going to hand him the real thing? Well, in
order to pull off the final twist, I had to make sure the seeds of
doubt and fear I'd planted over the last five days had all the
nourishment they needed.

"Luckily," I said, "the fooling's already been done for you. I've
told you a hundred times. Our replica is absolutely perfect."
I opened my purse and, carefully, pulled out the Heart of Envy—
the real one. Even under the dim streetlight, the emeralds
glimmered and the diamonds twinkled, casting a spell over him.
"Just *look* at it," I said, handing it over. "It's basically identical to
the real thing. Trust me. I've thought this through. Nellie and I
have as much riding on this as you do. More, actually. It *will*
work. It has to."

Reid turned the bracelet over in his hand, deep in thought. I
was convinced—for obvious reasons—that he was impressed by

what he was looking at. It looked so real it *had* to be real, right? Confirmation bias, a dangerous game.

His eyes flickered again to Theo, who—I think—nodded at him. Weird.

There was a tiny chance, now that things were looking a bit more precarious, that Reid would insist Nellie or I meet with Mr. L instead of him, which I definitely wasn't OK with. But because that would mean we'd end up being the ones holding the sixteen-million-pound USB at the end, I didn't think he'd risk it.

"And as long as Mr. L himself thinks the bracelet is real," I reiterated, "the agreement will stand. You'll get your Bitcoin and everything will be fine."

I looked at Nellie and couldn't help but feel a deep pang of longing for all this to be over. I was burned-out, exhausted, my nerves frayed. I wanted to be back home. I wanted to be with my family.

Reid stirred. "But . . . what if . . . what if he figures out the bracelet's a counterfeit later on? He'll track me down and kill me."

"How will he track you down?" I asked. "He doesn't know your name, where you live, nothing. You've only been communicating with him on Goods Exchange, and under your code name. Trust me," I repeated, "as long as the bracelet passes that first check upon handover, we'll all be fine." He stared at me ashen-faced, his lips parted. "It's this way or nothing. We're out of options."

"And time," Nellie added tensely. "We've got ten minutes!"

Sensing something was off, Theo got out of the MG and marched over. "What's going on? Where's the bracelet?"

We all ignored him. Reid, especially, didn't seem too keen to loop him in and say he was about to hand Mr. L a fake. I wondered why.

Reid continued to stare at me, his eyes narrowed and dark. If this had been a cartoon, there would've been steam coming out of his ears. He wrapped the bracelet in a wad of toilet paper (*toilet paper!*) and stuffed it inside his pocket.

"Don't let them out of your sight until I have that USB in my hands," he said to Theo. "Clear?"

Theo nodded, his eyes skirting in every direction.

"Fetch the laptop," Reid said, addressing me.

I rushed over to the MG, retrieved our laptop from under the front seat, and handed it over. Obviously, Dax had already cleared the hard drive and removed all sensitive and incriminating data, leaving only two installed apps on the desktop: the dark web search engine, Tor, to access the Goods Exchange platform, and an app for checking Bitcoin wallets.

Reid shoved the laptop into his haversack. "You're a few minutes away from freedom," he said, speaking mostly to me. "Don't fuck it up, yeah? Don't fuck it up for any of us."

I thought I had become numb to Reid's threats over the last few days, but somehow this last one hit a nerve. Because he was right, in a sense. Nellie and I were now so very close to being rid of the vile bastard and his two friends and putting this whole wretched ordeal behind us. Except we weren't, were we? Because if we let Mr. L walk off into the sunset with the Heart of Envy, my life would be over. Once the security guards at the gallery put the replica bracelet back in its glass box, the weight sensors would pick up a discrepancy immediately. The alarms would sound. Panic. Mayhem. And once the security lads and the gallery's management realized what had happened, the building's CCTV would be analyzed and every invitee called in for questioning. And let's not forget that Joel had actually seen me at the event and knew who I really was. There would be no

way—not even with all the luck and good fortune in the world—
that I wouldn't become the prime suspect. But apart from that,
there was another, even more important reason I couldn't let
Mr. L walk away with that bracelet, and it was morals. Yes,
morals.

Nellie and I were criminals—we knew that. But since starting the Games, we'd never swindled anyone without a good reason. And we weren't about to start now. I had no idea who would
suffer the consequences (apart from me, Nellie, and Dax) if the
Heart of Envy were to go missing. Maybe that poor old bat with
the bruised toe. Would she be interrogated and shunned and
her name splashed all over the morning papers? And what about
the security guard who was responsible for keeping an eye on
the bracelet? Would he lose his job, be arrested? And the gallery
owner, or the usher at the door who'd so kindly let me in? It was
safe to say that the unforeseen consequences of our actions were
too much for my conscience to take. And that's why I'd decided
days ago, right at the very beginning, that we weren't ever going
to steal the Heart of Envy. We were just going to borrow it.

GUN IN HAND, THEO RETURNED TO THE MG. NELLIE AND I
followed, and as soon as Reid had vanished into the darkened
street ahead, I pulled out my phone because it had been ringing
incessantly for the last two minutes. There were five missed calls
from Dax.

"What does he want now?" Nellie asked in an anxious whisper.

I was about to answer when a sixth call came through. As I
placed the phone to my ear, however, I felt a firm, cold hand on
my shoulder.

"No phone calls," Theo said. "Not now." He jerked his head
at the street corner, where Reid had stalled, turned around, and
was staring directly at us. "He'll think you're up to something,
then delay us. Just drive. We need to keep him in our sights."

Nellie adjusted the rearview mirror, gave him a look. "Listen,
bozo, just because you're holding the gun doesn't mean you're
the one—"

"He's right, though," I interrupted, squinting at the spot
where Reid had been standing just seconds ago but no longer
was. "We can't let Reid out of our sight." I drummed my hands

against the dashboard, dropped my phone back into my handbag. "Drive!"

WE REACHED ST. Leonard's Terrace minutes later, turned into Franklins Row, then Royal Hospital Road.

Nellie turned off the engine and headlights as we parked alongside the pavement, Burton Court to our right. A strange, tense quiet filled the air. The rain had died at last, as had the wind. But minute by minute, the air temperature dropped, and it wasn't long before it was so cold that my nose began to run and blotches of purplish blue popped up wherever my skin was exposed to the air. I blew into my hands and sank down deeper into my seat, trying to get myself as close to the warmth of the engine as I could manage.

"Here," Nellie said, handing me her Burberry coat, even though she was still wet from earlier and surely colder than I was.

I draped the coat across our knees. "Joel was there, inside the gallery."

Nellie turned to me, horrified. "No."

"With his new fiancée."

"No!"

"She was there as an influencer to cover the event for Instagram."

"Oh my God . . ."

"And he introduced me as his 'ex-colleague from the firm.'"

"OH MY GOD!"

I laughed softly. "It's OK, really. It was good, actually. I needed to see him again. Like closure, you know."

Nellie watched me closely, just to make sure, then mouthed, *"Love you."*

I turned my gaze back to the darkness. Up ahead, some-where near the middle of the street and directly opposite the Royal Hospital Chelsea, I could just make out the dim outline of Mr. L's Mercedes-Benz Maybach with tinted windows and num-berless plates. Several other cars were parked between us and the Maybach, though all appeared to be unoccupied.

Reid, however, was nowhere to be seen.

"I'd better get into position," Nellie said as she, too, caught sight of the Mercedes. She gave my hand a squeeze.

"You have it?" I whispered.

She nodded and tapped her pocket. "All set."

"What does that mean?" Theo asked nervously, leaning over from the back seat. "Have what? What are you talking about?"

"OK. Just be careful," I urged, as if I hadn't heard him. "Wait for a safe opening. And make sure you stick to the timings like we discussed. If you do it before the assessment—"

Nellie grinned at me. "I've got it, babe. No stress. See you in fifteen for the grand finale." She grabbed her bag from between her feet and opened the door.

"Hey!" Theo yelped. "Hey! Where you going? Wait!"

He scrambled to climb out after her, the gun slipping dan-gerously in his grip, but she'd dashed left and vanished, out of sight before he could even take a step.

"Where the hell is she going?" he asked, whirling round to face me, a vein protruding in his temple. "What's going on?"

"You don't need to know that."

"James is going to kill me! And then you. If he comes back and finds her gone, we're all dead. He told me to watch you!"

"Oh my God. Just relax! We've got this under control. Nellie will be back before Reid, I guarantee it."

Theo looked left and right, breathing weirdly, but after a few minutes he seemed to calm down. He plucked his phone from his pocket. The screen's backlight flashed on, lending a bluish-white hue to his already pale features. He started typing something while I drew out a pair of binoculars and examined the street ahead.

A large white utility van had pulled up at the end of the street, several yards from where the Maybach was parked. I adjusted the focus dial on my binoculars, trying to see who was sitting in the driver's seat. There was no way to tell if the van was part of Mr. L's setup or not.

But still, no sign of Reid.

When Theo tucked the gun under his trouser belt, I flinched. A look flashed across his face, one I didn't like. He was still edgy but now also . . . excited? Was that right?

"I want to be there to see it," he mumbled under his breath.

"What?" I asked.

He nodded at me, as if confirming something I hadn't figured out. "She's going to freak out when she realizes it's me."

I turned my focus back to the street. *She?* Who was he talking about? Nellie?

I got my answer as someone emerged from the Maybach, their face illuminated under the light of a nearby streetlamp. My eyes pressed tightly against the binocular lenses, I squinted, gasped softly.

Although I'd made Reid believe Nellie and I had worked with Mr. L several times before, we never had. We'd never seen him in person and had no idea what he looked like. I'd always imagined him to be a well-proportioned middle-aged man who donned a long black coat and a trilby hat, smoked cigars, and maybe wore a diamond-encrusted knuckle-duster like Nellie's. *Sopranos* mob boss Mafia-style. You can imagine, then, that I was just a little surprised when I discovered Mr. L was, in fact, a woman. A petite woman with cropped blond hair, carrying a bloodred snakeskin Birkin and dressed in a long gray skirt, ankle boots, a delicate white chiffon blouse.

She.

I turned to Theo, my thoughts swirling, nothing making sense. But while he'd been standing to my left just a second ago, he was now standing right in the middle of the road, arms pinned to his sides, eyes fixed dead ahead on the Merc. Actually, on Mr. L.

"Hey! Theo!" I snapped. "Get back here!" He ignored me. "What are you doing?" I leaped out of the car just as he started to move toward the Merc. I pulled him to a halt, spun him round to face me. Had he lost his mind? "What's going on with you?" He blinked, that odd look still on his face—satisfaction, or terror, or some combination of the two. I remembered then that he didn't yet know about my "failure" in the gallery and was therefore under the impression that Reid was about to hand Mr. L the real Heart of Envy. I'd have to enlighten him before he did something stupid, like take Reid's place. "The handover isn't . . . we lied," I said.

This, at last, seemed to snap him out of his trance. "What do you mean?"

We saw it at the same time: Reid walking slowly toward the Merc from the opposite end of Royal Hospital Road, hands in his pockets, hood pulled down over his face. He faltered as Mr. L stepped forward to greet him, her arms crossed, glasses slipping down her nose. He craned his neck to peer over her shoulder, clearly expecting someone who looked a bit more like the infamous Mr. L to materialize behind her.

Mr. L removed her glasses and smiled wickedly at Reid's

confusion, then said something that caused him to shove his hands deeper into his pockets and take a step backward.

Theo pulled from my grip and started walking toward the Merc again.

"It's a trick!" I called out, urgently trying to keep him from moving any closer and ruining everything. It *had* to be Reid who handed over the bracelet, no one else. "The bracelet's a fake," I lied quickly. "I couldn't get the real thing in the gallery. Reid's going to sell Mr. L the replica instead."

His eyes widened, mouth fell open. His lips were moving but I heard just a shallow croak. Now, I was sure, he looked only terrified.

I got back into the MG, checked the time, my fingers clammy and cold. Theo began to pace up and down the pavement, grunting and moaning softly, as if trying to make up his mind about something. But if he was thinking about putting a stop to the handover, it was too late. Reid had pulled out the bracelet, still wrapped in a wad of toilet paper, and given it to Mr. L. She inclined her head, then disappeared into the Merc and shut the door.

I scanned the street behind and in front of the Merc. Three men, dressed identically in black tracksuits, beanies, and leather gloves, emerged from the white utility van a few yards off. They surveyed the street, then parted ways. Mr. L's entourage, presumably. Hit men. Murderers. Getting into position in case things went south.

FIVE MINUTES PASSED. Ten. A brisk, cool wind had picked up again. The rain clouds parted, casting a dim streak of moonlight across the scene in front of me. Pedestrians moseyed past the

Merc, mostly uninterested. Cars zipped along the street without slowing.

While Theo continued to pace, Reid had begun to fidget, no doubt terrified at what Mr. L was doing with his supposed counterfeit. He shifted from foot to foot, drew his hands from his pockets, ripped off his hood, pulled it back on. At one point, he even peered over his shoulder at the MG. I wasn't sure he could see us parked there in the darkness so far away, but he must have at least known we were nearby.

Eventually, Mr. L reappeared from the Merc. Even though it was dark, and I was far away, I could see the fear course through Reid's entire body. His shoulders shot up to his ears; his arms stiffened at his sides.

Mr. L closed in, gestured at the white utility van parked at the end of the street. Reid stalled, staring at the darkness ahead of him, then hunched his shoulders and started for the van.

Cars and buses rumbled past; pedestrians came and went, some in large groups, others alone. And although I couldn't see her, I knew Nellie would now be in position, dressed in a baggy gray tracksuit and peaked cap, lingering at the corner of Franklins Row and East Road, awaiting her moment of opportunity.

Another minute slipped by before it came.

Chattering loudly, a group of seven pedestrians turned into Royal Hospital Road from Franklins Row, heading in the same direction as Reid—toward the white utility van. Gripping the binoculars so tightly I feared I might break them in two, I searched the group for its anomaly, the odd one out, the one who hung a few steps back from the rest, head down, hands twitching at her sides. At last I spotted her, and I held my breath.

Reid had reached the white utility van and was having a conversation with the driver—a burly, tattooed figure. Meanwhile,

Mr. L had reemerged from the Merc, the bracelet dangling from her thumb. But as the knot of pedestrians neared, she dropped the Heart of Envy into what appeared to be a large purse.

The pedestrians walked past the Merc, and as they did, one of them—the straggler—stumbled left.

Nellie hit the side of the Merc with a thump so loud even I could hear it. Mr. L flinched.

Focus.

Nellie and Mr. L crossed paths. Neither looked up. Without slowing, Nellie stretched out her right hand, her fingers reaching for the purse. And as Nellie merged back with the group of pedestrians, Mr. L—perhaps sensing something suspicious with finely tuned instincts—stiffened, checked to see that the bracelet was still in her purse. It was (sort of).

I chewed my lip, ignoring Theo's impatient grunts and nervous moans as I turned the binoculars back on Reid and the van. A stocky figure in a red wool jumper appeared from inside. He handed over a USB and a piece of paper, which I assumed contained the pin code and recovery phrase to access the wallet. Reid retrieved our laptop from his haversack, placed it on his knee, plugged in the USB, and tapped something out on the keyboard.

I checked the time—10:21.

SECONDS LATER, NELLIE—NO LONGER DRESSED IN HER BAGGY gray tracksuit and peaked cap disguise—dived into the MG.

"So," she said, out of breath, "Mr. L is a woman. Didn't see that one coming."

"Neither did I!"

She placed her hand on mine. Something cold and jagged dropped neatly into my palm. I slipped the Heart of Envy over my wrist, concealing it under my dress sleeve as quick as light. Theo snapped his eyes on me, but a moment too late.

"We've got ten minutes, max," I said, handing Nellie the binoculars. "Reid's already started checking the wallet."

"It'll do." She looked at Theo, who was still staring at me suspiciously and looked so jittery I was sure he was about to spew his guts all over the tarmac.

"Something's up with him," I explained in a whisper.

"Like?"

"Not sure, but he almost blew his cover and ruined the plan. He said something about wanting to 'be there to see it.'"

"What the hell does that mean? See what?"

"No idea." I had a horrible feeling we were missing something important, obvious, something that had been right there in front of us this whole time. Was this what it felt like to be on the other side of the fence, to be duped?

Nellie shook her head as if to clear it. She put the car into gear. "You better get cracking, babe. It's time." She turned on the headlights, and before Theo could say anything about it, I leaped from the passenger's side and tore off down the street back toward St. Jude. Theo bellowed after me, furious and bewildered, but I didn't slow, tumbling onward while my heart beat madly against my ribs, a sharp pain building in my side, almost winding me.

Several yards on, I staggered to a walk as I approached the walled garden and police barricade that ran along either side of the red carpet. A few photographers, camera crew, and fans remained. No one seemed to notice me.

I reached the entrance, which was still being monitored by the young woman who'd rejected Nellie's invite. I didn't want her to check mine in case she put two and two together and figured out Nellie and I were a team, so I wiped the sweat from my forehead and neck, smiled smoothly, and marched through the checkpoint without pausing.

I had one foot over the threshold when she called, "Excuse me, ma'am. Can I see your invite, please?"

I turned sharply to face her, my expression steely. "My husband has it and he's inside."

She smiled tightly. "I'm afraid I still—"

"And besides," I snapped, cutting her off, "you already have. I was here earlier, remember? You asked me if I was looking for someone."

I crossed my arms and waited for her to recall the incident. When I thought she had, I added, "But of course, if you'd like to go in and find my husband, then by all means, go. His name's Wane McBride," I explained, using the name of the gallery's curator, whom I remembered from my research. It was a risky thing to say, of course, especially since I had no idea if Mr. McBride had a wife or not. But I said it with such confidence that for a split second even *I* believed it was true.

It's the storyteller that counts.

The usher's eyes bulged slightly and she said, apologetically, "Welcome back, Mrs. McBride."

I WAS INSIDE. Now let me explain.

Reid had his USB, *check.*

Mr. L had her bracelet, *check* (or *a* bracelet, I should say).

Nellie, Theo, Dax, Sophia, and I were technically off the hook, *check.*

And yet there I was, back at the St. Jude gallery, about to engage in small talk with the very woman from whom I'd just swiped a multimillion-pound bracelet, the bracelet that was curled around my wrist, the bracelet Nellie had so neatly nicked from Mr. L at great personal danger and replaced with our second replica (sorry: forgot to mention we had two).

But why?

Nellie and I didn't want or need to steal the Heart of Envy. We only needed to borrow it for long enough to allow Mr. L to assess the piece, give Reid the green light, and hand over the USB. The second reason I was back at the gallery was because I didn't really want to go to prison for the rest of my life. Therefore,

I had five minutes to put the Heart of Envy back on the dear old bat's wrist and reclaim replica number one. If I took any longer than that, said replica was going to be locked up in a glass safe, the weight sensors were going to freak out, the gallery alarm was going to go off, the police were going to be called, and everything I had gone through would've been for nothing.

I wrapped my fingers around my wrist, touching the Heart of Envy. The only time in my life I had ever felt so sick with nerves was when I did this for the first time. I was lucky then. Everything had gone just as I'd planned despite Nellie's absence. But doing it all over again in exactly the same way—and getting away with it—seemed about as likely as being struck by lightning twice on the same day. And I didn't fancy calculating those odds.

I ran my thumb along the white-gold chain, over the diamonds and emeralds, thinking. How could I get close enough to the woman wearing my replica without raising suspicion or drawing attention to myself?

"This way please, ma'am," said a gruff voice, jolting me from my thoughts.

A security guard—a different one—was standing just ahead of me, ushering forward the woman wearing the Heart of Envy replica (who was still limping, by the way). I balled my fists and pressed them to my stomach to stop myself from throwing up. The security guard and the woman with the bracelet were already at the glass case, alongside a young brunette wearing the Napoleon breast pin and a redhead adorned with the Marie Antoinette choker. Six security guards stood between me and them, and, as if it could get any worse, I realized the woman who'd been wearing my replica no longer had anything encircling her wrist.

I froze, my gaze fixed on the glass case that was supposed to contain the Heart of Envy.

Nothing inside there either.

So the bracelet wasn't on its wearer's arm and it wasn't in the case. The only logical conclusion was that the counterfeit had been seen for what it was and I—standing in the middle of the gallery like an idiot with the real bracelet around my wrist—was about to be dragged off to the clink.

"They take them to the office afterward," a soft voice said from somewhere over my shoulder.

I turned slowly, my limbs heavy and numb. The redhead who'd been wearing the Marie Antoinette choker was smiling at me with a glass of Merlot in one hand and a turquoise crystal-studded purse in the other.

"Excuse me?" I croaked thickly.

She took a sip of wine, dabbed the corner of her mouth, and gestured at the glass case in front of us. "You asked where it was. I presume you meant the Heart of Envy?"

Had I spoken that question out loud instead of just thinking it? "Oh, oh. Yes. Right." I swallowed, took a shallow breath. "The office? What office? What for?"

She laughed, probably at the tone of my voice, which was reaching falsetto pitch. "The office down there, near the bathrooms. I presume they do it to check for damage before they put it back in the—"

Say no more.

I was probably halfway across the hall by the time Miss Marie Antoinette finished her sentence. Through the short marble corridor, past the bathrooms, past the staff room. A security guard was striding ahead of me, a small steel case bobbing at his hip. He turned into another short corridor, past a spiral staircase, and through a large, unfurnished, white-walled room that had probably once held an exhibition of its own.

Assuming we'd soon arrive at the office he was heading to, I realized I had to act. And now.

First, I had to get myself nice and close to that steel case. But strolling up to Mr. Security Guard while he was transporting his precious cargo would earn me a fist to the chin.

When in doubt, I heard Gran's voice whisper inside my head, *make them come to you.*

I loosened the Heart of Envy around my wrist, pulled it over my hand, came to a halt.

Then, wriggling the bracelet over my knuckles, I said, "Excuse me, sorry, hi."

The security guard paused.

I let the Heart of Envy slip from my grasp. It landed with a soft clink on the marble floor, and as it did, I took three long steps forward, muffling the sound.

"Yes?" the guard said, turning on his heel.

I gave him a quick smile. "I think you might've dropped something. Over there."

It took a moment for him to realize what I was talking about and another moment for him to realize that the glittering object lying on the floor was, in fact, the multimillion-pound bracelet he was supposed to be transporting.

His face turned as white as the walls around him. "What the—"

"The latch on that case of yours," I suggested smoothly. "It must have come loose while you were walking. Check."

For a few seconds he seemed unable to speak or move. We were completely alone, though the drone of chatter drifted out from the exhibition hall behind us.

At last the guard jolted into action. He put a finger to his ear and spoke into the microphone attached to his shirt. "Security backup needed, gallery 2A."

"Anyway, good luck," I said coolly. "I was just on my way back to the exhibition." I took one step back, closer to the bracelet, and he was on me like a dog, his hand seizing my arm.

"Ma'am, please. Don't move. I need you to stay right where you are until the backup arrives."

"Am I under arrest or something?"

"No, ma'am. But this is a very expensive piece of jewelry and I can't have you getting any closer."

"Are you serious? Listen, buddy, if I was going to steal that bracelet, I would've done so right after it fell out of your little carry bag. I also wouldn't have called you over to tell you about it." Undeniable logic, if you ask me.

I ripped my arm from his grip, glared at him, then the steel case.

Growing more confused by the second, he lifted the case to eye level, stared at it a moment. "But . . . it's locked," he murmured, incredulous. "It couldn't have fallen out."

I shrugged. No need to convince him that it had: the evidence was lying right there in front of him.

"Gallery 2A," he repeated a little more frantically into his headset as he continued to stare at the locked case, stupefied. "We've got a situation here." He tapped in a security code at the side of his case and it clicked open.

Perfect.

The next bit was like a dance in slow motion.

The security guard lifted the case lid toward him. I took a step sideways, realigning his focus. His eyes followed me, and in that moment I swept my right hand across the open lid while I used my left to swing my handbag gently into his stomach. In real time it would've looked like I'd shifted my position to see inside the case (I mean, who wouldn't want to get a look at *the* Heart of Envy?), which forced him to move around me in defense and, in doing so, bump into my handbag. Of course, by the time he'd snapped the case away from me, I'd plucked out the counterfeit and slipped it over my wrist.

AFTER BEING FORCED TO WAIT AROUND FOR THE SECURITY guard's backup to arrive—which set me back another five minutes—I ran. I didn't care if I looked suspicious or guilty as sin. I ran. Across the gallery floor, people starting to stare, out the exit, down the red carpet, past the checkpoint, past the police barricade, through the walled garden, and onto King's Road, dodging pedestrians and paparazzi and rain-filled potholes, my flamingo-pink frock trailing behind me like a cape. I turned into Cheltenham Terrace, across St. Leonard's, and onto Franklins Row, and finally screeched to a halt as I reached Royal Hospital Road, where the MG was parked.

"Tell me it's done?" Nellie asked as I hauled myself into the car and doubled over, heaving for breath and pale with adrenaline.

I nodded, eyeing Theo, who was standing stock-still on the pavement alongside the car, as if frozen.

"It's true," Nellie said, following my gaze. "He's being weird. Very weird."

"Right?"

"And he's been staring at his phone nonstop with this strange look, like he's terrified or something."

I shook the tension from my hands, too on edge to puzzle out the nuances of Theo's current mood. "I'm so tired. Can this just be over now?" I surveyed the street. "Where's Reid?"

Nellie handed me the binoculars, gestured at the strip of pavement a few yards from the white utility van. "He's just finished his verification process. You're bang on time."

I spotted Reid halfway up the street, marching toward the MG and away from the white utility van, his stride short and quick.

"All right," Nellie said. "Here we go. You ready?"

"Can I not be?"

"No."

"OK, then I'm ready."

It was time for the final stage—the most reckless and incalculable. As Reid was about to discover, there were only two ways this night could end, and I was pretty sure he wouldn't like the idea of either of them.

Nellie held out her hand. "I'll do the talking. I've got a few things I'd like to say while I'm at it."

But just as I was about to hand over our burner phone, a text was delivered with a soft ping. I looked at the time stamp—it had been sent fifteen minutes ago, while I was inside the gallery, but had only come through now that I had reception.

"It's Dax," I uttered slowly, my throat closing as I read the message: Send me that photo NOW. And don't do anything until I've called you back.

In all the haste and excitement of the past hour, I'd completely forgotten about the unsent picture in my drafts folder.

Nellie read the text over my shoulder. "Photo?"

"He texted just after we arrived at the gallery. He wanted a picture of Reid."

"What for?"

"Didn't say. Something about the background search he was doing." I scrolled through my drafts folder and re-sent the picture.

Swoosh. At last, it was delivered.

Nellie fluttered her fingers. "Gimme gimme. Let's get this over with."

I kept the phone tight in my white-knuckled grasp. "He said not to do anything until he calls—"

Nellie shook her head impatiently, took the phone from my hand. "Too bad. We don't have time to wait. If Reid gets to the end of this street and we lose sight of him, he'll walk away with that USB and your whole plan's toast."

"OK. Right. You're right." Still panting and cold with a dread I didn't quite understand, I pressed the binoculars to my face while Nellie dialed Reid's number.

After scanning the street for several seconds, I located Reid. He was striding up the right side of the pavement, just a few yards from where we were parked.

He paused, pulled his phone from his pocket, and stared angrily at my name flashing on his caller ID.

He hesitated a moment, like he was considering rejecting the call, then answered.

Nellie put the phone on speaker.

"What?" he spat, his usual tone—impatient and irritable—though this time colored with something else too.

"See that pretty old building on your left?" Nellie said coldly. "The one with the clock above the door?"

Reid halted, glanced left.

"That's the Royal Hospital Chelsea, and if you look carefully, you'll see a man in a black tracksuit pacing back and forth in front of the entrance. See that bulge in his pocket? Hate to say it, babe, but I think that's a gun. Now look to your right. At those three recycling bins. Your other right, idiot. There, that's it. There's another chap over there, leaning up against the lamp-post. See him? I've a feeling he's also got a gun."

"What do you want?" Reid snarled.

"Those are Mr. L's hit men," Nellie continued, unfazed. "There's one more hiding somewhere nearby. Might be on the roof or something like that. Good vantage point, don't you think? Nothing to worry about, though. They're just hanging around in case, I don't know, Mr. L suddenly realizes you sold her a fake." She sighed theatrically. "Anyway, here's the deal, babe: that USB you're carrying belongs to us. We did all the planning, all the work. We took all the risks. And now we get the reward. Karma. Fair and simple."

Reid brought the phone directly in front of his mouth, his face screwed up in a horrible scowl. "Piss off. I've got a gun, re-member?"

I heard a buzzing sound and noticed a flicker of bluish light to my left. I didn't turn to see what it was.

"How could I forget?" Nellie went on. "But still, it's one against three. And that's not counting Mr. L and whoever else she's got hiding out in that Merc."

Reid snorted. "So what? You're all working together now or something, setting me up?"

"Let's just say we have a common interest."

"You're dead! You hear me?! DEAD!"

"No, James, *you* are. In exactly three minutes and five sec-onds. You see, when you've been in the business as long as we have, you have a reputation to uphold. Which is why we've decided we're going to send Mr. L a message from our burner phone in the next three minutes. Burner phone means it's untraceable. Anyway, the message will suggest she does a quick double check on that bracelet she's just bought for sixteen million quid because we're pretty sure it's a fake."

There was a long silence. I watched Reid through the binoculars. Was he breathing? It didn't look like it.

At last, he stirred. He looked over his shoulder, across the pavement, then finally straight ahead at the MG. "You're lying. You don't have her mobile number. She would never have given it to you. To any of us."

"True," Nellie said. "But we have the number of the mobile phone I dropped into her handbag a few minutes ago."

His brow creased. "What?" Nellie didn't answer. Reid muttered something, then said, "And anyway, so what if you call her and tell her to check the bracelet again? It passed her appraisal the first time; it'll pass again."

"You're wasting time, James," Nellie said. "But no. It won't. The only reason it passed Mr. L's assessment the first time was because it really *was* the Heart of Envy. The real thing."

The phone in his hand slipped an inch. He brought it back to his ear.

"We told you it was a fake," Nellie explained, "but it was real. Emma is a master pickpocket—of course she managed to nick the thing, even without my help. The bracelet Mr. L is holding on to now, though? That's replica number two. I'll let you puzzle out how we made *that* swap happen."

"Mr. L will come after you too," he mumbled. "You wouldn't risk it."

"Come after us? How? She has no idea who we are. You're

the one who set this whole thing up. You're the one who's been communicating with her. You're the one who handed her the bracelet. Sure, we'd be the one tipping her off via an untraceable burner phone, but to be honest, James, I think she'd be quite grateful about that. Who knows, we might even end up best buds."

Reid was silent. I could see him thinking, hard, trying to find a loophole in our plan. "You're forgetting what I told Emma," he said at last. "If you screw me, I'll ruin you."

Nellie looked down at the diamond choker in her free hand, then at me. Naturally, we'd discussed this issue at length: Was Reid capable of exposing us to the public, or the police, or Mr. L? Did he know enough about who we really were? If he'd hacked our laptop or phone, like I'd originally feared, he would've had access to every bit of our personal information: ID numbers, driver's licenses, full names, legal addresses, crypto wallets. But thanks to Theo's confession and Dax's stringent security checks, we now knew he hadn't ever been a hacker. Just a stalker who'd read Dax's texts.

"Really?" Nellie said. "Then tell me what our surnames are."

No answer. He squeezed the back of his neck, worked his jaw. "What's in it for you, anyway?" he asked. "If you tell Mr. L I screwed her, she'll kill me and take back the USB. You'll have nothing."

"Well, not nothing. We'll have revenge. But you're right. We'd much rather you gave *us* the USB than have to watch Mr. L pry it from your lifeless hands. So if you want to live, here's what you're going to do: walk nice and casual up the street until you see that bench on your right. Sit down. Be cool. Take off that stupid hoodie. Place your gun and the USB, along with its pin code and recovery phrase, on the bench, cover them with your hoodie, then get up and turn right into East Road. And then start running. Run, run, run, and don't stop until you're out of this city, or preferably the country."

James lowered the phone to his side but didn't hang up. He stared off into the distance, then, slowly, turned to the right, toward the man with the gun leaning up against the lamppost.

They locked eyes. Reid shuddered, placed the phone back against his ear.

"You're bluffing," he said, toneless.

"You sure about that?"

"Yes."

"All right. Then I suppose we'll just have to prove it to you."

She hung up, punched out a text, and sent it to the burner phone lying in the bottom of Mr. L's handbag.

I held my breath.

Mr. L was leaning up against the Merc, puffing on a cigarette, her bloodred snakeskin Birkin hanging from her arm. I couldn't hear the message alert tone, but *she* did. Cigarette clamped between her teeth, she opened her bag, face screwed up in confusion, and drew out the burner phone.

For a moment nothing happened. Mr. L stared at the phone, her expression bewildered.

Reid continued to march up the street.

Nellie and I tapped our feet and waited.

Finally, Mr. L looked up, handed the phone to her driver, and ground out her cigarette on the tarmac. She got into the car. The Merc's lights flashed on, illuminating the street ahead.

Startled by the light, Reid swung round to face the car.

Doors snapped shut.

A strange beating sound caused me to peel the binoculars from my face. Footsteps? Someone running? I blinked at the dimness ahead, at the strip of road rolling out in front of us.

I turned to my left, then my right. My shoulders tensed. "Where's Theo?"

Having just redialed Reid's number, Nellie was too preoccupied to answer.

Frantically, I looked again through the binoculars. Reid was still walking away from us, his phone in his hand. But where the hell was Theo? Had he finally lost his nerve and bolted? Somehow, I knew there was more to it.

"One more chance, James," Nellie said as Reid answered. "We've told Mr. L to keep an eye on you, but we haven't told her why yet."

Reid raised his free hand to shield his eyes from the Merc's headlights. The engine purred to life.

Did he believe us? We knew he feared Mr. L; that was plain enough. But did he believe his two favorite con artists would go as far as framing him like this? Sentencing him to either a grim future on the run or a grisly death? If he'd taken the time to really get to know us, he would have his answer. He would know that the text Nellie had just sent Mr. L was simply to warn her there were cops in the area and it might be time to leg it. He would also know that as much as we despised him and what he'd done to us, we had no desire to witness what would happen to him if Mr. L discovered she'd just been conned. All we wanted was for him to doubt us enough to drop the USB and vanish.

"I'm going to hang up now," Nellie said as Reid watched Mr. L's hit men climb inside the Merc, which then began to move toward him. "If you haven't dropped that USB on the bench in the next thirty seconds, I'm sending another text to Mr. L. And after that, there's no turning back."

She cut the call, and almost immediately, another call came through.

Dax. *Again*. This couldn't be good.

I ripped the phone from Nellie's hand, suddenly aware of a horrible gnawing sensation in the pit of my stomach. Obviously, Dax had been trying to get through for as long as Nellie had been on the phone to Reid.

"Mate, where are you?" he blurted.

"In the car. Royal Hospital Road. What's wrong?" There was definitely something wrong.

"Where's Reid?" he asked next.

"He's here. I think we have him. He's about to take the bait. Mr. L's moving in and Reid's—"

Wait, what *was* Reid doing? He'd crossed the street and was now standing at the boundary of Burton Court. Was he talking to himself?

"And Theo?" Dax asked.

I scanned the street a second time—still no sign of him. "Don't know. He's run off somewhere."

Dax cursed, slammed something. Was that Sir Sebastian yowling in the background? Sophia tut-tutting?

"All right," he said, "look, just stay where you are. I'm on my way there now."

"What? No, you can't—"

"James Reid is Chris Keeling."

I obviously hadn't heard that correctly. "Umm, sorry, what?"

"'James Reid' is just an alias. Keeling was using a false name to try and protect Sophia. Or maybe Theo forced him to. Anyway, he's her father. And obviously still alive." He paused. "I'm about ninety percent sure."

"No."

"Make that ninety-five percent."

Nellie turned to me. "What?"

"No," I repeated. "No. That can't be! Keeling's dead. Theo told us he's dead. We even saw the body!"

"Yeah, man, of course Theo told us he's dead. He's been lying to us. About everything. *He's* ENT00X, not Reid. He's the one who's been communicating with Mr. L, not Reid. And that body in the warehouse . . . I don't know who it was you saw, but it definitely wasn't Sophia's father."

"But—"

"After we found out Theo had been playing me, I decided to do some research," he continued, cutting me off. "On Theo, on Nico, on all of them. Going on a hunch, I started with Theo's family. It would've been great if I'd done this earlier, but I guess when you're in love with someone you don't really feel the need to run a background search on them, or double-check everything they tell you. Won't be making that mistake again." I nodded. *You and me both.* "Anyway, it took me a while but eventually I found an article in *The Atlantic* from a year ago mentioning a pretty well-known Wall Street broker who was being investigated for shady dealings and something they referred to as 'attempted larceny' . . . of diamonds."

A well-known Wall Street broker. Wasn't that . . .

"Please tell me we're not talking about Theo's brother."

"Yeah, we are. But it gets worse. Michael Fletcher wasn't the only Fletcher family member involved in the ordeal."

I had a horrible feeling I knew where this was going.

"My suspicion is that Mr. L is Theo's father," Dax said.

"Mother," I corrected him with a sigh. "Mr. L is a woman."

"You're kidding. OK, well, anyway, I'm guessing that's what this whole thing is about. Theo's the black sheep of the family, he admitted that to us, remember?" I closed my eyes, hand to my mouth, wishing I could shut all of this out. "He just forgot to mention it was because he'd been left out of the family's black-market diamond-trading business. He wanted to prove himself, I guess, finally get the respect he felt he deserved and at the same time get back the cash his brother had squandered. So what better way to do both those things than by selling his beloved mummy the one item his golden boy brother, and the rest of the family, wanted more than anything else."

I gasped.

"You remember Theo told us his brother had conned him into investing into the family's failed start-up?" Dax explained, speaking faster than ever. "Well, I'm pretty sure that wasn't an app but actually the very same 'attempted larceny' Michael had been busted over. *The Atlantic* article said an ex-employee of a gallery in Hong Kong that was displaying the Heart of Envy at the time had been approached by Michael to leak some security information. The employee refused and went to the police, and so Michael's plan failed and whatever money Theo had invested in the heist—if that's what it was—went down the drain."

"But wait," I said, still clinging to the hope that Dax had got this all wrong, "if this is really Mr. L's family we're talking about here, surely they're as rich as Croesus?" Dax was silent so I went on. "Why would they have needed Theo to help finance the Hong Kong heist in the first place?"

"I don't think it was about the money," he said. "Not to Mr. L, anyway. It was a show of commitment. To prove he was one of them, Theo had to have some skin in the game."

I nodded to myself. "Right. Makes sense."

Nellie looked at me, muttered something, turned her eyes back to the street. Something or someone was hovering near the corner of Franklins Row, just a few yards away from Reid. Was it Theo?

Dax went on. "But then I thought, if this is just a family feud between the Fletchers, how do Kappas, Reid, and Keeling fit in? I tried to track down the gaming company Theo told me he worked for, but it took a while because he'd given me a fake address and company name, of course. Anyway, I found it eventually."

"OK . . ." I said impatiently. "*And?*"

"I decided to call and email some people and discovered that Keeling had worked there as a cleaner, though only for a two-week probation period."

"Of course, yes. Which is why you didn't find this out during your earlier background search on Keeling," I added politely.

"Exactly. His name wasn't reflected in the employee records, and if I hadn't known the company name and actually been able to speak to someone who worked there . . ."

"What about Nico Kappas?"

Dax cleared his throat. "He worked there too, just like Theo told us. And both he and Keeling quit around the same time Theo did."

"But Reid?"

"Doesn't exist. I emailed the HR department, the recruitment company they used, even some of the employees. No one's heard of a James Reid. I started to get this odd feeling we were talking about a group of four men when really it was a group of three. Theo Fletcher, Nico Kappas, and Chris Keeling. That's why I asked for the picture. To show Sophia, just in case my hunch *was* right." He paused, as if giving me time to process it all. "These were her exact words: *Oh, there's Daddy. You found him.* James Reid is Chris Keeling. That's a fact."

In something of a horrified daze, I pulled Sophia's stick-figure drawing from my purse. I'd always been so focused on her representation of me that I'd never really taken the time to look at the figure she called "Daddy." He was wearing a cape—that I'd seen before—and he had what looked like a medal hanging from his neck. No, not a medal, I realized with a jolt. A chunky silver chain.

"James . . . the chain . . ." I mumbled. "He's been wearing it this whole time . . . right in front of me!"

"Another fact," Dax said, talking over me, "is that Theo is dangerous and unpredictable and he really, *really* wants that USB. He's furious with his family, and making them hand over sixteen million pounds in Bitcoin without knowing it's going straight into his pocket will be all the revenge he's ever needed."

Dax was right. Theo was dangerous. And he was dangerous mostly because he was a brilliant liar. Instead of feeding us a list of complete fabrications, he'd simply reversed and altered the truth, misled us so subtly and so carefully that even now, looking back on the full picture, it was hard to separate what had been true and what had been a lie. He'd told us everything about himself and his family, revealed to us his motivation for the heist, and even told us the truth about Chris Keeling (save that he was alive and working under a false name). I wanted to kick myself for being so gullible.

Gran had warned us that one day we might meet someone who'd use our own tricks against us. Foolishly, I'd always thought I'd see it coming.

"I don't know what leverage Theo has over Kappas," Dax went on, "but we *do* know what he has over Keeling."

"Sophia." I gulped. "No wonder Reid didn't fall for our threats about Mr. L. If he gave up the USB, Theo would've gone after his kid." I felt a shriek of frustration building in the back of my throat. "Where is she now?"

"Safe, don't stress. I've moved her."

Nellie, who had been staring at me in stunned silence, spoke at last. "I'm not sure if I actually want to ask this, but . . . what's going on?"

Still holding the phone to my ear, I picked up the binoculars and examined the street. Mr. L's Merc sped up. Reid slipped behind a lamppost as the car flew past and turned the corner into Franklins Row. Reid waited. One second. Two. Then, throwing his haversack before him, he climbed the fence to Burton Court.

"OK, listen," Dax said after a pause, "I don't think Theo's a cold-blooded murderer, but he *will* kill if he has to. That stuff about him trying to stop Nico from shooting me in the hotel room was a lie, I'm sure of it. The minute he discovered Sophia was hiding out with me, he knew his cover was blown. Or was about to be, at least. If the two of us started comparing notes about him and realized the bad man and my boyfriend were the same person, he was done. He would've killed both of us if he got the chance."

I nodded to myself, shocked at how easy this was to believe. "OK, so that means . . ."

Dax huffed, like it was obvious. "Reid's about to hand over that USB to Theo, yes?"

"Well, if you're right about everything—"

"I am, this time. I really think I am."

"Then, yes," I said. "He probably thinks he has no choice."

"And in exchange," Dax added, "Theo's supposed to hand over Sophia. I'm pretty sure that was the deal."

"Except he can't!" I said, catching on, my insides churning. "He can't because he doesn't know where she is. But Reid—I mean Chris—won't give Theo the USB until he sees Sophia."

"Exactly. Which leaves Theo with only one way of getting what he wants."

28

11:05 P.M.

MY HEAD WAS SPINNING.

"Wrong person," I mumbled. "This *whole time* we were conning the wrong person!"

Nellie looked at me, bewildered, a small smile on her face like she thought this was all a joke.

"What?" she asked.

"James Reid is Chris Keeling," I blurted. "Dax just . . . he figured it out when . . . well, it doesn't matter right now."

Nellie recoiled like I'd struck her in the face. "But Chris Keeling is dead," she said simply, as if I might've forgotten this tiny piece of information. "We know he is. The body—"

"Wasn't him."

"But then who—"

"I don't know."

She scraped her hair out of her face, released a sharp breath. "OK . . . so then you're saying *Theo* is ENT00X?"

"Yes. He also planned everything. Set up *everything*. This whole time we've been working for him. Us *and* Sophia's dad."

"But why didn't Reid just tell us that, then? We could've

looped him in on our game plan and screwed Theo over together."
Before I could answer that, she figured it out. "Sophia . . ."

"He had too much to lose," I said. "But, as it turns out, so
does Theo." I briefly filled her in on Mr. L being Theo's mother,
to which she replied with a shriek so shrill my ears rang.

And in response my mind began to whirl. All the things we
had assumed, rather than known. The fact that the body we'd
seen was Chris Keeling, the fact that Theo's reticent, neurotic
character was a sign of incompetence and even innocence, the
fact that ENT00X and James Reid were the same person, the
fact that Mr. L was a man, the fact that Reid had been hunting
down Sophia to kill her rather than save her. Weren't *we* supposed to be the ones playing mind games?

While Nellie stared at the diamond choker wrapped around
her knuckles, muttering something about karma and mistakes, I
picked up the binoculars. Reid had vanished into the shadows of
Burton Court. Mr. L's Merc was out of sight.

But Theo . . .

I adjusted the focus dial. A slim figure was dashing across
the Burton Court cricket pitch, a gun in his right hand.

It dawned on me then that since Theo had started acting so
jittery only *after* I'd told him Reid had sold Mr. L a fake, it meant
he'd probably already told Mr. L he was ENT00X, the one behind the sale. It was a tiny relief, then, to know Mr. L would
blame *him*, not Reid, if she ever discovered the fake. But as sweet
as that thought was, I doubted it changed anything. Theo would
still be desperate to get his hands on that USB, maybe even more
so now that he believed his family would soon be hunting him
down. And one thing I knew for sure was that desperation plus
fear equaled violence.

I opened the door and scrambled to my feet as fast as I could.

"Wait! Where are you going?" Nellie said, reaching for my arm.

"I have to . . . We can't let them . . . Theo and Reid are meeting now to do the exchange. The USB for Sophia. That was the agreement all along."

Nellie cocked her head. "But—"

"But," I cut in, relaying what Dax and I had just figured out, "Theo knows he can't keep up his side of the bargain, which means he can't negotiate with Reid, which means if he still wants that USB, which I know he does, he's left with only one way of getting it."

"Oh," she said as it hit her. "Oh . . ."

"And if Theo kills Reid, it'll be all our fault. Sorry, all *my* fault. I even gave him the damn gun!"

I turned back to Burton Court. Theo had reached the middle of the cricket pitch. He stopped, staring at something on the other side. I couldn't see what, but no prizes for guessing.

"So what's the plan?" Nellie asked. "We use our bodies as human shields? Go down martyr-style? If Theo's happy to kill Reid for the USB, I hate to tell you, but he'll be more than happy to kill us too. Actually, we might even deserve it . . ."

Not for the first time that week, I found myself wishing I had Sophia's *Book of Good Advice* on hand, because I currently had a list of questions I urgently needed answers to:

1) Does conning the wrong person for the right reasons make me a bad person, or just a stupid one?

2) Would Sophia ever forgive me?

3) Was I about to die, and did I deserve to?

"We do it like a Switch," I said, blinking back into the present. "Version twelve."

Nellie looked incredulous, but she didn't stop to argue or ask questions. She picked up the phone, slipped it into her bra. We both hitched up our gowns and kicked off our heels. "Burton Court?"

I nodded. "I'll climb the fence this side, you get in from Franklins Row, and we'll converge somewhere near the pitch. Just . . . try to hurry. I don't know how long we've got."

She got out of the car. "On it. See you in a jiff."

29

NEXT THING I KNEW I WAS HAULING MYSELF OVER THE FENCE
with a shaky plan, trembling limbs, and the odds of survival very
much not in my favor.

*Sometimes it takes the scary things to show us how brave
we are.*

The events of this evening had certainly shown Nellie and
me what we were capable of. Could we pull off one more impossible feat? Mind racing, I landed with a thump on the damp
grass, then straightened. The air was chilled and dank, and although I was no more than a few feet from the bustle of Franklins Row and Royal Hospital Road, I could hear nothing but a
soft breeze through the treetops. I moved forward slowly, past
the tree line and onto the border of the cricket pitch. Theo had
been heading left, which meant he must have made it to the
main gate by now.

I tiptoed around the pitch perimeter, my eyes slowly adjust-
ing to the dimness and my ears to the eerie quiet. Gray shapes
came into focus: the towering trees above me, the pavilion on
my right, something moving in the distance. A person? I paused,

squinted against the dark. Nellie was walking hastily along the gravel path that ran parallel to Franklins Row, her rain-drenched frock and long golden hair making her look almost ghostly under the pale moonlight and shifting shadows. She stopped halfway up the path, turned to look at me. No, sorry. Not me.

A footstep crunched on the wet earth behind me.

I swung round.

"Where is it?" Theo asked, the gun trembling in his grip.

I thought he was talking to me, asking about the real bracelet and what I'd done with it. Then I noticed something shift to my left. Reid was standing about a foot away, a gun in his hand too.

"Where is it?" Theo repeated through clenched teeth. He looked as if he'd tripped and fallen somewhere along the way, his baggy trousers mud-stained and a bleeding graze on his right elbow. Despite everything, I felt a little sorry for him. "The USB. Where is it?"

"First tell me where Sophia is," Reid said.

Theo scoffed. "No, that's not how this works."

Reid cocked his gun but said nothing.

"You shoot me, you never find out where she is," Theo threatened.

"And *you* shoot *me*, you never get that USB. I don't have it on me. Pat me down if you want."

They glowered at each other, both determined to get what they wanted, neither willing to compromise.

"We know who you are now," I cut in quickly, addressing Reid. "Chris Keeling. Sophia Keeling's father."

Reid bristled. Oh good, I now had two guns pointing at my head. Could it get any worse? Stupid question . . .

"So the two of you are working together, then?" he snarled. "I always suspected it."

"No. No," I said. "Absolutely not. We're definitely not working together. We're just—"

"Where's Sophia?" Reid interrupted with a snap, addressing Theo. "You told me you had her locked up someplace safe. You told me you'd release her when I gave you the Bitcoin."

"I do," Theo said. "And I will. Go fetch the USB and I'll tell you."

"He's lying, Chris," I said. "He can't give you Sophia." Reid's face went pale and I realized I'd just made it sound like she was dead. "He told you he had her locked up somewhere because if he didn't, he'd lose his leverage over you," I explained quickly, hoping to rectify my mistake. "But Sophia escaped the night Nellie was kidnapped and we've been keeping her safe ever since. She hasn't been harmed. Theo has no idea where she is and if you hand over that USB he'll shoot you. And then me."

"Believe that if you want," Theo said. "Risky, though, because if she's lying—"

"I'm not lying! I'm sorry, Chris," I said. "I really am. But Theo told us *you* were the one who blackmailed him. He told us Chris Keeling was dead. We even saw the body!"

Reid threw a furious glance at Theo. "You told them I was *dead*?!"

"I didn't even need to," Theo said, nonplussed. "They assumed it right from the beginning."

"Because we saw the body! Who was it, anyway? The body? Who did you—"

"Didn't kill anyone," Theo said, then paused so long it was as if he was expecting us to fill in the blanks. "I needed a body, didn't I? Chris had to believe I was a killer."

Because you're not? I considered asking, but decided that was a stupid question to pose to someone when they're pointing a gun in your face.

"There'd been a hit-and-run near Paddington station," he explained. "Some pedestrian. Homeless guy no one knew."

I let out a soft shriek as I recalled the news story that had been circulating in the days before Nellie went missing.

"No family to claim the body at the morgue," Theo went on. "Except me."

"You're sick," Reid said.

Theo didn't seem to take that as an insult. "Or just an opportunist."

I looked over his shoulder at the dark strip of grass that ran along the border of the cricket pitch. Something shifted in the shadows.

"Look," I said, focusing again on Reid, "the point is: we wouldn't have done what we did if we knew the truth. Please just give me the gun and let's talk about this."

"Screw that," Reid spat. "You think I'm gonna trust someone who just tried to get me killed?"

"We weren't trying to . . . none of what we told you about Mr. L was the truth. We were bluffing the entire time. We never sent Mr. L a text. Not about you, anyway. She doesn't know the bracelet's a fake."

Reid gawked at this bit of news, but Theo screamed over him, sounding delirious. "That USB is mine, dammit! Tell me where it is or I'll kill you both and cut my losses!"

Reid's face slackened, and for the first time I saw the exhaustion, suffering, and fear he'd been hiding behind the mask of rage and authority he'd worn since the day we met.

"I'm tired, Theo," he said wearily. "You dragged me into this mess. You made promises. You lied. You tricked and humiliated me, and when I wanted to get out, you forced me to stay by threatening to take away the only thing in the world I've ever cared about. I've done everything you asked. I've lied for you. I've put my life at risk for you. All I'm asking is that you bring me Sophia and—" He broke off and turned to look at me, clearly still unsure to whom he should direct his plea. "I'm begging you, please."

Theo was quiet for a minute, though I didn't like the shift in his expression. He was plotting something.

I figured out what it was a second too late.

He lurched forward and grabbed me by the neck. Gun to my head, he growled, "Call Dax and have him bring Sophia here. Now."

"I don't know where he—"

"Do it! Now! Or I pull this trigger."

I frowned at the shadows beyond the tree line. One of them was moving. I caught a glint of something shiny. A spark of hope lifted in my chest. "All right," I said, stalling. "But I can't call him without a phone and mine's in the car."

Theo nodded at Reid. "Hand it over, Keeling."

Reid lobbed his iPhone at my face. I fumbled around on the keypad for as long as I could push it, praying Nellie would see me doing it.

"Hurry up!" Theo snapped.

The shadow beyond the tree line shuffled closer. A branch snapped. Reid flinched at the sound but didn't turn. Theo simply shoved the gun harder against my temple.

I punched in a number and pressed the call button.

Our burner phone ringtone—that good old Nokia tune—was so loud in the relative quiet of the park that everyone, me included, jumped a foot into the air.

Nellie dived out of the tree line while I spun out of Theo's grip.

"Nice to see you again, babe," she said, tapping him on the shoulder.

He whipped round to face her. I stuck a foot between his legs, unsteadying him. As he attempted to right himself, the gun slipped from his grip and landed with a muffled thump on the sodden grass. Nellie lurched for it, but Theo got there first.

A car screeched to a halt on Royal Hospital Road.

I turned to the noise.

Bang. Clang. A door opened and closed. Footsteps pounded on the pavement. Lots of huffing, panting. Someone yelling.

Theo—still dazed—couldn't seem to decide who to aim the gun at now. Eventually, he settled on me.

There was a soft *click.*

Nellie mouthed something but I couldn't make out what it was. Run? Duck? Pray?

I tried to ignore the pistol aimed at my head and turned my attention back to the road beyond the fence line. Who had just pulled up? Was it the Merc? Had Mr. L somehow found out about the bracelet?

I squinted ahead, but it was so dark by then I couldn't make out a thing. Theo's eyes bulged, seeing what I couldn't.

The footsteps beat harder, louder.

"Daddy! Daddy!" a small voice called out of nowhere. "Daddy, it's you! It's really you! Daddy! I told them you were alive. I told them!"

Sophia barreled over the fence and across the grass in a big dinosaur jumper and baggy trousers, her small legs moving in a blur, her eyes streaming. She flung her arms around Reid's neck and buried her head in his chest, squealing with delight. Reid—ignoring everything and everyone else—fell to his knees, dropped his gun, let out a long, low wail, and started sobbing.

"Great timing," Nellie said, breathless, as Dax appeared at my shoulder, gleaming with sweat, a backpack slung over his shoulder.

"I . . . I can't believe you're here, Soph," Reid croaked, cupping his hands around Sophia's face and pinching her cheeks. "I'm so happy you're OK. You *are* OK, yeah? They didn't hurt you?"

She shook her head spiritedly. "I'm fine, Daddy. Everyone's fine. These are my friends." She nodded at me, Nellie, and Dax. "Sorry, *family*."

"The USB!" Theo barked, interrupting the happy scene. For a second I—and I'm sure Reid—had forgotten about him and the fact that he still had a gun pointing in my general direction.

"Are you kidding me?" Reid snapped, picking up his own gun again and getting to his feet. Sophia scrambled to hide behind him. "You really think you deserve that USB? You're not the one who brought me Sophia."

Theo hissed something, turned the gun on Reid.

"No!" Sophia screamed from between Reid's legs. "Daddy, be careful!"

"I need that money," Theo said in what now sounded like the growl of a starved, rabid animal. "I needed it before, but I *really* need it now! I have to run, don't you understand? I have to leave the country! They *know*," he added more softly, almost regretfully. "They know it was me who organized the heist. They know I was the one behind the ENTOOX profile. And when they find out that bracelet is a fake, and they *will* find out, they'll think I screwed them over on purpose—" He broke off, shuddered.

The trees above us shivered. The air was crisp and felt weighted. My limbs were heavy, growing weak. I looked from

Reid to Theo, their jaws locked, shoulders hunched. But it was Dax my eyes fixed on.

His expression seemed thoughtful; his lips were moving silently. Then, out of nowhere, he turned to Theo with a look of pity and said, "The USB is buried in a box near the fence. I saw him burying it as I drove in."

"*Dax!*" I hissed. "What are you doing?"

"Five yards from the tree line on the other side of the cricket pitch," Dax said, ignoring me.

"Are you insane?!" Nellie shrieked.

"Five yards," Dax repeated. "He marked the exact spot with a cross in the soil."

"A cross . . ." Reid echoed, looking confused. He and Dax locked eyes. Something odd was happening that I couldn't decipher fast enough.

"I wish things could've been different, you know," Dax went on, now focusing on Theo. "I liked you and I really do think you liked me too. Love's just . . . it's never simple, is it?"

I couldn't believe it. Was Dax really pouring out his heart to this deranged weasel? *Now?*

"Dax!" I repeated, more severely. "This isn't the time . . ."

For a moment, Theo didn't move. Perhaps he, like the rest of us, was still trying to puzzle out what was going on. But eventually he nodded at Dax—a nod that might've said *Thank you* or more likely *You're as stupid as I pegged you for*—and scrambled off into the night.

"Dax!" Nellie and I snapped as soon as Theo had disappeared. "What have you done?"

"And what the hell is so funny?" Nellie added when he—unbelievably—started chuckling.

"I marked the spot with a cross, yeah?" Reid said. "Nice touch."

Nellie and I shared a bemused look as Dax unzipped his backpack and pulled out the USB.

Sophia slapped a hand over her mouth and started giggling.

"You bloody brilliant trickster!" Nellie said.

Dax smiled. "Learned from the best, I guess. Now, let's get out of here before Theo digs up that empty box."

We all stalled a moment, every single one of us (even Sophia), looking at the USB in Dax's hand.

"All yours," Reid said, lifting Sophia onto his hip and holding her tight. "I mean it. I never cared about the money anyway, so long as Theo didn't get it."

"There're sixteen *million* pounds on there," I said, dumbfounded.

"Family money?" Sophia suggested brightly.

No one seemed to know what to say to that, so I took the reins. "Or how about we go get a drink before we make any crazy decisions?"

"Good idea," Nellie said. "I vote the Lanesborough."

"It's nearly midnight," I said. "They won't be open."

"For a family with sixteen million pounds: trust me, they'll be open."

And so it was decided, and off we headed together, the five of us, side by side, the most unlikely family I could ever have imagined.

Nellie and I climbed into the MG, while Reid and Sophia caught a lift with Dax. The police barricades in the surrounding streets had been removed, so, just for the hell of it, we swung left into King's Road and zoomed past the gallery—top down, the chilled night air stinging our eyes.

"Some night, huh?" Nellie said.

I took one last look at the grand pillars at the gallery entrance, the red carpet, the knot of guests still lingering in the foyer. "It'll be a hard one to top."

She grinned mischievously. "But I bet we could."

THREE MONTHS LATER

30
VERONA, ITALY

THE SCENT OF FRESHLY BREWED ESPRESSO, THE CLATTER OF A bicycle down a cobblestone street, church bells chiming in the distance: sounds that had become the familiar background to our days in that long, languid summer.

The Palazzo Mongo—situated right in the center of old-town Verona—had been our home for the past five weeks. It was the seventh stop on our three-month whirlwind European holiday, including a ten-day sojourn in Greece to visit Nellie's parents (who were holidaying there) and one week in Amsterdam to see Jack. We were leaving Verona first thing tomorrow, though, and I would miss the views of the Piazza Bra, the constant hum of life from the streets below—laughter, anger, irritation, excitement—*the food*. But as I looked at Nellie, lounging on the couch, her long, tanned legs dangling over the side, Sir Sebastian curled up on her lap, I knew it didn't really matter where we went next, as long as we went there together.

I flopped down beside her, placed my brand-new laptop on my knees, and opened Janet Robinson's Facebook profile. It was the first time I'd done so since the heist, and, like always, I was immediately bombarded with photos of smiling couples, engagements, weddings, babies, happy families—people living their "best lives"—or so they claimed. I scrolled through it all, waiting for the inevitable ache of longing to hit me square in the chest. But it never came. *Family*, I thought with a smile, was something I knew now too.

I looked up to see Nellie watching me. She seemed concerned for a minute, then registered my expression and mirrored my smile.

"Well," I said. "I guess it's time. I'm doing it. Ready?"

"If you are." She gave Sir Sebastian a scratch between the ears.

I clicked on the settings tab in the top right-hand corner of my screen: REMOVE ACCOUNT. A prompt popped up, asking me if I was sure. *Yes or No*. I let the cursor hover for a minute. Nellie and I had already erased ourselves from Goods Exchange International, and this—Janet's Facebook profile—was the last tangible link to my swindling alter ego. In some way, letting her go felt like removing my own safety net, the only thing that would catch me if being Emma Oxley got to be a bit too much. Or maybe not the only thing.

I looked at Sophia's stick-figure drawing lying on the coffee table, the one she'd given me during the heist. *They* were my safety net now. I clicked *Yes*.

Nellie lit a stick of incense. Jasmine, this time.

"How does it feel?" she asked, waving a plume of scented smoke into her face.

I thought about all the other things I'd let go of over the past months: my resentment toward Joel and Rachel, toward my parents, toward myself. That last one had actually come first, the others following effortlessly in its wake. "It feels . . . I don't know. Natural, I guess."

She nodded, but there was something hesitant in her expression. Her gaze moved over the coffee table, her diamond choker lying in full view. It caught a ray of sun, flashed, almost blinding me.

"But, you know," I added gently, "letting go's hard. You've just got to do it when you're ready."

She opened her mouth but didn't seem to have anything to say. And instead we sat there in silence as the late sun streamed in through our hotel window, the smell of hot pizza wafting in from the street outside, mingling with the sweet scent of jasmine. It was the end of one day, but soon, seamlessly, it would be the start of another.

I closed the laptop and let out a breath.

Start again.

"WELL, WE SHOULD probably get going," Nellie said a short while later. She ground out the incense and helped me to my feet. "It's a bit of a walk and you know how the crowds get through town."

"True. And we must account for our stop-off at the *gelateria*."

"God yes."

I pulled on a pair of cream cotton shorts and a bright-orange blouse, fixed my hair into a high knot, and followed Nellie through the lobby and into the crowded cobblestone streets of the old town center. Maybe it was just my imagination, or maybe it was my brand-new technicolor wardrobe, but people seemed to notice me now. I didn't mind too much.

Under the sweltering June sun and sapphire-blue skies, the two of us ambled lethargically back through the bustling Piazza Bra, through the surrounding alleyways, and over the Ponte Pietra.

Finishing our enormous gelatos, we walked along the promenade and through several short, serpentine backstreets—home to honest vendors and the occasional pickpocket.

Nellie slowed as we approached a small group of tourists encircling a middle-aged woman who was shifting a ball around under bunch of plastic cups on a wooden dais. We'd barely been there two minutes when one of the tourists started jumping around in jubilation.

"Cento! Cento!" the tourist exclaimed, waving a wad of cash around for everyone to see. "I won. One hundred euro! I guessed correctly and I won! Can you believe it?"

Nellie and I shared a knowing look as a second tourist sat down opposite the middle-aged woman and bet fifty euros on a game she'd never win.

Nellie placed her Gucci handbag on the ground, said to me, "Shall we?"

I grinned conspiratorially and shifted into position while Nellie nudged the unsuspecting tourist out of the way.

"I bet five hundred," she said with a snap, handing the woman five hundred euros. "Middle cup."

The crowd gawked.

The woman happily slipped the cash into the bag she had tucked behind her. "Middle cup. Are you sure?"

"Positive," Nellie said, stretching out her legs beneath the dais.

Then, as the woman was about to lift up the middle cup (and undoubtably reveal that the ball had conveniently vanished) Nellie gave the dais a sharp kick and sent the whole setup tumbling to the ground. In the ensuing commotion, I dipped my fingers into the trickster's bag, scooped out the contents of her purse, and tossed it at Nellie.

"Thanks, babe," she said.

"My pleasure."

"*Ridammelo indietro, sobito!*" the woman squawked as she scrambled to her feet.

"What's that?" Nellie chirped, sidestepping her. "You want us to call the police?"

"On it," I said, and got out my phone. The woman stopped in her tracks, scowled at the two of us, exclaimed "*Cazzo!*," and vanished.

"Lesson number one," Nellie explained to the stunned crowd as she dished out the cash—less the five hundred euros she'd gambled. "If it's too good to be true, you've just been duped."

SLIPPING AWAY FROM the crowd as they chattered excitedly among themselves, Nellie and I made our way toward an old café tucked into a large stone tower that overlooked the Adige River. I looked down at the address on my phone, then up at the café. "This is it: Osteria Ponte Pietra."

I made for the entrance, but Nellie stalled. Her gaze was distant and unfocused; she was lost in a memory, or some tangled thought. I knew not to ask her which. She ran a finger along the scar above her left eyebrow, the one Kade had given her, then reached inside her bag and pulled out her choker. It glinted in the late sun as she threaded it through her fingers, the way I'd seen her do a hundred times before. She nodded, not at me, at the memory maybe, then, a beat later, tossed the choker into the river.

I linked her arm through mine. "Proud of you," I said as we found a table on the café's balcony, under the shade of a large red-and-white umbrella, and ordered a garlic-and-rosemary fo-caccia and two Aperol Spritz.

Twenty minutes later, the café door swung open with a soft creak, and I caught a whiff of familiar cologne.

Dax drew us each into a hug. "Sorry I'm late. Time flies when, you know . . ."

He settled in the seat next to me and ordered himself a Birra Moretti and plate of gnocchi with extra Parmesan. Dax, like us, had taken a well-earned break after the heist fiasco and had spent the past three months backpacking through Eastern Europe, working part-time on our new business venture.

"Well? Go on," I said enthusiastically. "What's he like? Spill!"

Dax took a sip of beer while he contemplated his answer. "Nice, I think. But we probably won't see each other again. He's just here on holiday, like us. Goes back to Munich next week."

"Next week? Like, in seven days' time?" I asked, plucking a slice of orange from my Spritz and popping it into my mouth. We were talking about Dax's latest fling, some guy he'd met here in Verona just last week. "And you like him, right?"

"Well, he's not a criminal out to kill me, so that's a plus."

"And you both have location-independent jobs, meaning you can live anywhere?" He nodded; I nodded back, splayed my hands. "I rest my case."

Dax smiled gratefully and I felt my chest thaw out a little more. Each day a little more.

"Oh, forgot to say," he added, "I finished the website. It's been live for less than forty-eight hours and . . . look"—he pulled out his phone and angled the screen toward us—"I think we've just got our first client."

Nellie and I read the email on his phone, one that had presumably come from the contact page of CodeRed.com, our new website.

Subject: PLEASE HELP! URGENT!
Date: 24 June, 2022 at 3:02 p.m.
From: maria.smith93@gmail.com

To Whom It May Concern,

I found your website on Google and am really hoping you can help me because I'm desperate!

I've been dating this guy on Tinder for the last five weeks and, long story short, he asked me to lend him £10 000 (which I did. IDIOT) and now he's disappeared (OF COURSE HE HAS).

The police say there's nothing they can do because I handed over the money willingly.

Judging from your About page, you've got a lot of experience in the conning department so I'm really hoping you can help me to track him down and get the money back.

Please let me know how much you charge for your services and what information you'll need. I've included my contact details below.

Thanks,
Maria

"Yikes," Nellie said, leaning back in her seat. "What a way to start."

"Let's set up a meeting for first thing tomorrow," I said. "With everyone. Then we'll give Maria a call and decide how to proceed."

"Good idea." Dax slipped his phone back into his pocket. "And, hey . . . you finished with Janet's Facebook profile?" he asked me. "Can I go in and clean up the footprint?"

I stared over the railing, at the urgent waters of the Adige River flowing below us, carrying with it twigs and leaves and various other debris—all the way out to sea, gone, good-bye. "Yep," I said. "I'm done. Time for new beginnings."

"Speaking of new beginnings," Nellie said with a wry grin, "look what the cat's dragged in."

Sophia barreled headlong toward us through the cramped café like a bull in a china shop, her face split in two by a huge, toothy grin. "Emma! Nellie! Dax!" she gushed, wrapping her arms around each of us in turn.

Emma, I thought happily. *Even if it's just a name.*

"It's so good to see you again!" Sophia went on. "What have you been doing? Have you had any gelato yet? Chocolate and pistachio is my favorite. Have you seen the arena? Do you like it? What about Juliet's balcony? I thought it was boring. And the Tower? Daddy says the touristy stuff is silly but you should still go see it all at least once, hey, Daddy?"

Arriving at the café seconds later, a haversack slung over his shoulder, was James Reid (I still called him that, old habit). He pulled out a chair, first for Sophia, then himself. He was almost unrecognizable, dressed in a clean, well-fitted golf shirt and linen shorts. He'd let his hair grow out and it was now a light, glossy brown. The transformation was extraordinary, and I had to stare at him for several minutes before I caught sight of that wayward glint in his eyes, one I knew so well.

Unbidden, I slipped back into the memory of heist night and everything that had happened as a result.

BY THE TIME Theo had dug up the empty box at Burton Court, the five of us were sipping drinks at the Lanesborough's Garden Room, which—as Nellie had predicted—they'd opened just for us. After bonding over our shared trauma and mutual bitterness toward Theo Fletcher, we decided to split the Bitcoin four ways (Sophia insisted she did not deserve a cut and would share with her father). All was hunky-dory until it dawned on us that Theo and his friend Nico Kappas, now sans sixteen million pounds, were still a problem we had to deal with.

And so, the very next day, game plan in hand, Nellie and I paid a visit to the Royal London Hospital. I did feel a tiny bit sorry for Nico Kappas when I saw him lying there in the intensive care ward, attached to all sorts of tubes and wires and high as a kite on morphine. He looked terrible: pallid, weak, miserable, and very, *very* displeased to see us. In fact, I figured the only person he'd be less excited to see was the person who'd put him in the hospital in the first place. So, going on a hunch, I offered Boss Thug an opportunity for revenge, retribution, and a fresh start: five hundred thousand quid in hard cash and all he had to do was talk to the police. Smiling like a fool, he signed on the dotted line and within two weeks and four days, Theo Fletcher had been arrested for attempted murder, body snatching (which is a crime—who knew?), and possession of an unregistered firearm (Boss Thug's firearm, but hey, details, *shmeetails*). Guess they weren't really friends after all.

Cherry on the top, Theo was also charged with fraud and possession of stolen goods because when the police raided his flat after the tip-off, they found an entire roomful of luxury watches and jewelry. I bet he tried to rat us out with that one, but since we'd relocated the Laundromat, and Dax had wiped all incriminating emails and texts from our phone and laptop, there wasn't any way he could prove we'd been involved in anything, or even that we existed.

As for Mr. L: we never heard if she tried to resell the bracelet, or whether she eventually discovered it was a fake, but a month after Theo's arrest, a new article sprang up in *The Atlantic* (and several other newspapers in the US and UK), revealing all the sticky details of the Fletcher family enterprise. Theo's parents and brother were subsequently arrested for fraud and a string of other charges, and if I had to guess I'd say—in exchange—Theo's sentence was reduced. Suppose he got his revenge after all.

NELLIE LIFTED HER glass of Spritz, jolting me back to the present. "Never in my wildest dreams did I think I'd say this, but it's good to see you, James. You look . . . happy?"

"Yeah, thanks, I am. People say money can't make you happy but . . . I dunno"—he pulled Sophia onto his lap—"it has with us. We've done all this traveling, we've got that apartment in London, we've got a car, new clothes, shoes, a real bed. One each." Reid grinned and ruffled Sophia's hair. "We'll stay here in Verona until the end of the school holidays. Then it's back to London to move into the new flat."

"We'll see you there," I said, then went on to explain. "Nell and I have decided to rent a place in Mayfair. Might not be forever, but we're keen for a bit of stability for a while."

"You'll come over for pancake breakfasts, then?" Sophia pleaded.

"Of course!" I said. "As often as you'll have us."

"You could even move in if you want," Sophia suggested. "To the flat. All three of you."

Nellie's eyes popped. "Well, sweetie, I'm not sure—"

"Oh, and here," Sophia cut in, undeterred. "I brought you something." She extracted a large green-and-gold hardback from Reid's haversack and slid the shiny tome across the table toward me: *The Book of Good Advice*, volume 2. "We printed one just for you," she said, "in case you need it someday. It's got some new chapters, too, like what to do when the bad men come for you. I hope you like it."

I burst into tears. "Thank you, Soph. I . . . I really—"

"We'll carry it with us everywhere," Nellie said.

"Also," Reid said a moment later, "thank you, again. For giving me a chance to work with you on CodeRed.com, I mean. I think we'll make a good team."

I nodded in agreement while Dax filled Reid in about Maria's email.

"So," I said, once he'd finished, "Dax, if you're able to track down Maria's fraudulent lover, then the three of us"—I gestured at Nellie and Reid—"can plot a Game to make him cough up that ten thousand quid."

"Should be a breeze," Nellie said. "James, what do you say? You up for another round of amateur dramatics?"

"Ha, yeah," Reid said, a little uncertainly. Then, after a pause, he added, "You know . . . I don't think I ever actually said it, but I wanted to apologize to you. I'm sorry you ever got pulled into things with Theo and I'm sorry for the part I played in it all. You know why I did what I did, yeah. But that doesn't make it right." He touched Sophia on the arm. "I want to teach Soph about the good things in life: how to be kind, how to treat others. But you can't teach your kids anything if you aren't that thing yourself. I realize that now."

Sophia looked up at him with large, wet eyes. "It's OK, Daddy. You were doing what you had to, to protect me. Same as everyone."

"Too true, Soph," I said. "We all did the things we did to protect the people we love." *And to figure out who we really are inside*, I didn't add.

SEVERAL HOURS LATER, the sun dipping low in the crimson sky, Nellie and I—now alone—ordered our fourth round of drinks and an enormous platter of cheese, plump olives, crispy bruschetta, and sun-dried tomatoes.

A Spritz in one hand, I set up our chessboard. Below the terrace, I heard the gushing waters of the Adige River and, beyond it, the hum of traffic and voices.

"Well . . ." Nellie said on a sigh, "I suppose you haven't forgotten what day it is."

"Twenty-fourth of June. Of course not. She would've been ninety-six today."

Nellie raised a glass. "To Janet Annie Robinson."

"The original swindler," I said, clinking my glass against hers. "Happy birthday, Gran."

Acknowledgments

Hayley Steed, thank you for your support, guidance, and stalwart belief in my dreams and ideas. Here's to many more years together.

Kerry Donovan, my brilliant editor at Berkley, who has been the loudest voice in cheering this book on right from the very beginning. Thank you for helping me shape, polish, and shine, for your insight, expertise, and passion. To everyone else at Berkley and Penguin Random House—the marketing, production, and sales teams, my copy editor and cover designer—thank you for your commitment and hard work in bringing this book to readers everywhere.

To my old team at the Madeleine Milburn Literary Agency and my new one at Janklow & Nesbit UK, I'm so grateful for everything you've done (and are doing) for my career.

To the experts who advised me on this project: Caleb McKellar at Barter McKellar for all things legal, Dr. Jade Evans for medical, and my supersmart tech friends for everything I didn't know about the internet—thank you for taking the time and effort to answer my (occasionally bizarre) questions. All errors and inaccuracies are entirely my own.

To the booksellers, librarians, bloggers, reviewers, and readers who have read and talked about this book: THANK YOU.

You are the beating heart of the publishing industry and I appreciate you all so very much.

To Will, my family, and my friends, who put up with me when I demand to be locked away in a quiet room, who bring me food and coffee and wine, who never say my ideas are too crazy or my dreams too big. You are all so wonderful and encouraging and understanding. Thank you!

Tess Amy was born in Johannesburg but now enjoys a nomadic lifestyle, living between Europe and South Africa. She holds a master's degree from the Durban University of Technology and is an outdoor enthusiast, an animal lover, and an unfaltering optimist.

Ready to find
your next great read?

Let us help.

Visit prh.com/nextread

Penguin
Random
House